COCKTAILS
BEFORE
MIDNIGHT

A **HOTEL HAMILTON** NOVEL

TANYA E WILLIAMS

Copyright © 2024 by Tanya E Williams

All rights reserved.

No part of this book may be reproduced in any form or by any electronic or mechanical means, including information storage and retrieval systems, without written permission from the author, except for the use of brief quotations in a book review.

This book is a work of fiction. References to real people, events, establishments, organizations, or locales are intended only to provide a sense of authenticity, and are used fictitiously. All other characters, incidents, and dialogue, are a product of the author's imagination and are not to be construed as real.

FIRST EDITION

Cover Photograph by David C Williams

Cover Design by Ana Grigoriu-Voicu

eBook ISBN 978-1-989144-30-5

Paperback ISBN 978-1-989144-31-2

Hardback ISBN 978-1-989144-32-9

Audiobook ISBN 978 -1-989144-33-6

For Aunt Irene

*You showed us how to live well, love much, and laugh often and you did so all the way to 101.
We will miss you dearly.*

CHAPTER 1

MONDAY, DECEMBER 5, 1927

*L*ouisa

My tired eyes scan the newspaper. Several days old, the paper is becoming tattered from my persistent perusal of the theatre headlines. Seeing my name in bold, black print alongside a grainy photograph of myself on stage sends a delightful river of chills down my spine.

Clara bustles into the kitchen, her nervous energy arriving ahead of her physical presence. Her disapproving glance toward where I'm seated at the table speaks volumes. "Louisa, you aren't dressed."

"Don't go getting your knickers in a knot. We have plenty of time." Less than eager to start the day of making beds and scrubbing bathtubs, I return my attention to the editor's comments and bask in the praise of my recent role as Mrs. Craig. With my name in the paper, perhaps I will be discovered soon enough, and then I can ditch the role of dutiful maid for good.

The theatrical production of *Craig's Wife* came to a close yesterday afternoon with a final matinee, and I am already missing the cast, the stage, the limelight, and Thomas. At the thought of him, a warm blush creeps up my neck from beneath the collar of my silky rose-coloured robe. His persistent belief in me is what pushed me toward centre stage. With the final curtain call now behind us, I feel the pressure to figure out what is next for both my theatre career and my relationship with Thomas.

My sister moves about the small kitchen, making breakfast while packing lunches for our shift at the hotel. Clara's usual hurriedness is amplified this morning by the arrival of her first official day as an eighth-floor maid at The Hotel Hamilton. Proud doesn't even come close to explaining how pleased I am to see her step up in the world, pushing aside her natural tendency to shrink into the shadows and daring to seek more from her life.

A clatter, followed by Clara's gasp, draws my attention. "What is it?"

"Mama's watch." Clara's voice is coated with worry. "It fell off my wrist."

Before I can stand and offer my assistance, Clara waves me off. "It's fine. I must not have clasped it properly."

"Perhaps you should take a moment to slow down and breathe." I avoid looking at my sister in an effort to restrain an eye roll. "You have nothing to worry about. You are trained and you are ready for this."

Clara steps forward, straddling the space between the kitchen and the dining table. "I suppose you are right. I just —I get so worked up about the responsibility of it all. I am accountable for an entire guest's experience. I mean, on the fifth floor we tend to more than one guest on any given day, but I never realized how sharing the load with other maids lessened the burden."

The corner of my lips quirks upward as I issue a knowing wink. "It's why you'll be paid the extra twenty-five cents a day. For all that obligation."

Clara concedes the point with a tilt of her head and returns to the kitchen to butter the toast she's made for breakfast.

I nibble at tea and toast, taking the time to reread the theatre reviews. Thomas hasn't mentioned another play. But then again, I chide myself, it has been hours, not days, since his last production ended. The man surely deserves time to gather himself. On the other hand, I can't expect him to cast me as the leading lady in every play he directs, sweetheart or not.

No, I think as I take another bite of toast, I will need to find the next director who can see what Thomas sees in me. That is the only way I will be discovered in this city. When I become truly famous as an actress, then I'll be able to call my own shots and won't need to rely on anyone else. Thankfully, I have a list of newspaper reviews to give my name the boost it needs. The sooner I secure my next role, the better. Today's headline ends up in tomorrow's waste bin, after all.

Though I plan to approach other directors, I will hedge my bets and speak with Thomas about his plans.

"Louisa." Clara glances at her watch. "We really need to be going."

I take my dishes to the kitchen, placing them in the sink to clean later. "I'll be ready in five minutes. That will give us enough time to take the long way to work."

Clara inhales sharply, I assume attempting to smother a

huff as I test her desire to arrive at the hotel far earlier than necessary. "Fine. Can you hurry up, though?"

Five minutes later, Clara pushes me out the apartment door and locks it behind us. The winter wind whips my jacket open the moment the door of our apartment building, The Newbury, opens to the day. As I tug my jacket closed while buttoning every single button, my lips twist at the thought of another dreary day spent within the confines of the fifth floor of the hotel.

"Blasted wind." I tuck my chin into my coat's collar while steering Clara away from our regular route with an arm hooked through hers.

"Are you sure we have time?" Clara leads with a forlorn expression. "I would hate—"

I cut her off with a wave of my hand. "We have plenty of time, and this will only take a few minutes." I tug her closer, letting her know she can trust me. "I promise. I just need a moment with Thomas and we'll be on our way."

We wait for the traffic to clear before stepping out to cross the street. I decide distraction may be the best approach, given Clara's anxious state this morning. "I've been meaning to ask you. Now that the play is finished, I thought we could spend a little of my earnings and enjoy an evening at The New Orpheum."

"You don't have to spend your money on me." Clara, still the frugal one, is quick to turn down my offer. She's unable to let go of her need to scrimp and save, despite our much-improved financial standing in recent months.

"I know I don't have to. But I want to." I steal a glance in her direction. "I am dreadfully sore that I missed the theatre's grand opening last month. I would have given half the dresses in my closet for a chance to see Phyllis Haver in person."

Clara smothers a chuckle behind her mitten.

"It'll be fun. Just you and me." I eye her knowingly. "You can't say no to me, Clara. I know you want to go just as much as I do. Besides, we could use a night out. I am sure Papa won't mind one bit. If it makes you feel better, we can have dinner with him before heading to the photoplay."

Stepping onto the opposite sidewalk, I can feel my sister considering an evening spent at Vancouver's newest theatre, so I nudge her a little further. "If I have to return to my regular life as a hotel maid until someone whisks me away to fame and stardom, then I am determined to have some fun in the meantime."

Clara rolls her eyes at me before issuing a subtle nod of agreement. "Fine. I'll go with you to the theatre."

"Excellent. Then it's all set. I will see about tickets during the lunch break. We might be able to go as early as tomorrow. How exciting!"

We continue walking straight on Thurlow. Thomas' apartment building is located a stone's throw from our own. Though I've yet to visit him at his home, our time spent together at the theatre and the occasional dinner between rehearsals has provided confirmation that we are smitten with one another.

The buildings set back from the sidewalk do a good job of blocking the wind, giving us a moment's reprieve. I run my fingers through my wind-tossed hair while considering how brazen I'll need to be to ensure I run into Thomas this morning. My desire to secure my next acting role pushes me forward, shoulders back and head held high.

I am contemplating whether I have what it takes to actually knock on his door when Thomas' familiar frame steps onto the sidewalk fifty feet in front of us. A smile emerges on his face as he turns and sees us walking toward him.

A few long strides later, he is beside me. "Well, this is a coincidence. I was heading to the hotel to see if I could catch you before you started work."

My stomach does a somersault at his admission. "You were?"

"Hi Clara, it is nice to see you." Thomas, ever polite, gives Clara his full attention as he greets her before returning his attention to me. "I was. I have news on an upcoming audition for you. The director and I know each other from a project a few years back. I've seen the part, and I think you'd be perfect for it."

I bite my bottom lip, eagerness and excitement ready to burst forth.

"I tried calling, but I must have missed you by minutes." Thomas runs a hand through his dark hair, distracting me. "I can walk with you, fill you in if you are interested."

I teasingly poke Clara in the side with an elbow. "I am quite sure Clara would appreciate any progress that gets us to the hotel in the least amount of time possible."

Thomas' eyebrows converge. I gesture for us to walk and explain, "Today is Clara's first day as an eighth-floor maid. She is eager to get started."

"Ah, I see." Thomas leans past me to direct his comments to Clara. "Congratulations must be in order, then. Well done for securing such a position. Lou mentioned that you were in the running for the promotion."

Clara smiles demurely but says nothing as the conversation returns to the audition.

Thomas tells me about the role, and my excitement grows with every word. "The lead actress has quite the task, as she is to portray two main characters. The costume changes alone will need to be carefully scripted." Thomas runs a hand through his hair again, and I assume he is lost in the directorial challenges that such a play will present. Shaking his head, he returns his attention to me. "The audition is this Saturday at two o'clock. Do you think you can make it?"

    I can barely contain my enthusiasm, my fretting over breakfast replaced by sheer glee at the new opportunity. "I'll be there with bells on." I meet his gaze with a dazzling smile and loop my arm through his, giving his arm a squeeze of appreciation.

CHAPTER 2

MONDAY, DECEMBER 5, 1927

lara

The Hamilton stands proud against the overcast skies. Though the building is not as tall or elaborate as its next-door neighbour, The Hotel Vancouver, it is stately in its own way. Approaching the building from opposite the usual direction provides a fresh perspective on the hotel and the immense promise within its walls.

A shiver of excitement mixed with a hefty dose of overwrought nerves rattles through me as I leave Louisa and Thomas to say their goodbyes and step into the alley that leads to the back entrance of the hotel. Thankful for a few moments alone to collect myself, I climb the steps, take a deep breath, and tug open the heavy door.

Warm air greets me like a hug, delightfully scented with cinnamon and sugar. Cookie's head pops out from the pastry kitchen. Spotting me, my friend's smile lights up like the Christmas tree, decorated with electric lights, in the Spencer's department store window.

"Clara, I've been watching for you." Cookie steps into the hall, a mixing bowl resting against her plump torso as she stirs its contents with a wooden spoon. "Wanted to wish you luck for your big day."

I remove my toque and mittens while peeking into Cookie's bowl. "Thank you." Glancing about the hall, I lower my voice to a whisper. "I don't mind admitting to you that I am a tad nervous. I'm not sure I've ever had this much responsibility. My only hope is to do Ms. Thompson and Mr. Olson proud."

"Nervous? It's all grand. You've got nothing to worry about." Cookie's hand pauses its circular motion as her eyes meet mine. "You've not only been trained by the most accomplished of maids, but you also have a heart that strives to succeed. I've no concern at all about your abilities." Cookie leans in closer. "And neither does Ms. Thompson or Mr. Olson. You can trust me on that."

Letting Cookie's words settle within me, I acquiesce. "You are right. I've worked hard for this opportunity. All I can do is my best."

"Now you are thinking straight, Clara."

The back door opens and closes hard, slammed by a gust of wind. Louisa steps into the hall, stamping her feet on the entry mat. "Good morning, Cookie."

"And a good morning to you, Louisa, or should I say 'Miss Louisa' now that your name is splashed all over the newspapers."

"Hardly all over." Louisa beams at the recognition, despite her attempt to play it down.

Cookie holds up a finger, indicating for us not to go

anywhere, before retreating to the pastry kitchen. She returns with an envelope and hands it to Louisa. "I had the staff who buy the papers clip the articles about your performance. I thought you might like extra copies for your scrapbook."

Louisa gushes her appreciation as moisture gathers in her eyes. "Thank you. This is so kind." Tugging the newspaper clippings free, Louisa flips through them before returning them to the envelope for safekeeping.

"You two better be off, and I've got a gingerbread recipe to perfect before the holiday season is upon us."

In the locker room, I dress in my crisp, new eighth-floor uniform. After checking my appearance in the small mirror mounted on the wall, I make my way to Ms. Thompson's basement office. The rustle of my freshly starched dark blue skirt makes me smile, knowing I am now one of the few maids who get to wear the much more flattering uniform.

Rounding the corner of the basement's staircase, cool air greets me. I pat the back of my head, ensuring my hair remains secure within its tight bun. Without the fifth-floor uniform's cap to hide my rogue tendrils, I have spent hours practicing my hotel-approved hairstyle in anticipation of this day.

The dank-smelling basement is far from my favourite floor of the hotel, but Ms. Thompson requested my presence in her office prior to my shift this morning. Her words ring through my head. *A well-run hotel is the result of everyone following the same rules.* I agree with the sentiment whole-heartedly.

Navigating the corridors, I remember a previous encounter within the cavernous brick walls of the basement. I smile at the memory of learning about William's identity as Ms. Thompson's younger brother. Oh, how terribly I behaved in his presence. I still feel embarrassment at the thought of it.

Thankfully, William is not only the forgiving sort, but also a kind-hearted individual. Since his return to Toronto barely six weeks ago, we have exchanged a few letters. Pleasant, cordial, and friendly is what I've convinced myself they are, choosing to draw no further assumptions when it comes to William Thompson.

Yesterday's telephone call, however, caught me by surprise. I was making biscuits when the phone rang. Hands covered in dough, I reached for the phone's handle, squeezing it between my forearms only to have it clatter to the floor. After releasing a slew of flustered words and using a dishtowel to clean my hands, I retrieved the earpiece to hear William chuckling through the telephone lines.

I hadn't expected to hear his laugh or his voice, and though I was embarrassed that he'd witnessed my clumsiness, my heart softened at the words he had called to say.

"I am sorry if I've caught you at an inconvenient time. My sister mentioned your promotion and indicated you will be starting your new position tomorrow. I wanted to wish you well."

The phone line went silent as I found myself unable to speak. I eventually recovered my voice and thanked him for his kindness. Our conversation was short, given the cost of such long-distance communication, but his thoughtfulness has stayed with me since.

My thoughts of William are abruptly interrupted as I near Ms. Thompson's closed office door.

"May I remind you that other maids have been let go for less serious infractions." Ms. Thompson's reprimand echoes past the closed door, bouncing off the brick wall like winter hail on pavement.

Instinctively, I step a few feet down the hall so I do not appear to be purposely listening to the goings-on inside.

Ms. Thompson's voice drops an octave, and I imagine her putting on her less rigid demeanour. "There are rules in place for a reason. They exist to protect both you and our guests. What if the shoe were on the other foot? You could have found yourself in a much more serious situation. Do you understand?"

I assume the maid either nods or whispers her understanding, as it is Mr. Olson's voice I hear next.

"Let me be clear on this." Though I've only known him to be a fair and honest man, Mr. Olson's baritone voice inspires me to straighten my own posture. "You had the opportunity to be truthful about the situation, but you chose to dodge the facts. The Hotel Hamilton will not allow any such shenanigans between maids and guests, and we certainly will not tolerate a maid who turns to untruths in order to avoid reprimand. Am I clear?"

A muffled "Yes, sir" is all I hear.

"You may go, then."

A whoosh of air follows a third-floor maid I've had little interaction with as she runs from the basement office and the scolding she's just received. "Excuse me," she says as she skirts around me. I count to ninety before stepping toward Ms. Thompson's office. I linger out of sight and peer around the fully ajar door.

"Well, I think that will stop anything further. If not, she'll certainly be out of a job before Christmas." Mr. Olson's sigh is laced with exasperation. "I may be old-fashioned, but honestly, what has gotten into these young women? Thinking they can be as brazen at work as they are at those nightclubs they frequent. Don't they realize the consequences of their actions? What will they do when they are left with no job, no prospects, and a damaged reputation?"

Ms. Thompson shakes her head. "Flirting with a guest. A married one at that. And then having the gall to lie about it. If it hadn't been for the wife, I suspect we wouldn't have ever heard a thing about it, and then where would we be?"

Mr. Olson's voice is muffled as he runs a hand over his face. "I'm afraid I made the mistake of believing the girl the first time the wife came to me with her concern. I won't make that mistake again."

Ms. Thompson lowers herself to her office chair. "Well, the couple has vacated the hotel, at any rate. I checked them out myself this morning and didn't charge them for their weekend stay, though I don't suspect we will see them again anytime soon. I can't help but wonder how much of a role the husband played in all of this."

"I don't imagine we will ever know for certain, but from what I saw, this was not his first indiscretion." Mr. Olson's lips quirk up in a bemused smile. "His wife grabbed him by the ear like he was a naughty four-year-old." He let out a sigh. "Boys will be boys, I suppose. In any case, it's no longer our concern."

"I am not sure I can agree with you, Robert, if you are suggesting the husband's involvement in all of this is in any way acceptable."

Ms. Thompson's voice is stretched tight, and from my vantage point, I sense another discussion brewing. At the risk of having my morning delayed, I step into view in front of the open door and knock lightly on the door's moulding.

"Ah, Miss Wilson." Ms. Thompson smooths the front of her dress as she stands. "I almost forgot we were to meet. The morning must be getting on." She examines the watch pulled from her skirt pocket.

"As should I." Mr. Olson turns to leave. "Thank you, Ms. Thompson, for your assistance with this matter."

I step aside to let Mr. Olson pass through the narrow doorway. "Miss Wilson." Mr. Olson dips his head in greeting.

Out of respect for the hotel's manager, or perhaps the stern words he recently issued, I fold myself into a quick curtsy as he passes.

"Please come in, Miss Wilson." Ms. Thompson gestures to the chair across the desk from her own.

I take the offered seat and fold my hands in my lap.

Taking her own seat, Ms. Thompson gives me an affirming nod. "Miss Smythe tells me you have gotten on well with training."

"Thank you, ma'am. Miss Smythe has been a good teacher."

"She is one of our best. You choose your friends wisely, Miss Wilson. That is something to be commended for." Ms. Thompson shuffles papers on her desk, tugging one from the stack. "We will start you with one guest suite today and see how you get on. Perhaps by the end of the week, you'll be ready for a second. For now, you will take charge of suite 815." She examines the list. "Mr. Barnes is staying with us for the duration of the week and will be checking in this afternoon. He enjoys fresh flowers in his room daily, a task I am certain you can manage well. Given the winter season, we have less floral variety than usual, but I am sure you can find something that will please our guest."

The hotel's matron eyes me knowingly. My help with

the flower arrangements throughout the hotel has been an enjoyable addition to my regular list of tasks and is something Ms. Thompson has applauded me for on several occasions.

"Yes, ma'am. I will be happy to ensure Mr. Barnes has fresh flowers daily." My mind riffles through last week's flower delivery. Mostly greenery and a few sticks of holly. I can work with that today, but I make a mental note to inquire with the delivery driver as to what is available this time of year.

"Excellent. We won't leave you stranded, Miss Wilson. Should you need anything at all, you know where to find me." Ms. Thompson stands, and I take the cue that our meeting has come to an end.

"Thank you, ma'am. I won't disappoint you." I stand to leave, thankful for the favour Ms. Thompson has shown me.

I am at the threshold when Ms. Thompson's voice calls me back. "I almost forgot." She steps around her desk, reaching for something within the folds of her skirt pocket. "My brother asked me to pass this on to you. He included it with a package he sent me last week. Saving on a bit of postage, I assume." She places a small envelope in my hand.

"Thank you." I take the envelope and sheepishly tuck it into my apron pocket.

"I understand you two are becoming friends."

The word "friends" hangs in the air between us, and I realize in this moment that my budding friendship with William may actually be a misstep on my part. Is exchanging letters with Ms. Thompson's brother considered hotel shenanigans? He was a hotel guest when we first met, after all. My face falls at the thought of having done wrong.

"No need to fret, Miss Wilson."

I do my best to recover. "He has written a couple of times, ma'am. Your brother is a kind gentleman."

Ms. Thompson's smile stretches at the mention of William's kindness. "Like I said, Miss Wilson. You choose your friends wisely."

"Thank you, ma'am." I turn to leave.

"Oh, and Miss Wilson, be sure to gather the maids together in thirty minutes. I will meet you in the large linen cupboard on the eighth floor. I have an important announcement to make."

"Yes, ma'am." I dip my chin and head toward the eighth floor.

Thirty minutes later, all nine eighth-floor maids are huddled together within the confines of the largest supply closet.

"Ah, good. You are all here." Ms. Thompson enters the closet, clipboard in hand, and closes the double doors behind her.

The matron's arrival has us straightening our posture and closing our mouths.

"Ladies, I have some exciting news for you." Ms. Thompson's gaze lands on each of us individually. "You may know it is considered standard practice for an exemplary employer to present each employee with a holiday gift during the Christmas season."

All heads but mine nod in understanding, so I follow suit despite being unaware of such a tradition.

"The Hotel Hamilton is pleased to present each one of you with a fresh turkey for your holiday meal."

The maids smile and nod in appreciation, with a few clapping their hands together in quiet celebration. I am delighted by such a gesture, knowing all too well the additional cost of a Christmas turkey over that of a chicken. The last time our family enjoyed a turkey feast was when Mama was alive and we lived on the Murray Estate. Mr. Murray always made certain that Mama had a fine bird to roast for Christmas dinner.

"But that is not all, ladies." Ms. Thompson's eyes twinkle with a hint of anticipation. "Mr. Hamilton has decided to reward one maid for each floor with a cash gift of a week's salary."

My jaw almost hits the plush, red carpet beneath my feet. A whole week's wages is more than generous. I take hold of Rebecca's arm to steady myself and see the excitement in her eyes.

"Now, ladies. This is meant to be a friendly competition and one in which doing your best will be rewarded. The holiday bonus will go to the maid who shows a strong ability to manage her daily workload here on the eighth floor while being polite, respectful, and helpful toward all hotel guests and each other."

All heads nod eagerly.

"The winner will be announced the first week of January, so it is up to you to excel, as I know you can, throughout the holiday season. Things will be busier than usual. Guests will be arriving in time for the Spencer's Christmas Parade next week, and there will be many holiday packages to stow and possibly gift wrap. Should any of you need assistance with a task you are unfamiliar with, please see me directly. The only way to succeed, ladies, is to admit what you do not know and take the steps necessary to learn."

I make a mental inventory of the additional tasks we may be asked to perform during the holiday season. Though I am the newest staff member on the eighth floor,

Ms. Thompson has instilled in me the knowledge that I am capable of more than I think. A few months ago, I may have counted myself out of such a competition before it began. But now I know that if I don't try, I have no chance at all.

CHAPTER 3

THURSDAY, DECEMBER 8, 1927

*L*ouisa

"Can you believe it, Clara?" I twirl in a circle, sending the skirt of my drop-waist dress billowing. "What a night. What a photoplay." My secret dream of acting on the big screen courses through me, spurred on by tonight's visit to the theatre.

Glancing over her shoulder, Clara beams in my direction before returning her attention to the framed poster of Phyllis Haver on the side panel of The New Orpheum Theatre's entrance.

"I am glad the theatre was sold out and the only seats available were the more expensive tickets. I know you were worried about the cost, Clara, but you must agree that the premier seating was definitely worth the additional twenty cents each. I can't imagine experiencing the theatre any other way now. We would never have known the luxury of it all if the lower-priced seats hadn't been sold out for the next month." I stride back toward my sister, excitement over tonight's events warding off the winter chill.

"This is a beautiful theatre." Clara steps toward the doors, shading her eyes with both hands as she peeks through the glass at the grand foyer, lit by three oversized chandeliers hanging from a decorative ceiling.

I join her to peer through the glass. "I poked my head into the ladies' retiring room on my way to the washroom." I jab a finger into Clara's side to garner her attention. "There were maids tending to ladies as though they had come to the salon instead of the theatre." I shake my head and laugh. "Can you imagine?"

"The plush high-backed seats were more comfortable than most, but even if they weren't, I can't imagine taking my eyes off the show to sit in a salon." The lighthearted note in Clara's voice confirms our attendance tonight was just the ticket to distract her from concerns over her new position. "What was your favourite part?" Clara tugs on my coat sleeve and moves toward the sidewalk.

"*The Wise Wife*, without a doubt." I pause at the film poster once more before meeting Clara on the sidewalk. "It is terribly funny, and Phyllis Haver has oodles of talent. I wonder if she will make her way into a talkie, now that Hollywood is heading that way."

"Miss. Excuse me, Miss Wilson." A young woman dressed in a theatre maid's uniform waves her arm overhead from the threshold of the lobby doors.

I turn toward the voice. "Are you calling me?" Stepping toward the girl, I do my best to place her. "I'm sorry. Have we met?"

The girl blushes from her uniform collar to the top of her wide forehead. "No, miss. We haven't officially met, but I recognized you earlier when you looked in at the ladies' room." She shuffles back and forth over the plush carpet. "Then again, as you peeked through the doors just now. I— I figured it was my only chance to say hello."

I offer the girl a sincere smile. "Well, hello then."

Though I wouldn't have thought it possible, the girl's face turns an even darker shade of red under the shine of the marquee lights. "I saw you in *Craig's Wife*. Well, if I'm being honest, I saw the play three whole times. I thought you were magnificent." The girls' words run together in a rush of enthusiasm. "I imagine with your talent, it won't be long until we are all watching you in a photoplay, maybe even here at The New Orpheum."

"Three times?" I feel my smile grow wider at the girl's gushing admiration of my performance. At her mention, thoughts of being in a photoplay instantly consume my thoughts, but I press on, not wishing to appear rude. "You must have camped out in front of the theatre, since the play only ran for two weeks."

"I've always dreamed of being an actress." A slight drop of her chin tells me she lacks belief in herself. "My father. He doesn't consider escapades in theatre to be worthwhile."

My eyes scan the Orpheum's plush lobby behind her. "Yet you work here?" My left eyebrow climbs toward my forehead.

"Yes. It's as close to the limelight as I can get without disappointing him. At least I can experience the shows. Glimpses really, but it's enough to keep me coming back."

Clara nudges me from behind. "Lou, we really should be getting home. We are due back at the hotel by eight, and I could really use a full night's sleep."

"Hotel?" The girl, clearly more forthright than she first appeared, directs her question to Clara.

"That's right. We work at The Hotel Hamilton." Clara

tugs on my coat sleeve once more. "We really need to be going."

"What do you do there? I thought you were an actress, Miss Wilson." Her concern is evident, and I feel my status as a potential photoplay actress falter.

Hitching my chin up defiantly, I hold my ground and infuse my words with false confidence. "I happen to be both a hotel maid and an actress at the moment." I extend my hand toward the girl, intent on drawing the conversation to a close. "It was lovely to meet you—ah, I'm sorry, I didn't catch your name."

She places a small hand in mine, offering a slight squeeze. "Gwendolyn Russell, but my friends call me Gwen."

"Well, it is very nice to meet you, Gwen. You have a lovely evening." I turn to join Clara, but then think better of it. I too, after all, was a nobody with a dream before *Craig's Wife*. "Thank you for coming to the play. Don't give up on your dream, Gwen. We all have to start somewhere."

Tucking my arm into the crook of Clara's, we stroll toward home, the joy of the evening making our steps light.

Gwen's brief mention of me on the silver screen races through my mind on repeat, mirroring my rapid cadence as we walk quickly down Granville Street. Papa only agreed to our later-than-usual outing on the condition that we remain on primary, well-lit city streets and arrive home in a timely manner. The city is still reeling from the shooting and subsequent death of Constable Ernest Sargent last month, and residents are wary and on the lookout for a man with a gun.

White clouds of breath form in front of me as the December cold urges us forward. While we walk, I contemplate my current status as a Vancouver theatre actress. I've been thinking too small. What if I am destined for more, for Hollywood? I've dreamed of California since it has been in my line of sight, making its presence known through the pages of my beloved magazines.

In a recent edition of *Motion Picture Magazine*, a headline announced that a new era was upon us. Given the advancement in talkie films, the time period is being labelled the Golden Age of Hollywood. My fingers tingle inside my gloves at the thought of being discovered during such a time. I mean, if Mary Pickford, a Canadian native, can become America's sweetheart, why can't I?

But how? I am mulling over how one may find herself being discovered when I remember a man from several years back who was looking for new talent. At the time, he was on a search for the next Mary Pickford. What was his name? Romaine? Yes, that is it. Romaine Fielding. I make a mental note to see if I can track him down. Perhaps Thomas or someone from the theatre knows how to contact him. He was, at least at one time, well known in the city, with his advertisements and auditions.

"A penny for your thoughts." Clara bumps me mid-stride with an unexpected hip check.

I stumble to the side, taking her with me and giving a boisterous laugh. "I'm not sure they are worth that much."

"They are to me." Recovering her footing, Clara doesn't miss a beat. "That girl back there. She didn't upset you, did she?"

"No. Nothing like that." We nod good evening to The Hotel Georgia's doorman as we pass. "She was actually quite sweet. A fan, apparently."

"That's nice. I am sure you will experience more of that with the recent newspaper reviews. But I can tell there is something more, Lou. What's wrinkling that brow of yours?"

"She got me thinking is all. For years, I've dreamed of being on the stage, and in the last few months, I've attained that goal. I owe so much to Thomas for putting me at the centre of the production, and I wouldn't dream of letting him down, but what if I am destined for more?"

We cross Hornby Street without having to wait for traffic. "I thought you were happy on the stage," Clara says. "What is bigger than that?"

"Promise you won't laugh?" I steal a sideways glance.

Clara removes the mitten from her left hand and lifts her little finger to me. "Pinky promise."

I do the same, clasping her little finger in mine before returning my hand to the warmth of my glove. "Hollywood." I force the word out in a rush of air. "I would like to be in the movies. Just like Phylis Haver and Mary Pickford."

Clara's head bobs in agreement, which both pleases and surprises me. "I can actually see you on the big screen."

"You don't think it's silly? To have a such a wild dream."

"If you had asked me six months ago, I would have said it was silly. But now, you've proven your talent and dedication to a career as an actress. How could I say otherwise? I'll support you, Lou. Honest I will."

I can't resist a jibe at Clara's expense. "You do realize that Hollywood is in California? I will have to leave Vancouver, eventually."

"Ha, ha. Very funny." Clara's mock laughter peters out as we turn onto Thurlow Street and The Newbury comes into view. "Though I'd like nothing more than to keep you close, I can't be the one to clip your wings. You need to follow your heart and your dreams. It's the way you move through the world." Clara's shrug tells me she has given significant thought to what our futures may hold. "I, on the other hand, am inclined to adhere to the typical parameters set in place. Don't get me wrong, I am not at all disappointed by the prospect. Neither one is right or wrong. Just different."

I tug on the door of the apartment building and hold it open for my sister. "Since I have your approval, all I need to do now is figure out how to accomplish such a feat."

"I'm sure you'll think of something." Clara steps through the door and begins climbing the stairs to our third-floor apartment.

Knowing my whirring mind will make it impossible to sleep, I kiss Papa, who has been waiting up for us, good night. Grabbing a blanket from the cupboard, I settle myself on the sofa with a stack of motion-picture magazines. Determined to glean through interviews how today's stars were discovered, I flip open the magazine on top and search for the featured interview. I take it as a good omen that Mary Pickford, born in Toronto, Ontario, Canada, stares back at me. Her warm smile and kind eyes tell me that anything is possible.

CHAPTER 4

FRIDAY, DECEMBER 9, 1927

lara

A yawn sneaks past my lips. Pushing my cleaning cart toward suite 815, the tiredness from our evening out at the theatre clings to me like a noon-day shadow.

"Miss Wilson, are you only getting started now?" The concern in my friend Rebecca's voice is difficult to miss.

I pivot to find Miss Smythe, as I refer to Rebecca while we are working as eighth-floor maids, a few paces behind me. "I am. Mr. Barnes remained in his room most of the morning, so I diverted my attention to the seasonal bouquets for the arriving weekend guests."

"That was good of you, but you know you'll be cutting it close to guest registration time?" Miss Smythe checks her watch. "Only three hours until they start arriving."

"I'll be ready in time." I give her a reassuring smile as we arrive at the door of suite 815. The sound of movement behind the closed door dashes my hopes and my promise.

"Or perhaps not." I push the cleaning trolley ahead several paces and whisper to Miss Smythe, "He is still in the suite. What should I do?"

"We should check with the front desk. They usually inform us if a guest has delayed their checkout, but perhaps his was a last-minute request." Miss Smythe places a hand on my cart's handle and helps me push it over the plush carpet to the nearest storage cupboard. "I'll go with you, in case something is amiss."

"Thank you." We scurry down the back stairs, our footsteps echoing through the cavernous stairwell.

Peeking into the hotel's lobby, I find myself squinting as my eyes adjust to the dimly lit space filled with dark wood. Today's weather offers little in the way of warmth or light. Miss Smythe ushers me forward once she has confirmed the registration desk is free of guests.

"Excuse me. I'm sorry, I don't think we've met." Miss Smythe extends a friendly smile to the desk attendant. "I am Miss Smythe. This is Miss Wilson. We are eighth-floor maids, and we have a guest in suite 815 who appears to still be in his room but is scheduled to check out today. I wonder if you can tell us if the guest has extended his stay?"

"Miss Smythe, Miss Wilson." The lanky man in a tailored hotel uniform inclines his head in greeting. "I am Mr. Reynolds. Mr. Olson has hired me to manage the registration desk, since the last person who held the position was clearly not up to the task."

I stifle a smile at the man's impertinent remark and shift my eyes downward to examine the gleaming wood of the registration desk.

He brushes aside his comment with a wave of his hand. "It is good to meet you both. Now, it was suite 815, you said?"

"Yes," Miss Smythe says. "Mr. Barnes is the guest there."

Mr. Reynolds flips through the daily register until he reaches the eighth floor. "I see. Mr. Barnes is departing today on a four o'clock train. There is no note for a late checkout. I imagine he will be vacating the suite within the next two hours if he is to catch his train."

"Mr. Reynolds, what is the hotel policy when a guest…" Miss Smythe's lips twist as she contemplates an appropriate way to deliver the question. "Overstays their scheduled reservation?"

"Well, for a guest such as Mr. Barnes, I believe the hotel will overlook his extended stay." Mr. Reynolds narrows his eyes at us, as though we are the ones out of line. "Given that he is to be a frequent guest on the eighth floor, I would think he is due such a courtesy."

I exchange a questioning look with Miss Smythe. "I see," she says to Mr. Reynolds. "Thank you for your assistance." Miss Smythe steers me by the elbow to the back-of-house corridor. "I don't think we will get anywhere with Mr. Reynolds. He doesn't appear to be the sort to concern himself with someone else's problem."

By the time we have climbed the eight floors, we have decided that the best course of action is to wait for Mr. Barnes to vacate his suite. We pool our resources, working on Miss Smythe's last suite of the day, and in exchange, she will help me right suite 815 as soon as it is empty.

Midway through cleaning Miss Smythe's suite, I venture into the hall to deposit the bedding and towels into the laundry cart stowed within a utility closet. Rounding the corner on my return trip, I find the occupant of suite 815 craning his neck from his suite's doorway.

"Ah, just the maid I was looking for. Miss…?" The man,

whom I presume to be Mr. Barnes, steps forward, a smile dancing on his thin lips.

"Miss Wilson, sir. Pleased to meet you." I incline my head in greeting and resist the urge to take a step backwards.

"Well, Miss Wilson, I've been wondering where you've been all day." He speaks with a light tone, and I sense his words are intended to be teasing. But I don't miss the hint of accusation.

"I'm sorry, sir. Was there something you needed?" My thoughts instantly go to the holiday bonus. I am very aware that if I am unable to meet the needs of the one and only guest in my care, I won't even be considered for the prize. Winning such an honour among the eighth-floor maids is a sure way to show Ms. Thompson I'm worthy of her belief in me, and earning the holiday bonus would prove to Lou that Papa and I will be just fine on our own. I can't be the one to hold her back from her acting career beyond Vancouver.

"I've been hanging around this joint"—he gestures behind him to his suite's door—"waiting to meet you." Mr. Barnes leans a little closer than I am comfortable with and winks. "You are the girl who's been taking such wonderful care of my room all week, aren't you?"

I feel his breath on my cheek, and I hesitate. It takes me a moment to realize the man is unsuccessfully attempting to be friendly. "Yes, sir. I am your suite's maid."

"Well then, Miss Wilson. I am pleased to meet you." Mr. Barnes lifts my wrist and presses his lips to the back of my hand.

Though the urge to withdraw my hand is immediate, I remind myself that hotel protocol is to treat the guest with the utmost respect, especially on the eighth floor. Despite the hall being on the cooler side, I feel a trickle of sweat snake down my back. I brush the unsettling feeling aside, blaming my perspiration on the work I was engaged in earlier.

Not wanting to pressure the man but also wishing to bring our meeting to a close, I press on. "Are you all set for your journey home, then? Is there anything I can get for you?"

"Now that we are acquainted, I am right as rain. Please have the bellboy bring my cases down." Mr. Barnes moves past me, his shoulder brushing mine as though we are squished together in a tight space instead of in the wide eighth-floor hall. I remain where I stand and am waiting for him to vacate the hall when he turns back to me. "Oh, Miss Wilson. I am not travelling home today. I will be back in town next week. I look forward to getting to know you better then."

I force into place the smile expected of an eighth-floor maid and clasp my hands in front of me. "Have a safe journey, sir."

With my heart beating fast, I dash toward the suite Rebecca is tending and let her know Mr. Barnes has finally vacated suite 815.

"I will get started on it right away," I call over my shoulder as I move quickly in the direction of the supply cupboard. Unable to tamp down the urge to run, I tug my cleaning cart free and move with hurried steps toward the suite, my sole responsibility.

I begin with the bedroom, aware check-in time will be upon us in less than one hour. I strip the bed with more force than is necessary, tossing the sheets into a pile on the floor. The thought of Mr. Barnes' lips on my hand sends a shiver through my limbs. I shake my head to dislodge the uneasiness, along with any notion that he meant to be anything but cordial, and focus on the room before me. With any dilly-dallying on my part, the suite will not be ready for the check-in hour.

The darkness of the room adds a claustrophobic weight to the space. I turn on both bedside table lamps and am drawing the curtains open, lost somewhere between my list of tasks and ruminating mind, when I am startled from behind. "My suite is all sorted, so I can help with yours."

I spin around to find Miss Smythe standing at the foot of the bed. "Sorry, you scared me."

"Don't worry one bit. Together, we'll get this done in a jiffy." Miss Smythe's eyebrows converge as she takes a step closer. "Clara, are you all right?"

The use of my first name snaps me back to the present. "I'm fine. Anxious about the check-in deadline is all." I press a reassuring smile into place and thank her for her help. "I'll start in the washroom, if you'll take the sitting area."

We each move toward our designated areas, ready to set the suite right.

My face in the washroom mirror is as white as the bedsheets I just tossed to the floor. I contemplate confiding in Rebecca about Mr. Barnes' forward actions but think better of it. I have little experience with the goings-on of the eighth-floor guests. For all I know, Mr. Barnes' behaviour was typical for a guest staying in the opulence of the hotel's most extravagant suites.

Another look in the mirror has me splashing water on my face. I am being silly, I tell myself. I am simply not accustomed to such attention, and besides, part of my job is to deal with guests and their needs. Some people are more exuberant than others. That is all there is to the situation.

I empty the dustbin and remove the towels for washing before focusing on the vanity's marble countertop. Eager to complete the suite ahead of the check-in hour, I move quickly as I sweep the black-and-white penny-tile floor.

As I contemplate the situation with Mr. Barnes, I remember fondly another grateful guest, the mother of a small child whose stuffed bear had been forgotten on the train, leaving the child inconsolable and the mother at her emotional breaking point. After I retrieved a stuffed bear from Spencer's department store during my lunch break, the mother squeezed my arm as she thanked me profusely.

Mundane tasks being the solution to a contemplative mind, I realize that my discomfort is due to my inexperience with receiving such attention from a male guest. The mother's friendliness wasn't so different from Mr. Barnes', and at the time, I was pleased about her appreciation. My lack of experience has resulted in an overreaction. I shake my head at my folly.

I scrub the bathtub clean, and by the time I've moved on to scouring the sink's basin, I've resolved the encounter with Mr. Barnes as nothing more than a misinterpretation on my part. I stand on tiptoe, left hand raised to steady myself as I move a dry cloth over the mirror's surface. The clatter of metal on porcelain echoes in the confined space. My gaze falls to the sink, where Mama's watch lays inches from the open drain.

Snatching the watch from danger, I grip it in my palm. My heart races and I force myself to take slow breaths. I am overtired is all. I tuck the watch into my apron pocket and retrieve fresh towels from my cart. With the towels lined up and ready for their next guest, I leave the washroom and meet Miss Smythe in the bedroom. Together, we make the bed, dust, and vacuum just in time for the check-in hour.

CHAPTER 5

SATURDAY, DECEMBER 10, 1927

*L*ouisa

With time to spare before today's two o'clock audition, I decide to visit a friend, certain he will be able to steer me in the direction of the Hollywood connection I am seeking. Taking a detour to the theatre feels like going home. After all, I all but lived there for the better part of a month. The aroma of last night's stale popcorn lingers outside the theatre doors. I step over the kernels left by a street vendor's cart and move toward the main entrance.

I tug the weighted door open and step inside the lobby. The floor gleams as though Mr. Johnson has been polishing it all morning. His whistling tune reaches my ears before he appears from behind the ticket booth.

"Well, I'll be." Mr. Johnson beams at me, mop and bucket in hand. "If it isn't Miss Louisa Wilson, in the flesh."

"Hello, Mr. Johnson." I take a careful step forward,

cautious of the slippery tile. "I was in the neighbourhood and thought I might catch you."

"Well then, I better consider myself caught." Setting down the cleaning supplies, the friendly janitor reaches me in a few long strides. "You know, me and my wife were just talking of you the other day. Wondering how you were getting on, now that the play has ended."

"It's been less than a week. Don't tell me you've missed me already." I tease my friend before placing a hand on his. "I told you I wouldn't forget you."

A hearty laugh tips his head backwards. "As you say, Miss Louisa, it hasn't even been a week yet." Recovering himself, Mr. Johnson inclines his head in the direction of the theatre's inner sanctum. "Would you like a peek inside?"

"Lead the way, fine sir." I place my hand in the crook of his arm as he guides me toward the theatre, so rich in colour and texture that it feels like we are stepping into another world.

As the large theatre doors close, the familiar hush of the enclosed space embraces me. The stage is waiting patiently for tonight's play to begin, with a makeshift kitchen set in place beneath the glow of a single spotlight. The only things missing are the actors and an audience.

We walk until the slope of the theatre aisle levels out. "You were sure something on that stage, Miss Louisa."

My smile is a shy one, given the many productions I am certain Mr. Johnson has witnessed during his time at the theatre.

"Did I tell you that I brought my missus for your final matinee performance?" His eyes twinkle in the low light. "After weeks of listening to me brag about you, she finally told me to hurry up and buy two tickets. She arranged for the neighbours to watch our boys just so she could get gussied up and see what I was going on about."

"I didn't know that." I feel the heat of exhilaration run through me.

"And she wasn't disappointed, despite being tucked out of sight, up there." Mr. Johnson points to the upper benches in the rafters, and my heart sinks at the reminder of the blatant discrimination within the theatre's luxurious setting.

"No, ma'am. She's been talking about the play since last Sunday, she has." Mr. Johnson lets out another hearty laugh. "Course, when everyone she tells about it asks when and where they can see it, she has to apologize and tell them it's already closed."

"Oh dear. I am sorry to hear that. It is good to know, though, that Thomas could have had another week's run had he known about Mrs. Johnson's advertising campaign."

Mr. Johnson slaps a hand to his thigh. "I suspect you could be right about that."

He fills me in on the current production, the cast, and its opening night, before heading back to the lobby and the midday light. "Now, I don't expect you came all this way just to listen to me go on about things." Mr. Johnson's friendly expression doesn't waver. "What can I do for you, Miss Louisa?"

"I do have a question for you."

"Yes, ma'am. Anything I can do to help."

"Do you happen to remember a man named Romaine Fielding? He is a Hollywood director who travelled through Vancouver several years ago."

Mr. Johnson's eyes spark with recognition. "I do remember him."

My heart beats faster at Mr. Johnson's recognition of

the Hollywood director. "I believe he was seeking fresh talent at the time."

"I was reading about him just yesterday."

"Yesterday? I didn't realize he was in the city. That is fortunate news." I can barely conceal my excitement at the happy turn of events. I hadn't expected to find the man in my very own backyard. "I am not sure if he is still actively looking for new actresses, but I thought it might be a good place for me to start."

"A good place to start?" Mr. Johnson scratches his head.

"I thought I'd try my hand at a bigger acting role. Hollywood has been on my mind a lot since the play finished." I blush at the candid admission of my secret desires. "I don't suppose you happen to know where I might find Mr. Fielding?"

"Oh, I'm sorry to say he isn't here." Mr. Johnson wrings his hands together.

"Do you mean he is expected to return soon?" I am hanging all of my hopes on a man I don't even know, yet I can't seem to stop myself from believing that Mr. Fielding may be the person meant to discover me for the silver screen.

"He isn't anywhere, really. I read about his passing in the newspaper yesterday is what I meant to say."

The words dash my hopes like a stone in a rain puddle. "Oh." My fingers settle atop my lips as I take a moment to regain my composure. "That is sad news."

"Newspaper said he experienced a blood clot of some sort and passed early in the week. He was about my age, I reckon." Mr. Johnson delivers his last words an octave quieter.

"I suppose that is that." A shrug of my shoulders is my unconvincing attempt at hiding my disappointment.

"I am sorry to be the bearer of bad news, Miss Louisa. Maybe someone else can help. What was it you needed from Mr. Fielding?"

"To be honest, I am not sure he would have even met with me. I suppose I was hoping he might recommend me for a Hollywood production." Saying it out loud, the idea sounds like a fanciful childhood wish rather than the plan I made it out to be. "I thought, given the play and all, that I might be ready for something more. Something bigger."

"Ah, I see." A quiet moment passes, both of us lost in our thoughts. "Miss Louisa, if I may."

I nod, encouraging him to continue.

"The way I see it, you don't need nobody to tell you that you're good enough for Hollywood, as you most certainly are well on your way. But as my mama used to say, just cause you want to be ready for something, doesn't mean it is ready for you. Keep on doing what you are doing, and you'll find your success."

I tuck my disappointment behind a sincere smile. "Yes, sir. Thank you."

Mr. Johnson reaches for my hand, giving it a reassuring squeeze as he guides me toward the exterior door. "Now, I don't want to keep you, and this lobby sure ain't going to clean itself. But I expect to see you again, real soon. And that offer still stands. The missus would love to have the one and only Miss Louisa Wilson at her home for dinner. You just let me know a suitable time."

I press my back against the cool door. "I certainly will. My mouth is already watering at the thought of Mrs. Johnson's biscuits."

As I stroll away from the theatre, Mr. Johnson waves at me from the open door. "You have yourself a blessed day, now."

"Goodbye." Even though my hopes of being discovered by Mr. Fielding have permanently disintegrated, my heart is warmed by the friendship I've found in Mr. Johnson. I wave a final farewell over my shoulder and head toward the audition and the new production waiting for me.

I arrive at the audition with twenty minutes to spare. A large notice board points me to the room where auditions are taking place. The door's hinges squeal softly as I pull on the handle and step into the room. Taking a seat in a chair positioned against the far wall, I scan the small gathering of actors and actresses.

The empty, elevated stage positioned at the front of the room is basic in design. Having joined Thomas' cast after auditions had taken place, the only location I knew was the theatre. It hadn't occurred to me that auditions for professional productions wouldn't usually happen within the grandeur of a theatre.

A bustle of activity at the door catches my attention. A gaggle of girls, presumably auditioning for a role in the play, chirp like birds as they survey the room. With a nod of one's head, all four march with confidence in my direction, smiles pasted on glossed lips. I am about to uncross my legs to allow them room to pass when the leader of the group leans toward me.

"Are these seats taken?"

"Not at all." I gesture to the vacant seats on either side of me.

Swishing her long blond hair over one shoulder, the petite but clearly self-assured girl sits down beside me while instructing her companions to do the same. "Thanks. I assumed you were here for the lead female role. This director prefers for us to sit near one another while we wait to be called. It's easier to save him the hassle of asking us to gather in our sets." A roll of her eyes tells me she finds this to be an unnecessary quirk. "You wouldn't believe how much time we waste as people try to organize themselves."

Titling my head to one side, I ask, "How did you know which part I was here for?"

"You're a dead ringer for the part." She extends a hand. "I'm Ana, and this here is Claire, Marie, and Helen."

I lean forward to greet the others. "Nice to meet you. I'm Louisa."

"You look familiar. Have I seen you around before?" Ana fiddles with her handbag, then tucks it discreetly under her chair.

A bubble of nerves rises within me, reminding me of how unfamiliar I am with this process. "I've recently moved into the city. This is the first opportunity I've had to audition."

The girl named Marie leans forward, an accusatory finger pointed in my direction. "Wait a minute. Didn't you play Mrs. Craig in *Craig's Wife*?"

I bite my bottom lip, unsure of whether a compliment or a criticism is heading my way. "I did."

"I knew I'd seen you somewhere before," Ana's lips curve into a smile. "Heck of a first role. I am assuming it was your first leading role."

"Yes, in a production of that size, that's right." I fold my hands in my lap, feeling the scrutiny of their eyes upon me. With my Hollywood prospects having taken a blow with the news of Mr. Fielding's death, I feel the urge to redeem myself by winning the lead role of this play. I have no idea what I am up against, but I am eager to prove myself.

I think back on Thomas' directorial notes, reminding myself to project my voice, regardless of how many people are in the audience. I remember his continual reminders to find something useful to do with my hands, even if it is simply being comfortable having them rest at my sides. His attention to detail pushed me to be better. I only hope I don't let him down.

Ana leans in. "I have to tell you, I saw you perform in *Craig's Wife*. You were stunning."

"Thank you. You are kind." Though technically my competition in this instant, I suspect that, if given the chance, Ana and I could become fast friends.

Our conversation ends abruptly as the director enters the room, striding toward the stage with pages of notes fluttering in his hand. Close on his heels is a young woman, practically glowing with a fresh face and bouncing brunette curls.

"Oh geez, we might as well pack up and head home now, ladies." Ana's words are delivered in a low mumble laced with disappointment.

"Pardon?" I look from her to the new girl. "Why would we leave before the audition?"

Ana's head tilts in the girl's direction. "That there is Eve Dumont, but we like to call her Daddy's Girl. Her father is in the entertainment business, and his connections seem to secure every single role she wants." Ana shrugs in defeat. "Looks like she has set her sights on this one. Well, what are you going to do? Can't win them all."

Ana and her friends all stand at the same time. "So, you are going to leave? Without auditioning?" My eyebrows knit together.

Tugging her handbag from beneath her vacated chair, Ana says, "Yeah. In this business, it all comes down to who you know. Sometimes you get lucky and nobody in the room knows anybody." She winks mischievously. "Then the audition becomes about talent. That happens less often than you'd think." Waving for the other girls to go ahead, Ana meets my eyes once more. "It was nice meeting you, Louisa."

Stunned by the actresses' quick departure, I consider my options and stand to follow them, but the director is calling the room to order. Not wanting to cause a scene, I take my seat again.

CHAPTER 6

SATURDAY, DECEMBER 10, 1927

lara

A gull screeches from beyond the closed bedroom window. Seldom do I find myself crawling out of bed after the sun has risen. Then again, I think as I draw the bedroom curtain back to reveal the day, the sun must have decided to sleep late too. The grey beyond the window causes me to wrap my housecoat tighter around my shoulders. Craning my neck, I look toward the sky. The clouds threaten rain, sleet, or perhaps even the city's first snowfall of the season.

Stifling a yawn, I pad to the kitchen and put the kettle on for tea. A note on the counter tells me Papa is working an extra shift with his parks crew. Vancouver features many green spaces throughout the city and preparing them for winter takes almost as much time as planting and trimming does come spring. My mind clears as I pour boiling water over tea leaves, the scent wafting up to wake me. Louisa must have left early for her audition, so that means I have a day full of household chores to contend with on my own.

I relish the quiet of the apartment and settle myself on the sofa with my cup of tea. There is no rush to get started, so I decide a slow start to the morning is precisely what I need to recover from the workweek. I wouldn't have thought an evening at the theatre would be enough to wear me out, but apparently I have become accustomed to the simple life of balancing a full-time work schedule with the tasks at home. Or maybe it is purely this dark, dreary December that has got me dragging my feet.

Louisa has left a pile of her movie magazines on the floor beside the sofa. Placing my cup of tea on the table, I reach for the glossy cover on top and flip through the pages. I can see the allure of the glitz and glamour. There is a sense of escape with each turned page, as smiling faces in vibrant gowns and top hats make me wonder if these actors' lives are truly this dazzling.

I pick up my teacup and alternate between small sips and page flips, the morning's obligations settling somewhere in the back of my mind. Teacup raised to my lips, my hand shakes and the splash of hot liquid startles me. An image of an older man kissing the hand of a young woman appears in front of me. In bold, bright colours, the advertisement turns my stomach, and the tea suddenly feels like a bad idea.

Returning the cup to the table, I take a closer look at the advertisement for soda pop. The advertised product doesn't offend my senses in any way. I read the words, trying to determine what has caused such a heart-jumping reaction in me. The advert is quite tame in nature, and the woman pictured shows far less skin than others in the same magazine.

I am about to blame my response on sleeping too late when the pictured man's beady eyes elicit another punch to my empty stomach. The way his flushed cheeks set off the gleam in his bright blue eyes sends an unsettling shiver down my spine. Without words to convince me of his intentions, all I see is an uncomfortable situation for the young woman.

My mind flashes back to my encounter with Mr. Barnes. I toss the magazine to the pile on the floor and stand with as much assuredness as I can muster. Don't be so silly, I tell myself as I empty my tea down the kitchen drain. The man was only being friendly and appreciative of my service.

Deciding that having food in my stomach is a sensible plan, I make a late breakfast of toast and eggs, determined to push any thoughts of Mr. Barnes from my mind. By the time I've finished breakfast, I have a task list written on a piece of paper and am eager to tackle the day.

Even after scrubbing the week's laundry, my thoughts are still as saturated as my hands. The more I consider Mr. Barnes' words, the deeper my spiral of uncertainty swirls. His parting comments play on repeat through my mind. *I will be back in town next week. I look forward to getting to know you better then.*

The damp winter weather forces me to put each piece of clothing through the wringer twice, which is, thankfully, physically exhausting and provides an outlet for my unease. I place the drying rack near the kitchen, butted up against our dining table. The apartment's compact size is a blessing and a curse. The small space will allow the warmth from the bread baking in the oven to speed the drying of clothes, but the position of the drying rack means I will be bumping into it for the remainder of the day.

The more I think about my encounter with Mr. Barnes, the more questions I have. Why in the world would a hotel guest need to get to know me better? As Hamilton maids, we are trained to disappear into the woodwork. Becoming invisible is part of the job and, when done well, is said to make a guest's stay that much more pleasant. I'm not sure why Mr. Barnes seems to want the exact opposite. All I am certain of is that if I want any chance of being awarded the holiday bonus of a week's salary, then I must ensure Mr. Barnes' stay at The Hamilton is precisely to his liking.

Though I know I must persevere in being the best eighth-floor maid I can possibly be, I can't help but sense something is amiss when it comes to Mr. Barnes. It is unusual for a guest to stay at the hotel more often than once every few months, and it certainly isn't typical for anyone travelling by train to return to Vancouver in such a short period of time.

I attempt to shake the troubling thought from my mind with a sharp jerk of my head. Louisa has told me on more than one occasion that my tendency to overthink things will not serve me well. Maybe she is right.

Hanging the last of Louisa's dresses on the drying rack, I consider how to best put my worries aside and do as an eighth-floor maid is expected. I check the time on my watch; the scent of the baking bread informs me it is ready to be pulled from the oven. I leave the oven door ajar to warm the apartment a degree or two more and relish the whoosh of hot air as it rises toward me. With the bread cooling and the hand-crank washer tucked in the closet, I try to distract myself with the mail that has gathered over the week.

A Spencer's holiday booklet featuring new winter styles for men, women, and children catches my attention. The ten pages full of colourful suits, dresses, shoes, hats, and winter outerwear reminds me of the small booklet Ms. Thompson gave me on my first day of training as an eighth-floor maid. I read through it quickly during my lunch break, vowing to reread the instructions every evening before retiring for bed. I kept the information close, tucked away for safe keeping in the bedroom I share with Louisa.

I leave the remaining mail sitting on the kitchen counter and head to the bedroom. Keen to find answers to my questions, I open my bedside table drawer, where the booklet is stashed, along with my notebook. I sit on my bed and pull them into my lap.

Tucked within the notebook is William's recent letter, handed to me by Ms. Thompson and hidden from Louisa's prying eyes. My fingers grace the envelope, the roughly torn edges leaving little question of my eagerness to hear from him. A pang of guilt grips me, knowing I have yet to reply. Between the announcement in his letter, his telephone call, and the growing awareness that our friendship may be tottering on the edge of something more, I have yet to find the right words to respond.

Despite my desire to read his words again, I place William's letter beside me on the bed and turn my attention to the booklet of instructions. With only twelve pages, the booklet is direct in nature. I can feel Mr. Olson's input in the wording of the policies, which assures me of their reliability, as I scan the final page of dos and don'ts for an eighth-floor maid.

1. Tidy uniforms and spotless aprons are required while tending to guest suites.

2. *Cleaning carts are to be kept out of sight and are never to be left unattended in the hallway. Keep your cart with you inside the suite, and store it in its designated cupboard when not in use.*
   3. *Hotel guests desire privacy. Do not assume a guest has vacated a suite. Always knock and announce yourself three times prior to entering a suite.*
   4. *An eighth-floor maid must be courteous and attentive to their guests' needs at all times. Each guest's experience is of the utmost importance and should be at the forefront of your mind.*

The list goes on, but the fourth item mentioned clears up any uncertainty about my duties. As a maid, I am to ensure a guest's needs are met at all times. My job is to put Mr. Barnes' needs first while he is a guest at The Hamilton.

With the decision made for me, I tuck the notebook back into the booklet. William's letter calls to me as though the man himself is standing before me, and I find myself unable to turn away from his attention.

The crisp page, filled with writing in William's hand, slides with ease from its cream-coloured envelope. My fingers grace the slightly raised edge of his barrister's company logo printed at the top of the page. I knew he was a lawyer from his previous letters, but this correspondence is the first I've received on formal letterhead. I question briefly whether the formality of the stationary contributed to the careful consideration I am giving his invitation.

Before William, no gentleman had ever paid me such attention. I am only seventeen, after all, but I also lack awareness of such things. In person, he is disarming and genuine and quite accustomed to putting others at ease. His manner may come from the seven years he has lived beyond my own, or perhaps from a career that requires such confidence. Either way, I find everything about William both exhilarating and terrifying.

I scan the few paragraphs of his straight cursive script, his tidy and assured hand only furthering the directness of the words written there.

Dear Clara,

I hope by this time, you will permit me to call you by your first name. If not, perhaps I have misinterpreted our previous communication. If that is the case, simply disregard the rest of this letter to save me from embarrassing myself.

At the risk of appearing too forward, I wanted to inform you that I will be visiting Vancouver over the holiday season. I will be staying at The Hotel Hamilton at the request of Mr. Olson, whom you should know is a long-time family friend. Though I am certain we will bump into one another at the hotel, the reason for my letter is twofold.

Though I am coming to celebrate the holidays with my sister, spending time with you is at the top of my list. I did not wish my arrival there to catch you unaware or to be misinterpreted. Clara, seeing you was the first thing that came to mind when my sister suggested the visit.

If you will allow me, it would be my great honour to invite you to dinner while I am in the city. I expect to be in Vancouver no later than the twenty-third, but if I can secure earlier travel arrangements, I am eager to do so, if only for the chance to spend more time with you.

I am looking forward to seeing you.
Yours sincerely,
William

Folding the letter and tucking it within the envelope, I consider his words. He surely sent the letter before telephoning last Sunday to wish me well for my first day on the eighth floor, yet he didn't mention his impending visit. I suppose even the dashing and self-assured William Thompson may be a tad shy when it comes to a dinner invitation.

    I am unable to suppress the smile that seems determined to lift my cheeks at the mere thought of seeing him again so soon. I contemplate returning his letter with one of my own, but I find myself in unfamiliar territory, uncertain of so many things when it comes to William Thompson.

CHAPTER 7

SATURDAY, DECEMBER 10, 1927

ouisa

Eve Dumont exchanges a few words with the actresses vacating the audition before setting her sights on me. A pleasant expression that appears forced stretches across her pretty face as she walks in my direction.

"Hello." Without any pretense, she settles herself in the chair beside me. "I'm Eve."

"Louisa." I offer a tight smile before returning my attention to my hands folded in my lap.

"Attention, everyone. Can I get your attention, please?" The director steps onto the raised stage and peers over spectacles sitting low on his nose. "Thank you all for coming to the audition for *All Souls' Eve*. I have a few notes, and then we will get underway."

As the director outlines the events of the afternoon, I mull over the idea that the girl seated beside me will be handed the role simply because of her father. The irony is not lost on me. Earlier today, I too was seeking success via another's influence. Perhaps that is the way of people looking for a step up. I release a slow breath and ask myself, Should I have left when I had the chance?

"All those prepared to read for the double role of Alice Heath and Nora O'Hallahan, please stand." At the director's request, I stand to be counted. Eve does the same. "Only two of you?" The director's hand scratches the scruff on his chin. "I suppose the lead is a tall order."

Without missing a beat, Eve speaks up. "Perhaps it is because I am destined for the role, given my name."

Appearing amused, the director waves a hand in her direction. "And what name would that be?"

"Eve. Eve Dumont." A flirtatious lift of her shoulders highlights her delivery. "Just like the play's name, *All Souls' Eve*." She laughs at her own joke and quickly covers a put-upon shy smile with the tips of her fingers.

This girl does know how to act, I think to myself as the director motions for us to return to our seats. Eve tosses me a sideways glance that feels like a challenge.

Thirty minutes passes as the director sorts the applicants by role. Ana was right; this need to have everyone grouped by character is a waste of time.

Finally, those present are called to the stage one by one. I watch the auditions unfold, marvelling at the variety of choices the actors make in interpreting the same characters. It doesn't take long to spot those who understand the amount of effort it takes to successfully embody another personality. I think back to the many days and nights spent rehearsing. I may not have the right connections for a quick ticket to Hollywood, but surely my talent as an actress will speak for itself on the Vancouver stage. I consider Eve from the corner of my eye. Daddy's girl or not, if she is going to get this role, she will have to work for it.

When the role of Alice Heath is called, Eve goes first, reading from the script with ease. I have to admit that she handles the audition well enough, but her free hand repeatedly stabs the air, making every line feel as if it ends in an exclamation mark.

You must become the character, I remind myself as my turn arrives and I accept the page of script from Eve as she steps down from the stage. I feel a slight advantage at having heard the lines in advance, during her performance. Once on stage, though, the butterflies warn me that success is far from assured.

I begin with an introduction. "My name is Louisa Wilson."

The director angles his head to the left. "As in Thomas Cromwell's recent production of *Craig's Wife?*"

"Yes, that is correct." I lift my gaze to the back of the room and catch the view of Eve Dumont's mouth dropping open in surprise.

"I read your review. Nicely done." His chin dips in admiration, boosting my confidence. "Thank you for coming out, Miss Wilson. Please proceed."

The audition sails by in a three-minute blur. I embrace the character's plight to save the boy and feel the real prick of moisture in the corner of my eyes as the scene escalates with emotion. I don't realize how silent the room has gone until I finish uttering the last line.

A single clap from somewhere to my right turns into several as those present applaud my efforts. I bite the inside of my cheek to prevent the spread of a wide smile.

Eve does an excellent job of ignoring me during the

auditions for the rest of the roles. I can't say I am concerned by her cold shoulder, given I am in a two-person race for the leading role. If the path to Hollywood requires being discovered, then I must continue to put my best foot forward on the theatre's stage. That is the only way I can think of to garner the attention of someone with clout.

"We will take a short break while I make some decisions. Let's resume in fifteen minutes, and then those who aren't required for a second audition will be free to go." The director takes his notes and leaves the room.

Eve and a handful of other actors follow suit. I stand to stretch my legs and am wandering toward the exit, in search of a breath of fresh air, when movement through a half-open door to another room catches my attention.

"Miss Dumont, may I remind you that I am the director of this production? It is my job to ensure the roles are suited to the actor." The director's voice is stern but hushed, causing me to pause mid-stride.

"May I remind you, sir, that my father's influence reaches further than you'll ever know? If you want this play to succeed, then you'll make the right decision. The choice may be up to you, but the guarantee of your play's success is not. Good day, sir."

"Miss Dumont, please." The director is still pleading as the door swings open and Eve appears, catching me motionless in the middle of the hall.

A slow smirk turns her pleasant features sinister. I feel as though a northern wind blows through me as she brushes past.

I should have known. My chin drops to my chest in defeat. Ana and her friends tried to warn me. Eve Dumont can apparently get any part she wants by holding her father's connections over the director's head. I was slow to realize it, but now I know that even my acting ability gives me no influence here.

CHAPTER 8

TUESDAY, DECEMBER 13, 1927

lara

The ornament is heavier than I expect. Perched two rungs up on the ladder, my balance wavers momentarily as I juggle the weighted glass ball in my hand. The hotel lobby's Christmas tree is coming along, with baubles of gold and crimson filling its branches.

Thankfully, George and the other bellboys strung the shimmering lights earlier this morning. Having never had the opportunity to use electric Christmas lights on our tree at home, I doubt I would have had the faintest idea of what to do with the constantly tangled strand. The rest of the decorating is up to Hazel and me, the only two maids without a full roster of rooms to clean on this quiet December afternoon.

Thankful for the reprieve from the usual tasks, I find it easy to let the holiday spirit take hold of me as the hotel transforms with the magic of the season. The scent of pine permeates the room, adding a festive touch against the backdrop of the snow that has finally begun to fall beyond the hotel's windows. Hazel hands me another ornament, this one long and tapered, with a sparkle of gold highlighting its sculpted centre.

"How about the tinsel?" Hazel holds up a fistful of silver strings.

I stifle a laugh as she eagerly pushes the tangled mess in my direction. "Maybe just a few strands at a time. I don't think I can stay upright on this ladder and sort the tinsel at the same time."

We spend the remainder of the afternoon shifting the ladder around the base of the tree as we adorn every vacant branch with decorations. Ms. Thompson keeps an eye on our progress, checking in twice an hour as she bustles around the lobby, hanging wreaths and adding a bright red poinsettia to each table.

I hear the doorman's greeting as a whip of winter wind steals inside. "Good afternoon, Mr. Barnes." The doorman holds open the hotel's large, glass-paned front door, ushering in the guest. "Welcome back to The Hotel Hamilton."

Having taken a break from the ladder, I duck behind the tree's expanse as George rushes to the bellhop's desk to sort Mr. Barnes' luggage. I admonish myself for my high-strung, knee-jerk response at seeing the man again, and I busy my hands with straightening the tree's decorative skirt.

I sneak glances in his direction from between the branches and remind myself of the expectations I must live up to as a Hamilton maid. Waiting at the registration desk for his room key, Mr. Barnes looks past the mahogany arches and into the interior lobby and sitting room. The Christmas tree's lights are sure to draw every guest's attention. I only wish I wouldn't be hiding beneath its boughs when it catches this particular guest's eye.

Hazel returns to the lobby with a square box in hand. "I found it," she announces as she places the box on the fireplace's stone hearth. Lifting the box's lid, her awe is evident. "I've never seen anything so beautiful."

I spot Mr. Barnes as he moves toward the elevator, room key in hand, and decide it is safe to remove myself from hiding. I stand beside Hazel as she lifts the large, glass star from its box. The tree's topper glimmers in the dancing flames of the roaring fire, mesmerizing both of us into silence.

"Now, that's a showstopper." Mr. Barnes' voice booms through the small interior lobby, making me clutch a hand to my chest in surprise.

I swivel to see him a few paces away, hands outstretched with his thumbs touching as he frames the view of Hazel and me, the large star between us. "Right there, ladies. Don't move. That is what we in the business like to call motion-picture magic."

Whether from the heat of the fire or Mr. Barnes' appearance at our side, my cheeks grow warm. I force a polite demeanour. "Mr. Barnes. Welcome back."

"Miss Wilson, it is good to see you again." Mr. Barnes lifts both bushy eyebrows and wiggles them in what I suspect is an attempt at humour. "And who have we here?"

Clearing my throat, I gesture to Hazel. "Forgive me. Mr. Barnes, this is Miss Greenwood."

The man bows gallantly, the girth around his middle covered by the broad rim of his winter hat. "A pleasure to meet you, Miss Greenwood."

On cue, Hazel blushes bright red, delivering a quick curtsy but offering no words.

"Ah, Mr. Barnes." Ms. Thompson's voice cuts through the room. "I was about to call on you. We have a message waiting for you at the front desk. From your—"

"Marvellous." Mr. Barnes cuts off Ms. Thompson with a dismissive wave of his hand. "I was just telling these young ladies what a wonderful job they are doing with the holiday decorations."

Ms. Thompson's polite expression is firmly in place, but I can't help but notice her hands clenching as she nods. "Yes, we are all very excited to celebrate our first holiday season at The Hamilton. Won't you come this way?"

Tipping his head once more—"Ladies."—he follows Ms. Thompson to the registration desk.

I shake off my discomfort and return my attention to the oversized star in Hazel's hands. "We should finish up here. I believe Ms. Thompson has some garland she would like us to string before the day is through."

As I reposition the ladder as close to the tree's base as possible, Hazel hisses in my ear, "Did you hear? He is from Hollywood. A director or something. He must be, with all that film talk. I've never met a real director before."

"Will you hold the ladder?" I etch the impatience from my words, adding "please" as an afterthought.

Hazel, undeterred by my abruptness, places her free hand on the ladder while keeping the star tucked safely against her abdomen with the other.

I climb the first two rungs of the ladder, balancing my weight with each step. A quick glance up the tree tells me that I will need to climb to the sixth rung in order to reach the top. I extend one hand behind me, careful not to rock the ladder. "Can you pass me the star?"

Hazel lets go of the ladder and carefully lifts the tree

topper with both hands, passing it to me before gripping either side of the ladder. "Careful, Clara."

With the star pressed close to my chest, I ready myself to take another step. Then another. By the fifth rung, I am reminding myself not to look down. I tune out the sounds and movements of the hotel lobby, as the distance between me and the floor has grown as far as I am tall. At the sixth ladder rung, I inch my feet outward for added stability before stretching toward the tree's crown. The base of the glass star slides onto the two short boughs standing straight as toy soldiers at the top of the tree.

A wave of relief washes over me as I pull my arm back from the precarious position. "Is it straight?" Not wishing to risk a tumble, I raise my voice instead of turning to address Hazel directly.

"Yes. You can come down now." I feel Hazel's hands grip and steady the ladder at the bottom. "I've got you."

The wood of the ladder is all I see as I move carefully down one rung after another. My palms are damp with sweat, forcing me to pause and wipe them one at a time on my apron.

"You're almost there." Hazel's voice is closer now, providing reassurance, since I've lost count of how many rungs I have yet to descend.

"I've got you, Miss Wilson." I barely register the voice before large hands wrap around my waist, tugging me backwards and causing the ladder to wobble.

"No." My hands slip from the ladder rails and I feel myself falling. I brace myself for an impact, squeezing my eyes shut while curling into myself.

"You are all right now." A man's laboured breathing against my cheek is suffocating. "I've got you."

It takes me a moment to recover myself, my heart

racing to catch up. I stretch my toes, reaching for solid ground, and when I open my eyes, I realize I am in Mr. Barnes' arms.

Seldom do I feel anger rise within me with such force. Who is this man to think he can lay his hands on me? What made him think I needed saving from the ladder I was almost down from? And why is he still holding me in his arms?

"Please, sir. Put me down at once."

When my feet touch the floor, I stumble into Hazel, her face ashen. I worry that I somehow struck her while being pulled from the ladder by Mr. Barnes. Hazel's hands reach out to steady me, pulling me close to her side with a protective sweep of her arm. She may be too timid to utter a word, but Hazel's reaction tells me more than any words could.

Ms. Thompson's frown is pulled tight with astonishment as she rushes toward us. "Miss Wilson, Miss Greenwood, are you all right?"

"We are fine, ma'am." I steal a glance in Mr. Barnes' direction and deliver a quietly pointed observation. "I was fine descending the ladder too."

The man clearly can't help himself. He pounces on the opportunity. "It was quite something, madam. Miss Wilson here was about to take a tumble from this ladder." Mr. Barnes grips the ladder rail, jostling it back and forth animatedly. "Thankfully, I was able to reach her in time and save her from a dastardly fall."

"Oh." Ms. Thompson is seldom at a loss for words, but none come forth as she looks from Mr. Barnes to Hazel and then to me.

Extracting myself from Hazel's firm grasp, I straighten my apron and uniform skirt with stiff movements, pulling taut the fabric that climbed above my knee during the commotion. I catch the matron's watchful eye and deliver a curt nod followed by a restrained shake of my head. Without verbal communication, I've informed her that I am well but that Mr. Barnes' story is far from accurate.

"Well then." Ms. Thompson's shoulders straighten, her matronly demeanour back in place. "Thank you for your assistance, Mr. Barnes. I think we can take it from here." Without waiting for his reply, Ms. Thompson waves George over. "Mr. Baker, please remove the ladder from the lobby and have Mr. Jones help you with these boxes. Let's clear the room so our guests can enjoy the festive decor."

As George collapses the ladder for its return to the basement, Ms. Thompson, noting Mr. Barnes' continued presence, adds to George's list of duties. "Mr. Baker, please have Cookie prepare a plate of sweets for Mr. Barnes. You can deliver them upon your return."

"Madam, that is very kind of you." Mr. Barnes' chest puffs out as though he has been awarded first prize at the county fair.

Though Ms. Thompson's voice has a slight edge to it, she conceals any emotions behind a polite smile. "It is the least we can do for your troubles, sir. Please have a seat. Enjoy the fire and this beautiful tree while you wait."

The matron directs her attention to Hazel and me. "Ladies, if you'll come with me, we have much more to accomplish, and the day is getting on." She turns to Mr. Barnes and nods once. "Thank you again. I hope you will find your stay an enjoyable one." Without another word, she turns on her heel, and we follow close behind her.

The moment we are out of the lobby, standing in the short hallway between Cookie's pastry kitchen and Chef's swinging kitchen door, Ms. Thompson stops abruptly and turns to face us. "Miss Greenwood, will you please let Mr. Olson know the lobby is ready for his inspection? I believe you will find him in his office."

"Yes, ma'am." Hazel's eyes shift to me with a worried glance before she pivots toward the back-of-house corridor.

Ms. Thompson's gaze follows Hazel's back until she is out of sight. "Now, Miss Wilson." Folding her hands together in front of her, she pauses. "I sense that all is not well with Mr. Barnes."

"Everything is fine, ma'am."

The matron's raised eyebrows tell me she doesn't believe me.

"I—I suppose I am not used to such exuberance from a guest, but I understand that I am to put the guest's needs ahead of my own." I square my shoulders to demonstrate my willingness to do so. "I will do what I can to ensure Mr. Barnes' stay is an enjoyable one."

"Miss Wilson, it is clear as day to me that Mr. Barnes has unsettled you, and I can't say that I fault you for feeling a little put out. I witnessed his attempt to rescue you from the ladder, and I dare say you were perfectly safe climbing down on your own. I've seen his sort before, and all I can gather is that he is accustomed to having all eyes on him." Ms. Thompson waves a hand. "Perhaps it is the Hollywood way."

Letting out a slow exhale, she lifts a hand to her forehead and begins pacing the short hallway. "The thing is, Miss Wilson, Mr. Barnes is well-regarded by Mr. Hamilton, or so I am told. Though I've no idea how they are acquainted, given that they appear to have nothing in common, I've been instructed to ensure Mr. Barnes' frequent stays at the hotel receive the utmost care and attention."

"Yes, ma'am."

"I'm afraid when it comes to Mr. Barnes, we will need to do a little more putting our heads down and simply getting on with it."

"Yes, ma'am. I understand."

"Very well, Miss Wilson. I will let you get back to the eighth floor. Thank you for helping with the decorations. I am quite sure they will be enjoyed by all who visit us this holiday season."

"Thank you, ma'am."

Ms. Thompson's brow softens. "Why don't you spend the remaining hour restocking the supplies in the linen cupboard? I am certain the evening maids would appreciate the assistance."

I dip my chin in acknowledgement, suspecting the matron's instruction is twofold, since it will provide me a quiet hour to collect myself.

George bustles into the hallway, stopping short when he spots us. "Sorry to intrude. I am fetching the sweets for Mr. Barnes."

"Yes, of course, Mr. Baker." Ms. Thompson steps aside to allow George room to pass into Cookie's pastry kitchen.

"Thank you, ma'am." I offer a final curtsy and turn toward the corridor and the stairwell beyond.

CHAPTER 9

WEDNESDAY, DECEMBER 14, 1927

Louisa

I've been in a mood since Saturday's audition. My sour disposition became even more apparent with this morning's telephone call. The director's assistant called moments before we stepped out the door to inform me that, though the decision had been difficult, the director has cast Miss Eve Dumont as the female lead for the production of *All Soul's Eve*.

"He didn't even give me the courtesy of telling me himself. Can you believe it?" I huff, creating clouds of frost-tinged air as we trek toward the hotel. Tugging my coat tight with one hand, I realize Clara hasn't uttered a word all morning. I feel a twinge of remorse. These past few days, I've done little except ruminate on and incessantly recount the audition. Even if she had something to offer, I haven't exactly given her the space to do so. "Is something wrong?"

She looks up from the sidewalk her eyes have been glued to. "Why do you ask?"

Her deflection of my question does not go unnoticed, but I take the hint and let it be. I've got enough on my mind without spending hours trying to pry a story from my reluctant-to-share sister. A gust of wind has us ducking our toque-covered heads together as we lean forward into the flurry of snowflakes.

Back to reality, I think glumly as we push through the biting temperatures. I am disappointed the play didn't pan out. It would have been a nice accolade to add to my accomplishments, in addition to being a happy distraction from my position at the hotel, especially since being discovered for Hollywood seems more out of reach than I first imagined. Every magazine article I read stated the same road to success. So and so was discovered by this Hollywood person or that Hollywood connection. Nowhere did I read that an actress made the decision to become a Hollywood starlet and then proceeded to become one.

"Darn this weather. Whoever said snow in December is idyllic surely didn't live in a city where it actually snows."

Clara's lips curve into a smile at my comment. I tug her arm, drawing her close as we cross the street toward The Hamilton.

By the time we round the corner into the shelter of the alley behind the hotel, I am making a concerted effort to locate a better mood for the day ahead. With the problem of how to get to Hollywood at the forefront of my mind, I lean into the knowledge that a day spent scrubbing is equal to a day spent considering my options. I tug open the door of the back entrance and stop Clara with a gloved hand. "Thanks for listening. I know I've been a bit of a bear these past few days."

Clara steps through the hotel's back entrance, an unconcealed smirk upon her lips. "Really? I hadn't noticed."

I am about to add a sarcastic comment of my own when I notice young ears in our midst.

"Well, hello there, Masao," Clara coos as she removes her hat and gloves while stamping her feet on the mat. "What brings you out in this weather?"

Cookie appears from the pastry kitchen, a genuine smile adding a shine to her already pink cheeks. "Ah, he's got a treat for you, he does."

I bend at the waist to greet our friend and ruffle his jet-black hair. "What sort of treat? Did you grow us an apple tree in the last week?" I wink in jest, knowing the boy's biggest ambition is to grow an apple tree from a seed as a gift for his grandmother.

A full belly laugh erupts from the boy. "Miss Louisa, I can't grow an apple tree in winter."

Cookie encourages him from behind. "Go on, then. Show them what you've got."

Masao pulls from his jacket pocket two tiny rounds wrapped in delicate green paper. "This is a Japanese mandarin orange. We give them to our friends in December to say thank you for being kind to us." Masao's words, though clearly scripted by his mother, speak to the truth of our friendship with the boy.

He places an orange in my hand, then one in Clara's. As I unwrap the tissue paper, the most perfectly shaped little orange peeks up at me.

"Masao, what a lovely gift. Thank you."

The boy beams as Cookie places an arm around his shoulders. "Wait until you taste them. There is nothing better than a Japanese mandarin at Christmastime."

Cookie eyes the clock on the wall. "Ms. Thompson knows Masao was waiting for you. I took him down to her office so he could deliver oranges to her and Mr. Olson, but time is getting on."

I follow Cookie's second glance at the clock and realize the lateness of the hour. Turning to Masao, I thank him again for the special gift and promise to savour it.

Waving a quick goodbye, I inhale the warm, sweet, festive concoction Cookie is surely responsible for as we move swiftly down the stairs to the locker room.

I say goodbye to Clara on the fifth floor, wishing her a pleasant day as she makes her way to the eighth. I sneak into the roll-call line just in time to hear Ms. Thompson call my name.

"Miss Wilson, I want to introduce you to our newest maid."

The girl from The New Orpheum Theatre steps forward at Ms. Thompson's urging.

"Gwen?" My surprise must be plastered across my face.

"That's right, Miss Wilson. I didn't realize you two knew each other." Ms. Thompson tilts her head in question.

"Not really, ma'am. We only met briefly at the new theatre last week." I glance in Gwen's direction, expecting to see a bashful reaction to my frank words, but she gives nothing away, wearing only a placating expression.

"I see. Well then, I am sure you won't mind showing Miss Russell how we do things here on the fifth floor?"

"I'd be happy to, ma'am."

Ms. Thompson directs her attention to Gwen. "Miss Wilson will be your guide for the remainder of the week. You will shadow her and learn from her." Ms. Thompson examines the papers on her clipboard. "You will do well to follow Miss Wilson's every lead. She is one of our most accomplished maids, having been with the hotel since its opening."

Gwen meets Ms. Thompson's eyes with a serious "Yes, ma'am."

Though I am certain Ms. Thompson meant well by her compliment, hearing the words aloud only fuels my desire to find a way toward the future I am dreaming of.

As the roll-call line scatters, with maids heading off to tackle their duties, I direct Gwen toward the linen cupboard where my cleaning cart is waiting.

"So, what brings you to The Hamilton?" I keep my tone light, despite being keen to learn the reason behind the girl's appearance here.

Gwen has the good sense to blush at my question, making me wonder if her reactions are more calculated than I first assumed. Perhaps she isn't the doe-eyed girl I pegged her as.

"You inspired me."

"Me?" I feel my left eyebrow lift toward my hairline.

"Yes, you." Gwen giggles and I feel myself warm to her once more. "When you said that we all have to start somewhere. I figured if The Hotel Hamilton is good enough for Louisa Wilson, then surely it is a good place for me to start too."

I gesture toward the linen cupboard, and we enter the small space. "You know the hotel has nothing to do with my theatre work? I work hard both on the stage and here in the hotel, and let me tell you, tacking a four-hour rehearsal to the end of work hours makes for a long day."

"I'm not afraid of a little hard work." Gwen's angelic expression does little to conceal the disparaging nature of her comment.

I bite my tongue and hold back further mention of the sacrifices I make in order to pursue a career on the stage: little sleep, no days off for weeks on end, and the immense and continual feeling of being unable to do either job well enough.

I change tactics and nudge her back toward her corner. "I thought your father didn't approve of a life in the theatre."

Gwen tilts her head to the side and smiles sweetly without saying a word.

Despite our somewhat stilted start, the morning goes by relatively well. Gwen follows close on my heels as we move from one guest room to the next. She is a quick study, and I am relieved to see the speed with which she learns. Even the bedding's hospital corners are no match for her dogged determination.

As the lunch hour arrives, I give Gwen a tour of the rest of the fifth floor before we retrieve our lunches from the locker room. I show her to the lunchroom and introduce her properly to the other fifth-floor maids, and they welcome her while accosting her with questions about The Orpheum's grand-opening celebration. Did she meet Phylis Haver in person? What is it like in the ladies' retiring room? Does she have a favourite act?

Gwen glows in the flurry of questions and attention, and I scan the room for Clara. I am not surprised when I don't spot her. Over the past few days, I've learned that the eighth-floor maids seldom eat lunch until the bustle of the morning is behind them, their duties being far more involved than those of the lower-floor maids.

Biting into my ham sandwich, the mustard Clara slathered on the bread hits my tongue with a delightful tang. Rosemary leans toward the centre of the table, a sure sign she is about to spill some gossip.

Her voice a touch above a whisper, Rosemary asks, "Did you hear about the Hollywood director who is staying on the eighth floor?"

My head snaps up. "What Hollywood director? Clara hasn't said anything about him." As the words tumble out, I am reminded that Clara hasn't said much of anything these past few days.

Rosemary leans in a little further. "Apparently this is his second stay in less than a week. My friend at the bellhop's desk overheard Mr. Olson saying Mr. Barnes is scheduled to stay on and off right through to the new year. Can you believe it? Our very own celebrity roaming these halls."

The girls chatter on as an idea begins to take shape in the corner of my mind. Maybe it is true that when one door closes, another is opened. The trick is to pay attention to the door that has opened in front of you.

One of the other maids teases Rosemary about the boy she has yet to name. "So, who's your friend at the bellhop's desk?"

A chorus of giggles erupts and I smile at the playful banter throughout the rest of the lunch break, but as we filter out to continue the workday, I know exactly what I have to do. I must find a way to meet this Mr. Barnes. I'd be crazy not to take advantage of an opportunity like this. Maybe he is looking for a fresh face to whisk back to Hollywood.

"They are a lively bunch." Gwen, whom I almost forgot I was responsible for, interrupts my daydream as we climb the stairs to the fifth floor. "Friendly, but lively."

"You'll get used to the banter. Don't worry." I pat her shoulder. "Though I do suggest you keep anything you don't wish to be shared throughout the hotel close to your heart."

She nods in understanding, but her pursed lips tell me she has something more to ask.

"Was there something else?" I pause at the top of the fifth-floor landing, giving the girl time to collect her thoughts as the other maids file past.

"I was wondering about the director." Her gaze falls to the cement landing, shyness emanating from her like a July heatwave. "You know, with you being a famous actress and all, I thought you might be able to introduce me to him."

I almost laugh at what I can only assume is her put-upon antics. I tilt my chin up and look down at her with scrutinizing eyes. So this little minx does know her way around a manipulative scheme. Bold for certain, but is she smart enough to know the difference between a fanciful girlhood dream and the reality of what it takes to succeed as an actress? Or for that matter, what it takes to succeed as a maid here at the hotel? I'll have to keep my eye on her.

"I wouldn't get your hopes up. We fifth-floor maids stay on the fifth floor. Ms. Thompson might show you the door if you were caught snooping around where you aren't permitted."

"Oh, I didn't mean to— Well, never mind. I wouldn't know what to say to a director from Hollywood, anyway." Gwen shrugs off her blunder and tugs open the stairwell door, checking for guests, as I instructed, before stepping onto the fifth floor.

I heed my own warning as I follow Gwen into the hall. Doing my best to appear subdued, I organize our next task of the day. I wait until we are separated by a wall before I invite the thrill of excitement to take over. I can hardly believe the solution to my Hollywood problem lies a few floors above me. For months, I've hoped my position at the hotel would result in introductions to celebrities, but The Hamilton hasn't had movie stars and musicians roaming its corridors like The Hotel Georgia.

I put Gwen in charge of scrubbing the bathtub so I can linger in my thoughts, mindlessly waving the feather duster as I consider the options that lie before me.

Running into an eighth-floor guest isn't as easy as one might think. They spend hours lazing about in their suites, with coffee service and daily newspapers being delivered to their rooms. Not to mention my uniform doesn't look anything like Clara's eighth-floor one.

I shake the obstacles from my mind. If I am going to succeed as a Hollywood actress, I will need to be much more brazen, less like a flatterer and more like the professional actress I am. Heaven knows the man must be accosted on a daily basis by those with little talent but plenty of dreams.

Thankful for my experience on the stage and my recent favourable reviews, I am confident my resume is enough to woo the man into at least listening to what I have to offer. All I have to do now is create an opportunity for us to meet.

I hear the final gurgle of water being drained from the bathtub. By the time Gwen appears in the bedroom, ready to help me make the bed, I have talked myself around the hurdles my plan involves. I am an actress, after all. If I have to act my way into a once-in-a-lifetime chance to secure my future in Hollywood, then that is precisely what I will do.

Catching a glimpse of Gwen's face, deep in concentration as she dresses a pillow with its case, I feel a twinge of guilt at having misled the girl. But there is something untrustworthy about her, and besides, she has freely admitted that she has no experience when it comes to the stage.

I weigh the challenges of the situation and decide Gwen's lack of acting chops are reason enough to keep her hopes at ground level when it comes to our Hollywood guest. I will take some of my own advice and keep my plans regarding Mr. Barnes close to my heart.

CHAPTER 10

WEDNESDAY, DECEMBER 14, 1927

lara

My heart sinks at seeing my name scrawled on the guest room roster list, in Ms. Thompson's cursive script, next to suite 815. After yesterday's events, I am not at all inclined to see Mr. Barnes, let alone tend to his suite. But as Ms. Thompson said, I must put my head down and simply get on with it. As Ms. Thompson promised, she has added a second suite, 812, to my responsibilities. I have little time to waste if I am to show the matron I am capable of the workload.

"Miss Wilson, are you feeling well enough? After yesterday's tumble, I mean." Miss Smythe stands at the threshold of the expansive supply closet, genuine concern written on her face. "I was going to telephone you last night, but it was my father's birthday, you see, and there was a cake and—"

"I am quite well." My lips twist in contemplation before

adding, "And I didn't tumble. I was perfectly safe descending the ladder." I stifle an exasperated sigh and soften my expression. "I hope you enjoyed your father's celebration."

"Oh, I thought…" Miss Smythe's eyes leave mine to scan the shelves lined with soaps, lotions, and towels. "Mr. Barnes has quite the knack for storytelling, it seems."

My hand pauses as I reach for a stack of towels, my head tilting in question. "Go on."

"I overheard him regaling several of the other maids yesterday afternoon. He spoke of rescuing you from a dire situation." Miss Smythe's cheeks colour in what I assume is a rush of embarrassment for me. "He said you were standing at the top of the ladder and you fell backwards." She examines the floor for a moment before continuing. "He said that he saved you."

I am unable to contain my humourless laugh. "Hardly. I was a step or two from the ground when he lunged forward and grabbed me around the waist. I was in no need of rescuing. Honestly, the man does have a vivid imagination."

"I should not have assumed." Miss Smythe steps forward and squeezes my shoulders with both hands. "I am relieved to know you are fine."

"You aren't the only one making assumptions, it seems." I peek over her shoulder to ensure our privacy. "Rebecca, can I ask you something?"

"Of course."

"Have you ever had a guest make you uncomfortable? No, that isn't the right word. I mean, I am not sure how to interpret Mr. Barnes." I clasp my hands in front of my apron.

My friend offers an understanding smile. "He is an attention seeker, that is for certain. I've not seen another guest of the eighth floor out and about in the hall as often as he is. If that answers your question."

Always discreet, Miss Smythe affirms my suspicions about Mr. Barnes' behaviour being unusual. "Thank you. I wanted to be sure I wasn't imagining something that wasn't there."

"Not at all, Miss Wilson. I expect he is a handful. At least he appears to be a jovial handful."

With Rebecca's words to settle my nerves, I gather my cleaning cart and head toward suite 815. Three knocks on the door while announcing my presence go unanswered. Thankful for small mercies, I use my master key and enter the suite, eager to set it straight and move on to the second suite requiring my attention today.

Two hours later, I am sliding the completed checklist back into its slot on my cleaning cart and preparing to vacate the suite when the door opens with a whoosh. I startle at the sudden intrusion, my hands gripping the cart's handle.

Mr. Barnes saunters into the living area, his winter coat draped over one arm. "Miss Wilson," he bellows, making me wonder if he is hard of hearing or simply a fan of listening to himself speak.

"Good day, Mr. Barnes. I'm all done here. I'll leave you to enjoy the suite." I offer a polite nod and lean into the cleaning cart in an effort to nudge it forward on the thick carpet.

"I am delighted to see you up and about. You had me worried after yesterday's fall." The man steps forward, hanging his coat and hat on the rack near the writing desk. "I am so glad I was nearby and able to be of service."

I clear my throat, preparing to respond, but I find my desire to set him straight to be overruled by my duty to follow hotel protocol. "I am fine. Thank you, sir." I lean into the cart again, but as soon as the wheels inch forward, Mr. Barnes steps in its path.

The slight tilt of his head unsettles me, and I feel his eyes as they travel the length of me. Flustered and hardly acquainted with such overt attention, my hands grow clammy atop the cart's handle.

"You know, Miss Wilson, I think I could help you with many things. I am a man of the world, you know." He steps around the cleaning cart, and on instinct, I shrink back. "I'm considered quite a powerful man in many circles. I could show you things you've never imagined."

"Thank you, sir." The words stumble from my lips as my eyes fixate on the closed door that lies between me and the eighth-floor hallway. "I wouldn't wish to burden you."

"It's no trouble." Mr. Barnes places a single finger on my bent elbow and slides it down the length of my bare forearm. "No trouble at all, Miss Wilson."

My head spins from the view of the door, and I force myself to meet his beady eyes. "Mr. Barnes." My voice wavers as I reposition my hand on the cart, intending to move his finger away from my arm. "Your suite is tidied and ready for you to enjoy."

I thrust the cleaning cart forward and, without looking back, pull open the suite's door. I step into the quiet and presumed safety of the hall.

"I'm sure we'll see one another soon, Miss Wilson." His pointed words are muffled by the closing door.

A droplet of sweat trickles down my spine, while a surge of pride courses up it. I am even more grateful for the guidance provided by the hotel's management. In a few short sentences, the maid's booklet directed me in dealing with a challenging situation while maintaining my professional conduct.

I run through the checklist in my mind. I was courteous and attentive to my guest's needs. Mr. Barnes' suite was properly cleaned and stocked. I did not interrupt the enjoyment of his stay and tended to his suite's needs at the most convenient time for him. Yes, I tell myself, I am being the best eighth-floor maid I can be. Surely this type of attentiveness will keep me in the running for the holiday bonus.

With my movements fuelled by adrenaline, my cleaning cart's wheels glide smoothly over the thick carpet. I don't stop moving until I am sequestered in the solitude of the brightly lit supply cupboard. Closing the door behind me, my assuredness with the way I handled the interaction falters. I let out a wobbly breath and lean my back against the wall to steady myself. Within moments, my short-lived burst of energy subsides and I feel my legs give out, shaking as I slide down the wall and come to a seated position on the floor.

I force myself to take slow, deep breaths. Being brave does not come naturally to me, and though I am acutely aware of my current frazzled state, I know I am able to do what is necessary in the moment.

I contemplate my next steps. I need to prove that I am capable of doing my job well. Being cast out of the running for the holiday bonus is not an option. With Louisa's sights now set on California, the bonus would be both a financial cushion and proof for my sister and myself that I am capable of taking care of things on my own.

Besides, I remind myself, Ms. Thompson was clear enough in her directive. Mr. Barnes is to be treated with the utmost care and attention.

Mr. Olson's words about shenanigans ring in my ears, reminding me of the consequences for untoward behaviour. Though I was certainly not flirting with a hotel guest, I am uncertain of how it might appear if Mr. Barnes is called to discuss the matter. What might a powerful man, who is seldom at a loss for words, say when backed into a corner? That is a risk I am unwilling to take.

I inhale another steadying breath. My job includes behaving in accordance with the hotel rules. When it comes to Mr. Barnes, I'll simply have to be vigilant and do my best to ensure I stay on the right side of hotel policy.

Checking my watch, I realize the eighth-floor lunch hour is upon us. The girls will be coming back shortly to park their cleaning carts and gather for the midday meal. Using my hands, I push myself up off the floor and straighten my uniform, determined to continue my day as though nothing has happened. With any luck, Mr. Barnes will have taken my quick exit as a clear indication that I am not interested in being anything other than his suite's maid.

CHAPTER 11

WEDNESDAY, DECEMBER 14, 1927

ouisa

By mid-afternoon, Gwen seems to have broken free of her shell. The girl may not have any experience when it comes to the stage, but she certainly has the lungs to carry on a conversation non-stop for several hours. A headache is brewing at the back of my skull as she prattles on, barely pausing for breath.

In the middle of positioning a sheet atop a bed, I stop and interrupt her incessant chatter. "Do you sing?"

"Sing?" The girl's large round eyes peer up at me from behind the bedsheet she's raised in the air, and I instantly regret my less-than-becoming thoughts. "No, I don't sing. Not well, anyway."

"Too bad. You have lungs that are well-suited to opera."

A hesitant "thank you" is her only response. Surmising I have not offended the girl with my interruption of her monologue, I relish the quiet, if only for a few moments.

With another room ready for its occupants, we push the cleaning cart to the sixth and final room of the day.

"May I ask you something, Miss Wilson?" Gwen's voice is steady, if a tad subdued.

"Please, call me Louisa. When guests aren't about, that is." A shrug of my shoulders indicates for her to continue. What's another question, I think as I move about the room, preparing it for vacuuming.

"Do you ever worry about being rejected?" Gwen strips the bedding, avoiding my gaze. "I mean, when you audition for a role. Are you afraid you won't be chosen?"

My heart softens for the girl. In that one question, I can feel her desire for something currently beyond her reach, and I understand. More than she probably realizes. All I can assume is today's talk of the Hollywood director has both inspired and terrified her. If I had to guess, I would say she is a year or two younger than me in age, but perhaps more in terms of life experience. I suspect hers has been a sheltered existence.

"Listen, Gwen. The stage isn't meant for everyone, but anyone who craves a presence on it must come to terms with the reality that you won't be everyone's pick. You won't be right for every role. And even if you are chosen, every actress in every role has a ton of hard work and obstacles to overcome. It isn't as easy as you might think. I know it all looks spectacular and glamourous from a seat within the audience, but in reality, acting is a gruelling and oftentimes pride-squashing endeavour."

The girl nods her understanding, but the moisture gathering in her eyes tells me that she too covets a life in the limelight.

I take a few steps toward her. "But if you want it more than air itself, you owe it to yourself to do whatever it takes to succeed. My mama used to say that anything worth having is worth working for. The stage requires even more from you than work. You may have to disappoint those you love, including your father." I tilt my head to the side in an attempt to meet her eyes. "You can be certain you'll break your own heart along the way, as well, by wanting something beyond your reach. But if being on the stage is all that you dream of, then you can't let anyone or anything stand in your way."

I have no idea if the girl has what it takes to follow her dreams and attain her goals. But even if my words do little more than make her feel better, it's the least I can do after the hard work she's put in during her first day as a Hamilton maid.

A sniffle followed by a shy smile is confirmation that my words have helped ease her worries, at least momentarily.

"Let's finish this room, and then we can get you your very own cleaning cart and stock it with supplies so it's ready for tomorrow."

"Thank you, Louisa. I'd like that very much."

With the guest rooms situated for the day, I leave Gwen stocking her cart in the supply cupboard while I seek guidance from Ms. Thompson about her plans for the girl. I am certain Gwen will feel more at ease once she learns what is expected of her for the rest of the week.

The snow is falling fast. I catch a glimpse of the weather through the back door as a delivery driver exits the hotel, returning to his truck parked in the back alley. Chill bumps rise on my bare arms as the winter air sweeps a dusting of snowflakes onto the mat positioned inside the door.

Popping her head out of her pastry kitchen, Cookie gives me a questioning look. "Are you lost, Miss Wilson?" Her expression transforms into a teasing smile. "Fifth floor is thataway." She points a whisk toward the back corridor as a giggle bursts forth.

"Very funny." I chuckle at her antics. "I am looking for Ms. Thompson. I've been with the new maid all day and was hoping to get her information about what to expect for tomorrow."

"Ah, the first days are always the hardest," Cookie says with a nod. "You've just missed her. She went in the direction of the lobby a few minutes ago."

"Thank you." I slip through the panelled door to the front lobby, hugging the wall with my back while assessing the activity within. If the space is filled with guests, I will have to retreat and wait for Ms. Thompson to reappear out of their sight.

With only one guest in the lobby, moving from the registration desk to the elevator, I take the chance to walk quickly past the registration desk toward Ms. Thompson, who is speaking with the doorman near the front entrance.

Her hands move animatedly as she inclines her head toward the tiled floor. The section of patterned tile is a beautiful and welcoming feature of the grand two-story lobby, with its gleaming chandeliers and rich wood accents. The hotel's large glass door, trimmed with gold, swings open, casting a blinding reflection as I step onto the tile.

I lift a hand to shade my eyes from the piercing ray of light as the doorman issues a friendly "Welcome back, sir."

The moment my shoe touches the tile, slippery with melting snow, I realize my mistake. I slide across the floor, my foot twisting hard beneath me as I crash into the sturdy legs of the man who has just entered the hotel.

Stunned into silence and shocked by my body's severe contact with the hard floor, I lay limp, my face inches away from a pair of expensive-looking black oxfords. A groan slips past my lips as several pairs of hands reach out to help me stand.

"Miss Wilson, are you hurt?" Ms. Thompson's voice is stretched tight with concern as strong male hands lift me by my shoulders to an upright position. Ms. Thompson's voice trails off as she turns toward the doorman. "This is precisely what I was worried about, Mr. Davies. Mr. Baker, go to the basement and get as many floor mats as you can find. We can't have our guests skating across the lobby floor." Ms. Thompson's rapid instructions fade into the shadows as my head spins.

A soothing voice beside me whispers in my ear, "There, there. Easy does it. Let's see if you can put weight on that foot of yours." The man's voice is strong, reassuring, and calm.

"I'm sorry," I apologize, but my words seem quiet to the point of not existing at all.

"No harm done. Don't you worry your pretty little head. Let's see if that ankle is any worse for wear." A steadying hand wraps around my waist.

"Here, Miss Wilson." Mr. Davies places the stool from behind the bellhop stand in front of me. "Have a seat and we'll take a look at that ankle."

After issuing all her orders for remedying the slippery situation, Ms. Thompson returns her attention to me. "Miss Wilson, do you think you can make it to the kitchen? We wouldn't want you to catch a chill in the entranceway."

Though I know the matron is concerned for my well-being, I sense the urgency for her to remove me from sight of incoming hotel guests. Embarrassed by my less-than-graceful dive to the floor, I too am eager to remove myself from view.

"Yes, ma'am. I can try to walk on it." I steal a quick

glance at the man who has rescued me and give him my most appreciative smile. "Thank you, sir. I think I'll be all right now."

Ms. Thompson steps beside me, wrapping her arm around my waist. "Lean on me now, dear. Together, we can do this."

"Thank you, ma'am." I hobble and hop a few paces before taking a brief rest. "I am so sorry, ma'am. I didn't see the wet floor. I was only hurrying so I could be out of the way as quickly as possible."

"No need for apologies, Miss Wilson. I am sorry to say you proved my point about the danger of slippery tiles at a cost to your poor ankle."

"Madam, can I assist you in getting Miss Wilson here to the kitchen?" The gentleman's voice is behind me now. "I assure you I am not offended by the inner workings of a hotel, but I can avert my gaze if that is more suitable for you." I catch a glimpse over my shoulder and see the kind man's teasing smile.

"Thank you, Mr. Barnes. We will be fine from here." I feel Ms. Thompson tense beside me, and I assume I have disappointed the matron more than she is letting on. "I apologize for another disruption to your stay."

Another disruption? I wonder what else this poor man has witnessed during his stay. *Mr. Barnes.* The realization lands heavy on my heart, and my chin falls to my chest. The Hollywood man I've been hoping to meet has witnessed my less-than-dainty crash. I wear my embarrassment like a weighted cloak as Ms. Thompson guides me toward the warmth of the kitchen. One hop, hobble, and step at a time.

CHAPTER 12

WEDNESDAY, DECEMBER 14, 1927

lara

I've been ruminating over the situation with Mr. Barnes all afternoon, but those thoughts all vanish the moment the swinging door of the kitchen flies open. "Miss Wilson, can you lend a hand, please?"

I drop the pine-scented greenery I was cutting for the holiday vases and hurriedly retrieve a chair as Lou and Ms. Thompson shuffle into the kitchen. "What happened? Louisa, are you all right?"

"I'm fine, but ow." My sister's face contorts in pain. "I've twisted my ankle."

"Miss Wilson, fetch that crate." Ms. Thompson points a bony finger toward the corner, where an empty crate is waiting to be swapped out with the next produce delivery. Hu and Chef watch from the other side of the kitchen, their faces twisted with unease as Ms. Thompson guides Louisa into the chair. "Easy does it. That's right, settle yourself here, dear." The matron's voice is calm and soothing, but as I return to her side, with the crate in hand, I notice her forehead is riddled with deep lines of concern.

Ms. Thompson gestures to the floor in front of where Louisa is sitting. "Set it down there, upside down, please." She turns to my sister while softening her voice a touch more. "Now Louisa, I'm going to ask you to lift your leg and rest your heel in the middle of the crate. This may hurt, but you can squeeze my hand." Louisa takes Ms. Thompson's hand and nods once, stoically.

I've always known our matron to be a kind woman. Stern, rule-abiding, and perfectionistic, but kind as well. This level of care, though, I've never witnessed from her. The fact that she uses Louisa's first name likely has more to do with simplicity than intimacy, given both Wilson sisters are present, but I am grateful all the same for her ability to add a much-needed mothering tone to the tense situation.

Lifting her leg, Louisa winces, her eyes clamping shut. I let out a sigh of relief, thinking it must not be too bad, since I am familiar with the words Louisa can spew when distraught.

When her heel touches the wooden crate, I become instantly aware of how wrong that assessment was.

"Bloody hell." Louisa's voice is strained and loud.

"Louisa," I admonish. I feel my cheeks warm at my sister's outburst.

Ms. Thompson glances up at me from her bent-over position. "It's quite all right, Miss Wilson. Your sister is in a significant amount of pain." A small smile tugs at the corner of her mouth. "The occasional curse word won't improve the situation, but it surely can't hurt."

"Apologies, ma'am." Louisa sucks in a breath of air as her calf relaxes against the edge of the crate. Louisa's stocking does little to hide the swelling beneath its dark wool.

Cookie appears through the swinging door. "What have we here?" One glance over Ms. Thompson's shoulder at Louisa's propped-up foot and Cookie bustles into motion. "That's going to need some ice." Looking up at the two other people in the kitchen, my friend doesn't hesitate to take charge. "Well don't just stand there. Chef, boil water for tea. We are going to need a few stiff cups, it seems. And Hu, use that towel there and collect a handful of snow from outside."

Hu and Chef do as they are told, scattering to accomplish the tasks. I marvel at Cookie's ability to direct the men into action. She leans over Louisa's rapidly expanding ankle. "Let's get some ice on it, and then we can assess the damage. Nothing to do but give it some time."

Cookie places a comforting hand on Louisa's shoulder as she rises. She exchanges a knowing look with Ms. Thompson before murmuring, "We might need to add a nip of something to that tea."

With a subtle nod from Ms. Thompson, Cookie moves toward the kitchen door. "I'll find something suitable. Back in a jiffy."

Hu returns with a dishtowel filled with a packed ball of snow. "For you, Miss Louisa. I hope it makes you better."

I smile at the man's kind gesture. Cookie told me about his family's Chinese restaurant, where he works double time to feed his friends and neighbours. I wonder if his famous dim sum will be featured at the New Year's Eve celebration, like Cookie mentioned it might be. I've only heard murmurings about the event, scheduled to take place in the hotel's lobby and banquet rooms.

"So you do know my name, Hu." Louisa flashes a mischievous smile in the shy man's direction. "Thank you."

Ms. Thompson helps Louisa position the snow on her ankle while Hu backs away, bowing slightly.

Cookie returns, pausing in the doorway with a glass bottle of dark liquid. "Nicked this from the bar trolly. Should do the trick." A quick wink in my direction tells me she's pleased with her mock thievery.

The back door opens and closes with a thud, thrusting cool air into the kitchen. Cookie leans back into the hall, and a delighted expression lights up her features.

"I dare say, I've always thought you to be the respectable sort," a male voice teases, making Cookie grin even more. "Drinking already. It can hardly be past four."

"Well, look what the cat dragged in." Cookie's retort is in jest, the smile never leaving her face as the man steps forward and places a kiss on her cheek.

"It's good to see you, Cookie."

My heart thumps wildly in my chest as the man's voice and profile elicit an unfamiliar, humming response within me. Feeling a touch guilty at such thoughts, given my sister's current state, I drop my gaze to Louisa and crouch beside her, whispering that all will be well.

"William." Recognizing her brother's voice, Ms. Thompson stands and rushes toward the door. "Is that you?"

Cookie steps back to allow the siblings to greet one another with an embrace.

"Eliza." William steps back to take in his sister. "You look well."

"I thought you were going to telephone." Ms. Thompson swats William's arm lightheartedly. "I've got nothing prepared for dinner." Concern draws creases on her forehead. "Where are your bags? Have you checked in yet? I am not certain the room is ready."

"I caught an earlier train than expected. Keeping you on your toes is a younger brother's job. Don't worry about the room. I know what a tight ship you run, and I am quite certain my room will be ready in good time. I can stow my bags in your office until later." William's chuckle feels as though it has warmed the chill from the room. "As for dinner, I thought I could take you and Cookie out for a meal. It is the least I can do, since you'll be putting up with me right through the holidays."

"Listen to him," Cookie chimes in. "He's only buttering us up for the holiday treats that are about to come."

"You know me too well." He tilts his head back to examine the bottle in Cookie's hand. "What's with the whisky?"

Cookie gestures past the open kitchen door. "We've had a bit of an accident."

William's joy turns to concern as he takes in Louisa with her elevated foot. When his eyes land on me, a slow smile emerges on his face, sending a jolt of electricity through me.

"Miss Wilson." William's eyes never leave mine as he steps forward into the kitchen.

His gaze lingers, making me feel as though we are alone. He tears his eyes away only when he kneels in front of Louisa's injured ankle. "May I?" William points to the snow-dampened towel covering her foot. "I've experienced my fair share of sprained ankles playing hockey on the frozen lakes back home."

I sense Lou bracing herself in anticipation of more pain, but she assents with a silent nod.

Lifting the towel allows the remnants of snow to escape,

landing with a plop on the hard floor. William puts the towel aside and gently prods my sister's foot. "I don't think anything is broken." He looks to Ms. Thompson, who has moved to Louisa's other side. "But she shouldn't put any weight on it for a few days, or at least until that swelling comes down."

As she smooths the front of her skirt with both hands, Ms. Thompson's matronly manner reappears. "Well, Miss Wilson, it seems you will be at home resting for the next few days. I will make arrangements to cover your shifts and will speak with Miss Greenwood about continuing Miss Russell's training."

"Yes, ma'am." Louisa's downcast eyes tell me she is more than a little disappointed to be in this predicament. "I'm sorry, ma'am. I didn't mean to cause all this trouble."

"You've caused nothing of the sort, dear. The snow should not have been left to gather on the tile. I'll see to it that it does not happen again," Ms. Thompson asserts with conviction.

"How about that tea?" Cookie, having busied herself with filling a cup halfway with boiling water and tea leaves before filling the other half with whisky, offers Louisa a sip.

Louisa's face pinches at the taste of the brew. "This is awful."

"The first sip is the hardest." Cookie pats Louisa's shoulder, sharing an amused glance with Ms. Thompson. "By the third, you'll be feeling less pain."

I want to speak up, to tell them Louisa shouldn't have whisky, given our father's past trouble with the drink, but shame at our family's darkness keeps the words locked tight within my head. I am trying to weigh the potential harm to my sister against the chance at reducing her pain when Cookie's intentions are accomplished.

Three sips into her tea, Louisa smiles, and Cookie, without hesitation, takes the teacup from her hands.

Relief washes over me. I should have known that my friend would always have my sister's best interest at heart. I feel William's eyes on me, full of concern, and I realize he's been watching me watch Louisa. The worry etched into his expression warms me through.

Louisa's words, though soft and slightly slurred, hit me like a freight train, pulling me from the contentment I feel under William's gaze. "If it weren't for that kind Mr. Barnes, I fear things could have been far worse."

"Wh—what did you say?"

Louisa meets my eyes. "Mr. Barnes caught me when I fell. He was quite sweet, given the fact that I tumbled into him like a bowling ball." Louisa giggles. "A very tall bowling ball."

I feel the floor shift beneath my feet and a cloud of unsteadiness overcomes me. How is it that this man is everywhere? Did Louisa really slip, or did this man somehow orchestrate the whole thing? Something inside me whispers not to put it past him. I bite my lip to stop myself from saying more. All I want is for him to stay away from me, and now my sister.

Louisa's question tugs me back to the present situation. "How will I get home?"

I swallow hard, doing my best to shrug off Louisa's mention of Mr. Barnes. "If I can borrow the telephone, ma'am, I can call home and have our father come to assist. Between the two of us, I am sure we can help Louisa manage the streetcar."

"Yes, you can use the phone in my office." Ms. Thompson taps a finger to her lips. "Though I do suspect the streetcar may be a challenge in her current state. Either way, we should inform your father."

William speaks up. "Has Robert, I mean, Mr. Olson brought his motorcar with him today?"

"I imagine so, though I'm not certain." Ms. Thompson hesitates, then glances once more at Louisa's swollen ankle with a frown.

"If he is in his office, I'd be happy to speak with him. He may very well suggest the same thing, given the situation." William lifts his eyebrows, and I find myself touched by his thoughtfulness.

"Yes, that is a sensible idea." Ms. Thompson gathers herself up once more. "Miss Wilson, telephone home and then gather your and your sister's belongings from the locker room while we sort out the best way to get you two home."

"Yes, ma'am." I squeeze Louisa's shoulder in solidarity as I pass her on my way out of the kitchen. Before ducking out the kitchen door, I sneak a sideways glance in William's direction and catch him with his eyes on me again.

CHAPTER 13

WEDNESDAY, DECEMBER 14, 1927

*L*ouisa

By the time I am positioned in Mr. Olson's automobile, the effects of the tea are wearing off. My embarrassment follows me all the way home.

Barely after learning of Mr. Barnes' stay at the hotel, I have ruined any chance of properly introducing myself. What a fool I was to not see the melting snow. I shake my head at my current predicament.

What a mess I've made of things. I have humiliated myself in front of the one person who might have offered me a future in Hollywood, and I've cost my family several days of wages. Despite having had little expectation of earning the fifth-floor maid's holiday bonus, any chance I might have had has vanished now. I can only imagine the worry coursing through Clara's head as Mr. Olson's car pulls away from The Hamilton's front entrance and turns into traffic.

Usually, the opportunity to ride in a fancy automobile such as Mr. Olson's would be the highlight of my week. Sadly, the brief ride is riddled with bumps and turns. With a slicing pain running through my ankle, I barely open my eyes to enjoy the wintery view.

Clara sits beside me in the back seat, one hand clutching her bag, the other gently supporting my leg stretched across the seat. She winces every time I do, and though I suspect she would like to comment, she holds her tongue.

Mr. Olson and Mr. Thompson chat in the front bench seat as we rumble down Georgia Street, the late afternoon gloom doing little for my mood. Ms. Thompson's brother insisted on accompanying us home, mentioning the three flights of stairs he assumed we needed to climb in order to reach our apartment.

I am contemplating this bit of information when Mr. Olson asks over his shoulder, "Which building did you say you were in?"

Before Clara or I can answer, Mr. Thompson speaks up. "The Newbury. Corner of Thurlow and Robson."

My eyes grow wide. I turn to Clara in time to see her face, illuminated by the street lamps, quickly turning a shade of red I've never seen her wear. She looks away, avoiding my gaze by staring out the window. There is definitely something going on here. I can't imagine how I missed it.

As we pull up to the apartment building, I release an anxious sigh, knowing the next few minutes are likely to be uncomfortable if not downright unbearable. Clara gets out first, reaching one arm back for me. I slide my uniform-clad body, injured foot first, toward the open door. As I near the edge of the car's rear seat, I am met by Mr. Thompson's friendly face. His grey-blue eyes are striking this close up. No wonder my sister has been keeping mention of him from me.

Mr. Thompson offers me a shy smile. "The way I see it, we can struggle up three flights of stairs with all of us squished together, with you in the middle to lean on us. Or, if you are comfortable, Miss Wilson, would you allow me to carry you up the stairs with the utmost care?"

Even I see the potential disaster of having all of us crammed into one stairwell. A twinge from my ankle nudges me to let go of my shame and accept Mr. Thompson's offer with a quick nod of my head.

Clara pauses inside the lobby as Mr. Olson holds the front door open while Mr. Thompson slides through sideways with me in his arms, careful not to bump my dangling leg in the process. With my arms wrapped around his neck for security, his eyes barely stray from Clara's as we pass through the small entrance of the lobby.

I am certain the man is smitten with my sister, and the thought allows my mind to wander from the torment my ankle is experiencing while he carries me up three flights of stairs.

At the top of the landing, Clara rushes around us with the apartment key in hand. She twists the knob and pushes the door wide. I imagine her doing a mental inventory of the state of our apartment. Given her steadfast nature and the work she puts into keeping our home in spotless condition, I am confident she has nothing to worry about.

"Maybe we should lay her on the sofa. That way, she can stretch out." Clara walks into the apartment and turns at the end of the hall, bypassing our shared bedroom before entering the living room. "Just in here." Clara's cheeks flush again as Mr. Thompson moves past her and gently lowers me to the sofa.

"Clara. Lou." Papa's voice echoes through the quaint quarters of our home. "Why is the door open?"

"Papa," Clara says as she moves quickly to head him off in the hall. "We tried to telephone. Everything is fine, but—"

"Clara?" Papa steps into the living room and stops abruptly at the sight of two men he's never met standing in his living room. "Hello." Papa extends a hand, though his automatic politeness doesn't quite reach his usually kind eyes. "And you are…?"

Papa shakes Mr. Olson's hand and then Mr. Thompson's as they introduce themselves before his gaze moves to me on the sofa.

"Lou." Papa kneels beside the sofa. "Are you all right?"

"I feel a fool." My guard crumbles as he takes me in his arms. "I've twisted my ankle." Though I hold the tears at bay, ripe emotion laces each word.

"Don't worry, darlin'. We'll get you fixed up in no time." Papa squeezes my hands in his. "It'll all work out."

Papa stands and faces the men again, relief replacing his wary expression. "Thank you for bringing them home." His eyes shift toward the telephone on the wall. "I suppose that contraption only works if I'm here to be on the other end of it. I appreciate your effort in getting them home safely. Can I offer you a cup of tea or water?"

The men decline Papa's offer, and after a few more explanations of the day's events, he walks them to the door, thanking them again for their help.

From my vantage point on the sofa, I watch the exchange between Mr. Thompson and Clara. Neither utters a single word to the other, but one would have to be oblivious to miss the connection between them. I look forward to hearing what my sister has to say on the topic.

An hour later, Clara has placed my injured foot on a pillow and wrapped the rest of me in a blanket. Tea and a light dinner of toast and eggs is all my overwrought stomach can handle.

I am wallowing in the ramifications of today's events. My chance to be discovered by a Hollywood director was within my reach, and now I'm left to stare at the four walls of our tiny apartment for who knows how long. I can hardly believe my bad luck.

I shake thoughts of the setback from my head. The best thing I can do now is recover. The sooner my ankle is healed, the sooner I can revisit properly introducing myself to Mr. Barnes. He was kind and helpful. I can't imagine he would be so unforgiving as to not wish to speak with me. Besides, I am at least memorable to him now. That is something. It's not ideal, but perhaps it is something I can work in my favour.

The smell of dinner wafts through the apartment as Clara cooks a proper meal for herself and Papa. The telephone rings, startling me from my all-consuming thoughts.

"Hello, Wilson residence." Clara answers the phone with a lift to her voice, despite the weariness I know she must be feeling. "Oh, hello, Thomas." She turns in my direction as I swivel my neck to see her better. "Louisa can't come to the telephone at the moment." Clara lifts her shoulders in question, a strained expression stretching her lips. "She is here. But she has twisted her ankle and isn't able to make it to the phone."

Disappointment pushes me back into the sofa cushions

as I consider all the things I am going to miss while my ankle heals.

"Come here? I'm sure that would be fine. We are about to have dinner, so perhaps thirty minutes or so. Okay, we will see you then. Goodbye."

A hand covers my face. As soon as I hear the click of the phone being returned to its handle, I press Clara. "Why did you say that? I am a mess. He can't come here."

Clara stands over me. "He said it was important. He needs to see you tonight. Besides, I don't think you look a mess. You are stunning, just as you are."

"What's this?" Papa enters the living room after freshening up from his day's work. "Company is coming?" His soft chuckle does little to lighten my mood. "I'm not sure this apartment has ever seen so many guests, all of them arriving in one day. You know I've not met the boy properly yet, Lou. You can't hide him from me forever."

"I'm not hiding him from you," I grumble. "I'm not sure I have much more in me tonight is all."

Clara, clearly having lost her mind along with all sympathy for me, turns on her heel. "Well, I guess you'd better find a little more, because Thomas will be here in half an hour."

While the rest of my family eats dinner and cleans up, I run a brush, which Clara reluctantly deposited on my lap, through my hair. I haven't seen Thomas since before the audition. We spoke on the telephone once, and he mentioned a busy week planned, with work at the theatre club and some housekeeping items.

Perhaps he has good news and wants to tell me in person. Maybe he has another role for me. My spirits lift at the thought of seeing him, and I concede that maybe Clara knew what she was doing after all by inviting him over.

A small smile lifts my cheeks. It would be just like Thomas to take my bad day and turn it into something wonderful. After my disastrous introduction to Mr. Barnes, it would be far better for me to approach the Hollywood director with a lead role tucked up my sleeve. If he is in town long enough, I could invite him to the play and let him see my talent for himself.

The knock at the door startles me, and I spread the blanket over my legs while stowing the hairbrush beneath the pillow behind my back.

"I'll get it," Clara announces, graciously keeping Papa from being the first to greet Thomas.

"Hi," she says at the door. "Come on in. She's in the living room."

Thomas enters the living room, holding his wool cap in front of him. His eyes meet mine, and all my worries about seeing him tonight disappear like melting snow.

Papa stands from his chair and extends a hand toward Thomas. "Good to meet you, Thomas. Louisa has told us lots about you. Please have a seat."

Papa gestures to the only other chair in the room, and Thomas takes it, eyeing me with concern. "How are you feeling?"

A gush of flutters rises in my chest at his genuine concern for me. "I'll be fine. I suspect my ego might be more bruised than my ankle." I do my best to downplay the discomfort I am feeling.

Clara sets a pot of tea on the coffee table and serves each of us a cup before settling herself at the far end of the sofa, careful not to bump my ankle as she sits.

Realizing we aren't about to be afforded any privacy from my family, I push forward. "Clara mentioned you had something important to tell me."

"Yes, I do." Thomas hesitates, buying time with a sip of tea. "I have been asked to travel to California to work with a new production company."

I feel my smile drop as quickly as my heart. "California?" All I can think is that I was supposed to be the one going to Hollywood to become a film star. Though silent, the admission is no less selfish than it would be if spoken out loud.

Silence fills the room as I wade through my thoughts for an appropriate response. Perhaps, in time, Thomas' connections in California will be an asset for my future, but right now, in this moment, all I feel is sorry for myself.

Clara senses my disappointment and does her best to save me from myself. "What exciting news, Thomas. What kind of work will it be?"

Thomas' eyes appear imploring, but my mind is spinning so fast I can't determine what he is trying to say. "It is a temporary position. I don't expect to be gone much longer than a month or two, but it means that I will gain experience in the production of film. There are advantages with this type of advancement, given the anticipated expansion into talking movies."

"Oh, I see." Forcing a pleased smile in place, I tilt my head and ask the question I'm dreading. "How soon do you have to leave?"

Thomas examines his hands, and I know the answer before a single word falls from his lips. "I'm booked on tomorrow's train to Seattle."

CHAPTER 14

THURSDAY, DECEMBER 15, 1927

lara

I stifle a yawn. Walking to the hotel by myself this morning allows me time to think over yesterday's events. The evening slowly rolled into early morning as Louisa struggled to find comfort with her ankle. By bedtime she was able to put a small amount of weight on her foot with support but doing so did not ensure a restful sleep. I tiptoed around the apartment this morning after she finally succumbed to sleep in the wee hours of dawn.

An exasperated sigh sneaks past my lips. Louisa's lost wages can't be helped, but still I make a mental note to scan a copy of the newspaper during today's lunch break in the hopes of finding a few grocery items on sale. With a little luck, I'll be able to make up the difference with a few frugal meals. Papa tells me not to worry myself over the family finances, given how we've managed to pull ourselves out from the depths of poverty, barely avoiding eviction. But something deep within me refuses to let go of the fear. I suppose once you've known poverty intimately, you are forever shackled to its lingering effects.

My spirits lift when I remember the possibility of being awarded the holiday bonus. All I have to do is ensure my guests are happy with their stay. So far, with the exception of Mr. Barnes, the few guests I have tended to seem pleased with the touches of holiday cheer I have been leaving in their suites. With many of our guests arriving for a little holiday shopping and the Spencer's Christmas parade this weekend, I've taken extra care to draw up an itinerary of events happening around the city, and I plan to leave a neatly printed copy in each room I tend to.

Upon arriving at the hotel, my first stop is to Ms. Thompson's office. I move through the kitchen hallway and head straight to the basement, coat buttoned and toque firmly in place atop my head. I slip my mittens into my jacket pocket before knocking on her office door.

"Come in." Ms. Thompson looks at me over the glasses perched low on her nose. "Ah, Miss Wilson. How is you sister feeling this morning?"

"It was a long night, ma'am. She finally managed to find sleep as the dawn was rising. I peeked at her ankle before leaving for the day. The swelling has gone down some. I imagine it will take a few days though."

Ms. Thompson's lips purse at my news. "Will she be all right on her own?"

"I suspect she will sleep most of the day. I've given her aspirin for the swelling and to help make her more comfortable." I think back to my makeshift obstacle course of dining chairs leading from our bedroom to the bathroom, hoping they will help Louisa steady herself and serve as spots to rest in between careful steps. "I've left soup in a flask and a glass of water at her bedside. Our father is planning to stop by midday to check on her as well."

"Thank heavens for family." Ms. Thompson delivers a sympathetic smile. "I appreciate the update, Miss Wilson. If there is anything we can do to assist, please don't hesitate to ask."

"Thank you, ma'am." I dip into a quick curtsy and head to the locker room to ready myself for the day ahead.

On the eighth floor, with a feather duster in hand, I move from one end of the hall to the other, dusting the ornate picture frames, mouldings, and any other items with enough of an edge to gather dust and debris. The dark burgundy of the walls absorbs the light of the chandeliers, shadows playing hide-and-seek with the grooves of the intricately flocked wallpaper.

I am lost in an oil painting of a French countryside when a voice startles me from behind.

"Good morning, Miss Wilson."

Given that I am standing at the opposite corridor from Mr. Barnes' suite and his accommodations are not on my roster today, I can only assume he has been searching for me. Forcing a polite smile into place, I turn to greet the man who has quickly become a thorn in my side. "Good morning, Mr. Barnes. I hope you enjoyed a pleasant evening."

"A pleasant evening indeed. I ventured out to one of those clubs down the way. You know the kind? With dancing and jazz music loud enough to rattle your bones." Mr. Barnes lifts his arms as though he has a partner and does a quick twirl around the floor. "A most entertaining time, though it was a pity to do so on my own."

My hands fiddle with the handle of the duster as I consider an appropriate response.

COCKTAILS BEFORE MIDNIGHT

Clearly not interested in any response I might have to offer, Mr. Barnes presses on. "I don't suppose you would be interested in joining me for a spin around the dance floor?" His wink does little to endear him to me. "Friday evening, say seven o'clock?"

I snap my mouth closed when I realize it is hanging agape. My instinct is to flee, but I command myself to maintain my composure, just as hotel policy dictates. "I am sorry, sir. I do not frequent clubs." With a thought of preventing any further invitations, I look him directly in the eye. "Nor is it permissible by hotel policy for me to accept any such invitation from a guest of The Hamilton." I stride past him in two steps. "Good day, Mr. Barnes."

"I imagine your sister would be more appreciative of such an invitation. She's the sort of girl to enjoy an evening on the town, or so I've heard from a couple of the fifth-floor maids. Of course, she isn't likely to be in dancing form for a few days yet." Mr. Barnes speaks in a low but steady tone. "She *is* your sister? The one who took a tumble in the lobby yesterday afternoon."

I turn slowly and take in his smug expression. The unsettling nature with which he regards me gives rise to chill bumps along my arms. Not wishing to lose my decorum or, worse, my temper in front of the man, I spin around and walk in the opposite direction.

Several minutes later, I am returning the feather duster to the supply cupboard, with the intent to gather myself and my cleaning cart, when Rebecca startles me as she opens the supply cupboard door. Clutching a hand to my heart, I say, "Oh, Miss Smythe, it is you."

"Were you expecting someone else?"

I drop my gaze to the cleaning cart I've been pretending

to restock and fiddle with the hand towels I've placed on top.

"You look flushed. Are you feeling ill?" Miss Smythe takes a step closer, concern lining her face.

"Tired is all." I try to shrug off the question, not wishing to divulge the less-than-hospitable thoughts running rampant through my mind. Any idle chatter about indiscretions between me and a guest would be a direct route to losing my chance at the holiday bonus. "Lou was awake most of the night."

"I heard she took a nasty spill. Is she feeling any better this morning?"

"Where did you hear that?" Try as I might, I can't etch the accusatory tone from my question.

Miss Smythe places a calming hand on my shoulder. "Easy there, Clara. You must not have slept a lick if you are this jumpy." My friend watches me with scrutinizing eyes. "If you must know, Mr. Barnes was in the hall yesterday afternoon, regaling us with tales of his heroism, though I suspect it was less heroism and more happenstance." Rebecca lifts both shoulders. "But that's just me."

"Ah, so you are immune to Mr. Barnes' charms, then?" I cross my arms across my chest, waiting for a reply.

"Ha. Charms." Rebecca shakes her head. "I've learned a thing or two about how he acts these past few days, puffing out his chest like a proud peacock. I don't put much stock in antics such as his. Best advice I can offer, since he seems to have gotten under your skin, is to do your best to avoid him."

"Avoid him? That is an impossible feat. The man seems to be everywhere."

"True enough." Rebecca's lips turn up into a sly smile. "But there are plenty of closets, cubbies, and stairwells at our fingertips. I suggest you find one anytime he pokes his head out."

"I'll keep that in mind." I laugh, thankful for the camaraderie and understanding as I gather myself and my cart and prepare to tackle the three suites on my roster today.

After lunch, I return to the eighth floor to vacuum the hall, as assigned to me this afternoon. I am making long sweeping strokes with the mammoth of a machine when I sense someone behind me. I immediately power off the vacuum and pull it out of the way against the wall, as is protocol when a guest is present.

I turn my head and see Mr. Barnes entering the elevator. "Miss Wilson." He nods a cordial hello and disappears into the caged box.

Befuddled at the change in the man's demeanour, I am motionless for a moment as relief leaves me feeling a little jelly-legged. I let out a slow exhale and commend myself. I must have finally managed to get through to the troublesome guest. My confidence is restored, and now I know that the holiday bonus is not as far out of my reach as I worried it might be. I celebrate by circling the vacuum with a little dance. "Everything is going to be okay," I whisper to myself.

"Don't tell me. You are practicing your dance steps in anticipation of New Year's Eve."

Startled by another's presence, my back connects against the wall with more force than I intend. I steal a glance upward but keep my head down in an effort to hide my embarrassment as I'm reminded of my place among the guests of the eighth floor.

William strides toward me, barely concealing a cheeky

grin. "I am sorry. I couldn't resist, and you looked quite pleased with yourself."

"Mr. Thompson." I feel my cheeks flame. Of all the people to spot me dancing a jig, it had to be him. "What are you doing here?" I swivel my head from side to side, ensuring the hall is free of other guests.

"No need to panic, Clara."

Heat rises within me at hearing my name from his lips, and his own cheeks colour.

"May I call you Clara?" William's expression softens as he steps closer, his voice dropping an octave as he almost breathes the question.

"You may." My eyes dart about the hall and I rethink my response. "But perhaps not here."

"Not to worry, I came up the back stairs." He raises his palm before I can protest his presence. "With the permission of my sister, I'll have you know."

"I see." I fiddle with the vacuum's long, thick cord while imploring my mind to come up with something clever to say. Louisa's charm I do not possess, so without a better option, I press forward. Straight forward. "What brings you to the eighth floor, Mr. Thompson?"

William's warm smile crinkles the corners of his grey-blue eyes, their colour drawing me in. "I came to see how your sister is recovering. That ankle of hers had a nasty swell to it. I can't imagine it was a comfortable night for her."

I feel my cheeks lift at his genuine concern and do my best to hide the stab of disappointment that his presence here has to do with anything other than seeing me. "The night was not a comfortable one for Louisa, but I am quite certain she will recover completely. Thank you for your concern and for helping us home yesterday."

"It was my pleasure, though it wasn't exactly how I imagined I might meet your father."

A flutter of delight courses through me at his words. Not wishing to give myself away, I steer clear of William's mention of meeting Papa and attempt to usher the conversation to neutral territory. "I hope you will enjoy the holiday season here. I imagine the weather is different than in Toronto this time of year."

I feel myself rambling, but I am unable to stop. "Do you get a lot of snow at home? Ours has only started to arrive. Though it is pretty when the city is a blanket of white."

William glances back over his shoulder before answering. "The snow in Toronto is dryer and more plentiful, but Clara—I mean, Miss Wilson—the other reason I wanted to see you this morning is to ask if you've had a chance to consider my dinner invitation?"

"Oh." I have barely uttered a sound when we are interrupted by the opening of the lift's gate and the attendant announcing the arrival on the eighth floor.

Much to my disappointment, Mr. Barnes, hat in hand and smug smile firmly pressed up against his flaccid cheeks, appears in the hallway. I recoil inwardly as he swaggers toward us.

"Miss Wilson, I see you do make the time for some of your guests." I feel the rebuke as he extends a hand in William's direction. "Harold Barnes, and you are…?"

William sneaks a questioning look in my direction before offering a charming smile along with his outstretched hand to Mr. Barnes. "William Thompson. It is a pleasure to make your acquaintance, Mr. Barnes."

"What brings you to this fair city, Mr. Thompson?"

Silently, I urge William to put the man off. The last thing I desire is to have Mr. Barnes knowing anything more about me or the people I spend time with. The realization that I've just added William to the short list of people important to me makes me want to tell him yes. Yes, I'll go to dinner with him, and yes, I'll spend as much time with him as he has available for me while he is in Vancouver.

My delight over my decision to accept William's dinner invitation battles with my disappointment over Mr. Barnes' intrusion. William engages in mundane but polite banter with the man as I consider whether to wait for Mr. Barnes to take his leave.

"I am in town visiting family. And you, Mr. Barnes? What brings you to the city so close to the holidays?"

Mr. Barnes' expression is slippery at best. "Work, mostly. I am in the movie business, and as you may have heard, Hollywood seldom sleeps."

The men chat a few moments longer about the city and the weather as I coil the vacuum's cord, tucking it out of sight at the back of the machine.

With no apparent intention by Mr. Barnes to vacate the hallway, I excuse myself politely and tell the men I must be getting on.

Pushing the vacuum down the hall to its home within the supply cupboard, I can feel William's gaze on me. We'll have to pick up our conversation at another time, away from listening ears.

CHAPTER 15

SATURDAY, DECEMBER 17, 1927

Louisa

Our slow shuffle toward the hotel is more difficult this morning, with the slippery sidewalk. Snow mixed with sleet enveloped the city yesterday, leaving behind a low-hanging fog and icy streets that are sure to put a damper on today's Christmas parade.

"Slow and steady, Lou," Clara, tucked in close beside me, coos as we skirt icy patches in the frosty air. "There is no need to rush."

"I hope not, since you woke me a full thirty minutes ahead of schedule," I tease, shooting a bemused glance at Clara's ducked head.

"Well, I suppose I could let you walk there on your own," Clara chides me in return. "Though, I imagine getting home might prove to be more of an issue."

"You know I am grateful." I squeeze her arm in my gloved hand. "I am sorry that I have caused such a fuss. I never meant for you to have to work extra shifts to make up for my missed ones."

"As long as your ankle is feeling better, that is all I am concerned with." We reach the corner of Howe and Georgia and situate ourselves near The Hotel Georgia's covered entranceway for a brief rest. "Besides, I would have had to help get you to work either way. I might as well earn a wage for the day too."

Clara allows me to rest a few minutes more before wrapping her arm around me for support as we cover the final distance toward the warmth and safety of The Hamilton.

"I am actually looking forward to returning to work."

Clara eyes me suspiciously.

"Truly, I am. Two days sequestered at home has made me appreciate the hustle and bustle of the hotel. Besides, I am keen to apologize to that kind Mr. Barnes. I don't know what would have happened had he not been there. I might have slid right out the front door and onto the street." A laugh erupts from within me at the thought of such a scenario.

We turn left down the alley toward the employee entrance at the back of the hotel.

"Louisa, I've been meaning to talk to you about that. People aren't always what they appear to be at first glance. I —I want you—"

I interrupt my sister mid-sentence. "Does this have anything to do with Mr. Thompson? You can't hide it from me, Clara. I saw the way he looked at you."

"No, this isn't about…" We are at the base of the steps when the back door opens and Cookie appears. Clara's words rush out of her as Cookie descends the first step, arms outstretched in what I interpret as an offer of assistance. "I am not hiding anything from you, Lou, but we can't talk about this now."

"Here we are, then." Cookie meets us halfway. "I've been watching for the likes of you. Figured you might need a hand navigating these stairs."

"Thank you." I take hold of Cookie's arm as she helps me from above, while Clara ensures I do not tumble backwards.

Once inside the warmth of the kitchen hall, I rest long enough to take off my winter wear, handing Clara my coat and toque to deposit in the locker room.

"Ms. Thompson has got you set up in a corner of the lobby. With everyone expected to head out for the parade, it should be fairly quiet in there for most of the day."

"Thank you, Cookie. I am grateful to be able to return to being useful." I sit on the offered stool to rest my foot while I wait.

Cookie chuckles, clearly knowing more about the tasks ahead of me than I currently do. "Tell me that once you've polished every piece of silver in the hotel's storerooms."

"Do you need me to help get you situated?" Clara, arms full with both her and my belongings, moves toward me while discreetly checking the clock on the wall.

"No need to worry about that." Cookie shoos Clara with a wave. "The new maid, Gwen, will be here shortly to lend a hand. You go about your day, and we'll make sure Louisa is taken care of."

Clara meets my eyes, and I flash her a reassuring smile. "Okay then, but please fetch me if anything changes."

"Not to worry. Louisa will be just fine." Cookie's control of the situation is enough to set Clara in motion, and she is off without another word.

Cookie was right. The morning passes quickly as Gwen and I, partially hidden by a makeshift screen in the far corner of the lobby, polish silver platters, bowls, and teapots.

I positioned myself with a view of the space between the registration desk and the lift, hoping Mr. Barnes will feel the need to venture out from his suite today. I am eager to apologize and thank him for his kindness.

I never intended our first meeting to be one of such spectacular and dreadfully embarrassing fanfare, but now I've got to use what I have available to me. The man just might be my ticket to Hollywood. I rehearse my planned apology in my head while polishing.

Quietly, I convince George, the bellboy Ms. Thompson tasked with transporting the silver between its storage room and our polishing station, to leave the screen a little more ajar, allowing me a wider view of the lobby beyond. As we move on to polishing some sort of tiny forks, Gwen pauses her continuous chatter about her family's upcoming holiday plans to inform me they are seafood forks.

"Seafood forks?" I ask, turning the delicate utensil in my hand.

Gwen points to a squat, seven-tined fork. "This one is for sardines. See how it is shaped? It is wide enough to pierce a single sardine at a time."

I wrinkle my nose at the thought of the fishy smell. Gwen has confirmed her upper-class status with her knowledge of fine silver, though I suspect this is the first time she's polished any.

"So, is it true?" Gwen asks, head bent over the small table holding dozens of silver pieces.

"Is what true?"

"About Mr. Barnes, of course." She looks up at me with a wrinkle in her brow. "That you ran right into the

Hollywood director? At first, I didn't believe it, but the story kept getting repeated."

My face warms with humiliation.

"It was a brilliant plan, you know. I'm just sorry I didn't think of it myself." Gwen tilts her head to the side, her look of pure innocence conflicting with the casual manner in which she schemes.

I clench my jaw. "I didn't plan the collision. I slipped on the wet tile." I am considering mentioning the very real injury to my ankle when I catch sight of Mr. Barnes stepping out of the lift.

I tamp down my frustration with the girl and summon my sweetest demeanour. "Gwen, would you be so kind as to find Ms. Thompson and ask her where I should eat my lunch this afternoon? I'm afraid I won't make it up the stairs to the lunchroom, and I'm beginning to feel hungry."

Still new to the job and accustomed to doing what she is asked, Gwen puts her cloth and tiny fork on the table and slides past the screen in search of the matron.

I wait a moment to allow Gwen time to vacate the lobby before tugging the screen open a fraction more to reveal myself. The movement catches his eye, and when Mr. Barnes looks up, I offer a timid wave in his direction.

"Miss Wilson, it appears you are on the mend." His voice booms as he crosses the floor.

"Mr. Barnes, I was hoping to see you today." His chin lifts in question, but the jubilant expression lining his rounded face does not change. "I wanted to thank you for your assistance and apologize for crashing into you. I feel such a fool for not seeing the wet tile."

"Nonsense, Miss Wilson. It was my pleasure to be of assistance." He leans a little closer, delivering me a knowing wink. "It isn't every day that a man gets to become someone's hero."

A laugh flutters from my lips, and I am rewarded with the knowledge that I have captured the man's attention. "I thank you all the same, sir." I tilt my head and widen my smile, ensuring his attention remains on me.

"How is your ankle feeling?" The man makes a show of bending down to peer under the small table at my stocking-covered ankle, a feat that can't be easy, given the girth around his middle. He returns to standing, his face a touch redder than before.

"Much better. Thank you." Movement behind him catches my attention, and I see our conversation is about to be cut short, as Ms. Thompson and Gwen are heading in my direction.

"I am glad I got to thank you properly. I truly am grateful." I push the words out in a hurry as Ms. Thompson arrives beside Mr. Barnes.

"Mr. Barnes, how nice to see you out and about." Ms. Thompson is polite, though I sense a hint of reservation within her words. "Is there anything we can assist you with today? Perhaps you'd enjoy a tray of goodies sent up to your suite?"

"I won't decline such a generous offer, madam." He steps to the side, gesturing for Ms. Thompson to accompany him. "Do you suppose you could arrange for spirits to be sent up to the suite?" Though he lowers his voice, it's far from a whisper. "I'm afraid we are still under prohibition laws in California, and I understand the fine folks of British Columbia are far more sensible than that."

"I am sure that can be arranged. I'll have one of the bellboys bring up a selection for you to choose from." Ms.

Thompson nods politely. "Well, if you'll excuse us. Miss Wilson, will you come with me, please?"

I use my arms to lift myself to a standing position before taking the first cautious step with my recovering ankle. I deliver a radiant smile in Mr. Barnes' direction and follow the matron slowly out of the lobby, my thoughts turning to how I might meet with the man again.

Cookie greets us in the kitchen hallway. "It's not every day I get to dine with the illustrious Louisa Wilson." Cookie beams as she waves me through to her pastry kitchen. "Clara has dropped off Louisa's lunch, so we are all set."

Ms. Thompson nods. "I'll leave you to it then."

In the warmth of Cookie's pastry kitchen, a small bench and two stools are tucked against the back wall. "So, this is where you eat your lunch?" Until this moment, I hadn't actually considered where the other employees commune for the noonday meal.

"Welcome to my humble abode." Cookie gestures for me to take a seat. "Clara left your sandwich. In a bit of a hurry, she was." Cookie's face scrunches in what I interpret as concern before transforming once more into her familiar jolly state. "Chef has been so kind as to pour you a glass of milk."

"Oh my, I am to be spoiled, then. Usually, it is just plain old water." I unwrap the sandwich and bite into it.

Cookie leans in with a mischievous grin. "You may even be graced with a delicacy for dessert, since you're in my domain."

I chew and swallow before asking, "What kind of treats have you been busy concocting, given the holidays are right around the corner?"

"Mr. Olson has got me testing five different types of cakes for the New Year's Eve celebration. I swear the man can't make up his mind. He says each one I present is the best he has tasted yet."

I cover my mouth as a laugh sneaks through my lips. "I'd take it as a compliment. Though I don't suppose it helps you determine which cake you are to make for New Year's Eve."

"Well, he'll have to make a decision soon or there won't be any cake at all." Cookie takes a bite of her lunch, a homemade roll with roasted chicken and sauce that oozes out the sides.

"What are the plans for New Year's Eve at the hotel? We don't work in the evenings, so we haven't heard much about the festivities."

"Oh, it is going to be glamourous. A long day for sure, but it will be wonderful to see the lobby and reception area decorated with candlelight. And the food. Oh, Louisa, you'll never believe the array of food. Hu is making his famous dim sum, Chef has got his hands full with appetizers, and I am helping out with puff pastry filled with crab and shrimp. Then, of course, there will be delicate slivers of the cake Mr. Olson selects."

Despite being halfway through my sandwich, my mouth waters at the planned meal. "That sounds wonderful."

Before I have finished the last of my milk, Cookie places a slice of cinnamon-swirl coffee cake in front of me. "No wonder this room always smells so good." I thank her by diving into the cake with a generous bite.

As I enjoy my cake, Cookie bustles about the small kitchen, leaving me to think more about Mr. Barnes. He is a friendly sort, and given his animated response toward me, I can tell he enjoyed our brief chat. In my experience, few men can let my charms go unnoticed. It's amazing what a coy smile and a demure glance will do when it comes to holding the attention of men, hopefully including this Hollywood director. As I take the last bite of cake, I find myself contemplating how I might orchestrate another meeting with him.

Cookie tells me she is going to the storeroom and that Gwen will be back to collect me once she has finished her own lunch. I frown at the idea of needing someone to collect me, but I keep the disappointment to myself. I'll be back at full capacity soon enough, and then I'll use every advantage at my disposal to ensure another meeting with the man who could whisk me away to Hollywood.

The more I think about it, the more confident I am that Mr. Barnes is just the sort of gentleman who would be happy to help me with my journey toward stardom. Once he is aware I am an actress, I am quite sure he will know precisely what steps to take.

I sit up straighter as conviction courses through my veins. All I need to do is figure out how to get up to the eighth floor without putting my job at risk.

"Louisa, are you in here? Ah, there you are." Gwen pokes her head into the pastry kitchen. "Are you ready? We've only got the chocolate spoons to go."

"Chocolate spoons? I hope you are joking."

A puzzled expression is painted across Gwen's features. "No, I'm quite serious."

"Well then, we must not dawdle."

My sarcasm is lost on the girl, so all I can do is stifle a giggle and follow her to the lobby. As we continue polishing, I consider how I might make an unnoticed visit to Mr. Barnes' eighth-floor suite.

CHAPTER 16

SATURDAY, DECEMBER 17, 1927

*C*lara
  I am dragging my feet. As the lunch hour nears, it is all I can do to muster the energy to trek down to the locker room for Louisa's lunch. I trudge back up the stairs to the lobby to help my sister to the pastry kitchen.

Before ducking my head into the lobby, I take a moment to collect myself. I lift a hand to my head, ensuring my hair is neatly tucked into a bun. The heat emanating from my forehead catches me by surprise. I've been so busy pushing through my weariness that I haven't considered I might be coming down with something.

Smothering my displeasure at the thought of falling ill, I let out a slow breath and gently push the door open. I slip through the small opening and glance around the room. With only a couple of guests engaged at the reception desk, I stride into the lobby, doing my best to remain out of sight with the help of the oversized, dark wood columns that anchor the lounge area.

I am halted in my tracks by the sight of Louisa chatting

animatedly with Mr. Barnes. I suppress the urge to call out to her. There is little I can do without making a scene. I didn't make it clear to my sister what kind of man Mr. Barnes is, and now here she is, on full display, seeming to enjoy his attention on her.

When Mr. Barnes lowers himself to inspect Louisa's ankle, I feel the fire of outrage grip me by the throat. I am unable to say or do anything as I catch the disapproving glare of Mr. Reynolds, the new registration desk manager, who has clearly asserted himself as head of everything when it comes to the lobby and quite likely anywhere else his eagle eyes may fall. I turn on my heel and push through the door, into the comfort of the back-of-house hallway. I narrowly miss a collision with Ms. Thompson as I march into Cookie's pastry kitchen and unceremoniously drop Louisa's sandwich on the counter.

Knowing my emotions are far from in check, I offer a subdued apology and a quiet excuse of being in a hurry, and then I head toward the stairs, back to the eighth floor. Climbing one floor at a time, I remind myself that Louisa is more than capable of taking care of herself. But her misplaced admiration of Mr. Barnes concerns me. That and his status as a Hollywood director, which is sure to overrule even the most sensible thoughts in my sister's head.

By the time I reach the third-floor landing, I am out of breath and feeling decidedly unwell. I grip the stairwell railing as the chilled concrete space causes my head to spin.

I have barely recovered myself when the stairwell door opens. Seeing me, William steps forward and places a steadying hand on my shoulder.

"Clara, are you all right?"

"Yes. Yes, I am fine. What are you doing here?" I move

toward the next set of stairs, William's hand dropping from my shoulder.

Ignoring my ill-mannered question, he presses on. "You don't look so well." He joins me on the stairs. "Are you sure—"

"Yes. I am quite sure." My tone is unusually sharp and riddled with impatience. I don't meet his eyes, instead focusing on the steps in front of me.

"I am glad I ran into you, then. I was hoping we could finish our conversation. About dinner?"

Even though I know I shouldn't be angry with him, my head swims with contrary emotions and I find myself unable to locate a suitable response. The image of Mr. Barnes and Louisa dashes through my memory, and I am gripped by the fear of something beyond my comprehension.

"I have to get back to work."

"Surely, you have a minute to—"

I stop moving and meet his eyes, cutting him off once more. "This is my job, William."

He drops back a step, lowering himself away from me. "Of course. I apologize for overstepping."

Stomping up the stairs, I feel far less bold than I imagined I would. Instead, guilt at my harsh words and unkind manner consumes me. By the time I reach the eighth floor, I am winded and full of regret.

I spend the remainder of the workday trying to stay upright as fatigue and remorse thrum through my veins.

I've never been so grateful for five o'clock to arrive. I push my cleaning cart into the linen cupboard and spend the final few minutes of my shift restocking the cart while explaining to the evening maid the events and requests of the day.

Given that most of the hotel's guests braved the weather in order to attend today's parade, they are now quietly settled in their suites with warm drinks and happy memories.

Miss Smythe stops me on my way to the locker room. "You look a tad pale, Clara."

"I'm sure it is nothing. I just need a good night's rest is all."

"If you say so, but I think you should know that Miss Roberts went home early today. Ms. Thompson thinks she may be coming down with the flu." Rebecca shrugs as though to say, "What are you going to do?"

"Winter is definitely upon us now. Anyway, get that rest, even if it is simply to ward off a potential illness."

"Thank you. I will."

I gather Louisa's and my things from the locker room and head toward the pastry kitchen, where I expect to find my sister waiting for me.

Instead, I find Cookie with a hand on each hip. I sense I've done something to perturb my friend, though I haven't the slightest clue what it could be.

"There you are, Clara. I've been waiting for you."

I place my things on the small table nestled against the wall and tug my toque onto my head. I smother the exasperated sigh that is ready to unfurl and force on a pleasant expression. "Was there something you needed?"

"No, but I think there is something you need."

"Cookie, it's been a long day, and I'd really like to get Louisa and head home."

My friend holds up a finger to stop my protest. "William mentioned that you might be falling ill. He said he bumped into you in the stairwell and suspected you were feeling poorly."

I feel my cheeks warm at the mention of my less-than-friendly interaction with Ms. Thompson's brother.

Chef pokes his head out of the kitchen, passing Cookie a large flask. "Thank you, Chef. I am quite sure we will be needing plenty of this, since we are already down three staff members today."

Chef bobs his head in acknowledgement and returns to his kitchen without so much as a word.

Cookie hands me the flask. "As soon as I heard you were looking out of sorts, I went straight to work and made up a batch of my chicken soup."

My heart warms at her generosity. "That is very kind of you."

"You should drink that"—Cookie points to the flask in my hand—"and go straight to bed."

"Aye, aye, captain." I tease her with a mock salute before tucking the flask into my bag.

"I also recommend thanking a certain someone who wanted to ensure you were well." With a twinkle in her eye, Cookie steps backwards into the shadows of her pastry kitchen as William appears from beyond the lobby door.

My heart flutters at the sight of him standing before me with a sheepish expression.

"I hope you don't mind." He steps forward, closing the gap between us.

"Don't mind what?"

"Me telling Cookie that you may be falling ill."

My chin drops to my chest. "I imagine it is you who should be upset with me. I am sorry for my rudeness earlier."

I sneak a glance upward as his smile lights up his features. "I didn't mean to pressure you, Clara. I suppose eagerness got the better of me. I will give you the time you need to consider my invitation."

"Thank you." I contemplate how much to share with him, given his connections within the hotel. "There is something else I am dealing with, and I suppose I overreacted when you saw me in the stairwell."

William steps closer and leans his body against the wall beside me. "Is it something you wish to talk about? I am a very good listener."

I hesitate, placating him with a meagre smile. "I'm not sure that is wise."

"Ah, you are wondering if you can trust me." His words tease, but his eyes convey seriousness. "Anything you share with me will remain between us, if that is what you wish."

I check my watch and briefly wonder what is keeping Louisa, before returning my attention to William. "I have a guest who is causing me some challenges. I am uncertain of how to navigate his attention, and he often feels something like a pebble in my shoe."

"Can you elaborate?" William's eyes refuse to leave my own, the alarm in his voice barely restrained. "Has he harmed you?"

I shake my head lightly. "Nothing like that. Honestly, I could be misinterpreting the situation. I suppose I am not used to such attention." I try to appear untroubled, but I sense he does not believe me. "On top of it, there is this holiday bonus competition." Making the admission feels like revealing my soul to him. "A week's wages is a generous prize."

"I heard about the holiday bonus. Quite the prize indeed, but I did wonder about the ramifications of such a contest. Whether it would be detrimental to the symbiotic nature of the staff." William raises his palms. "But that is probably the lawyer in me, examining things from all sides to ensure fairness prevails."

I smile at his assessment of himself.

"Are you worried that you will be excluded from the competition if you say something about this guest?"

William Thompson is an exceptional listener with the ability to fill in the blanks with what I haven't said. I lift my shoulders in concession.

"I understand. That is a bit of a predicament." He is quiet for a moment as he considers the situation. "What I will say is your comfort should never be disregarded by anyone, including yourself. You don't have to reciprocate anyone's feelings or attentions, Clara. You have every right to stand up for yourself, even if it means disappointing another person."

Louisa appears in the hallway, fatigue weeping from every inch of her. "There you are. I was beginning to wonder if you'd decided to stay the night." Feeling a touch lighter after hearing William's advice, I find a teasing tone for my sister.

"Honestly, if that were an option," Louisa says, taking her coat from my outstretched hands, "I would happily collapse in a guest room."

William chuckles at Louisa's response before helping her into her jacket.

"Thank you, Mr. Thompson." Louisa angles her head to one side, appraising the man. "You seem to be our resident knight in shining armour."

I spot the flush of colour as it rises on his face and find I am unable to hide my smile.

"Ready to go?" Louisa turns toward the door, bracing herself for the gust of cool air that is sure to greet us.

I follow her lead. Before reaching the door, I pause, turning to meet William's gaze. "How did you know?"

"How did I know what?" His brow knits together.

"How did you know I wasn't angry with you when I behaved so poorly in the stairwell?"

His eyes crinkle as boyish delight commandeers his features. "You called me by my first name."

A small laugh slips through my lips. "That I did." I turn once more to leave but am tugged back in a rare moment of knowing precisely what I want. "Actually, William, I would very much like to have dinner with you."

CHAPTER 17

MONDAY, DECEMBER 19, 1927

*L*ouisa
With my ankle fully recovered, I arrive at the hotel well before my shift is to begin. By late Saturday evening, Clara was in bed with a fever and a cough. She dutifully sipped Cookie's soup all day Sunday, but the raspy cough is keeping her at home, at least for a day or two.

Though I am not delighted to see my sister under the weather, I can't help but appreciate the timing. Clara's cold means there is a temporary opening on the eighth floor.

I didn't mention the idea brewing in my head to my sister. I doubted she would see the wisdom in my plan, and besides, lengthy conversations had been far from possible this weekend, given her continual coughing.

If I am going to make my way to Hollywood, I will have to be bold and daring. Mr. Barnes' stay at the hotel may be a coincidence, but I am choosing to view it as serendipitous.

My first stop is Ms. Thompson's office. Yesterday afternoon, when it became apparent that Clara would not be in any condition for work today, I telephoned and left a message with the slightly uppity registration desk manager. He promised to convey the message, though he seemed to do so unapprovingly. Since I haven't spoken directly with the matron, I am confident she will appreciate the visit, which will also create an opportunity to put my plan into action.

Outside her office door, I steel myself and gather my courage with a deep inhale. A quick rap on the door gains me instant access.

"Miss Wilson, how is your sister feeling?" Ms. Thompson places her spectacles on the desk in front of her. "It seems the Wilson household has been on the receiving end of some unfortunate luck these past few weeks."

"She is feeling a bit better today, though that nasty cough seems to tire her out quickly."

"I am sorry to hear it. Especially since Miss Roberts is yet to return to her duties." The matron stands to move around her desk. "Was there anything else, Miss Wilson?"

"I wanted to offer my services. To the eighth floor, that is. I figured, being two maids down, you might require someone to fill in, and I wanted to let you know that I am happy to do whatever I can to help."

Pleased with the delivery of my rehearsed inquiry, I hold my breath in anticipation. A place among the eighth-floor suites as a fully authorized maid would be the perfect way to arrange another meeting with Mr. Barnes.

Ms. Thompson hesitates only a moment before turning me down. "That is very kind of you to offer. For now, I think we can manage."

Deflated by Ms. Thompson's response, I steer myself toward the locker room. My lips twist in disappointment as my mind tumbles back to the problem I was certain I had solved. How will I arrange another meeting with the Hollywood director?

Jane is the first to spot my sour disposition as I remove my winter wear, carelessly tossing my toque and gloves into the bottom of my locker, among the wet of my wool-lined granny boots. I change out of my dress and pluck the fifth-floor uniform off its hanger, sliding it over my head.

"What's got you in a huff?" Jane leans over, her bright red lipstick highlighting the porcelain white of her face.

"I am fine. Just another glamourous day at The Hamilton." I slip my feet into my black oxfords and sit down on the bench to tie them, determined to keep my aspirations regarding Mr. Barnes to myself.

Jane, ignoring my mood, reaches over me and plucks my hat and gloves from the bottom of the locker. "You'll be even less delightful if you come back at the end of the day to discover everything damp and cold." She plops the items on the top shelf and sits down beside me.

A gentle nudge from her shoulders tells me she is listening. "I don't want to bother you with any of it. I am being silly and stubborn and, oh, never mind. Let's just get on with our day." I try to shrug off my disappointment.

"Why don't we work together today? Ease the burden and all." Jane's invitation is kind and well-meaning.

Though we were unlikely friends in the beginning, Jane Morgan has become someone I respect and, from time to time, have confided in. But this is one secret I am not willing to share with anyone. At least not yet.

I catch Gwen watching us and decide that working alongside Jane is just the thing to turn my unpleasant mood around. "I'd like that." I give an affirming nod, and Jane and I head toward the fifth floor.

Ms. Thompson is tardy for roll call, so we busy

ourselves with readying our carts, rather than loitering in the hallway.

Ten minutes past the hour, Ms. Thompson arrives with her clipboard in hand and an apology lining her features. "My apologies, ladies. It seems we are falling prey to the influenza season. We are down another three maids as of this morning. The hotel hasn't slowed any in terms of guests arriving, so we will all have to pull together to do our best."

With a murmur of understanding, we maids file into a straight line for roll call.

Ms. Thompson informs us that Cookie has prepared enough chicken soup to feed an army, so we are encouraged to enjoy a bowl along with our midday meal in an effort to keep ourselves healthy and upright.

With tasks delivered and guest rooms assigned, Ms. Thompson excuses us to get on with our day.

George arrives on the fifth floor as we are about to depart. Though he has become quite comfortable with us maids on an individual basis, his youthful blush returns at the sight of the lot of us.

"Hello, George." I smile warmly at the young man, hopeful a friendly face will put him at ease.

"Oh, hello Lou—Miss Wilson." He corrects himself when he becomes aware of Ms. Thompson's attention on him.

I stifle a giggle and turn to follow Jane to retrieve our cleaning carts.

"Miss Wilson." Ms. Thompson waves me over.

"Yes, ma'am." I approach with hurried steps.

"It seems we have lost another eighth-floor maid. Miss McKinley was sent home this morning. Are you still prepared to assist on the eighth floor?"

I conceal my eagerness behind a stoic expression. "Yes, ma'am. I am happy to help in any way I might be useful."

"Thank you, Miss Wilson. Why don't you head to the laundry for the appropriate uniform, and I will meet you on the eighth floor in a few minutes."

"Thank you, ma'am." I scurry over to Jane, who is waiting for me, and give her the short version of the situation. "Another maid is sick. I'm heading to the eighth floor to help fill in."

Jane barely has time to wish me luck before I am out the door and dashing down the stairs to the laundry.

Once changed, with my hair pulled back into a brain-numbing bun, I climb the eight floors with slow, methodical steps, ensuring I arrive well put together instead of a sweaty, panicked mess.

I poke my head out of the stairwell. The deep, lavish burgundy and gold of the eighth floor welcome me. Stepping onto the plush carpet, I feel as though I am walking on a cloud, my oxfords sinking slightly with each step. The floor's decor is quite opulent, and it strikes me as interesting that Clara seldom speaks of the grandeur she spends her days in.

Ms. Thompson finds me near the lift, its polished brass far shinier than that I've seen on the other guest floors. "We've settled on a two-person approach for efficiency and to ensure we don't leave you stranded in a position you've not been trained for."

"Yes, ma'am." I follow close on her heels, aware that I will have to seek a moment alone to locate Mr. Barnes' suite and, with any luck, the man himself.

"You will work with Miss Smythe today," she says as Rebecca joins us in the hallway, "as I believe the two of you are acquainted with one another."

"Yes, ma'am."

"All the maids are doubled up on duties, so you may be called to assist with a multitude of tasks today, Miss Wilson. These may include fetching newspapers, securing extra pillows or blankets, and since it is the holiday season, wrapping guests' Christmas gifts."

"Where does that take place, ma'am? The wrapping of gifts."

"We have taken over a small banquet room for the time being. There is a table, paper, scissors, ribbon, and the like. To be honest, we didn't know what to expect when we started offering the service, but we have found that our eighth-floor guests are happy to hand off a great many tasks to our staff."

Ms. Thompson stops in front of a set of large double doors. She tugs the handle, and the doors open to a linen closet four times as big as the ones on the fifth floor. Shelves are lined with lavender soaps, plush towels, fleecy robes, and every other convenience one might expect at a luxury hotel.

"I must be getting on, so I will leave you in the capable hands of Miss Smythe." Ms. Thompson inclines her head in a quick motion and is out the door before I can say thank you.

"I am sorry to hear Clara is unwell," Rebecca says. "I suspected she was catching something when I saw her last." She piles towels onto the second shelf of her cart as we talk. "I am certainly glad for the help today. We're short three maids, and the suites are fully booked all the way through New Year's Eve."

"How can I be of assistance?" I decide that having the lay of the land before attempting to locate Mr. Barnes is both prudent and necessary, given the extra work heaped upon the maids this morning.

"We'll start with my suites, and then we will move on to Clara's. Once we're done with those, we will see who needs an extra hand. It's going to be a busy day. I sure hope that ankle of yours is good as new."

"I am happy to report that my ankle is indeed fully recovered."

"Off we go, then."

Miss Smythe tours me from suite to suite, directing me in how to handle rooms and furniture I've not encountered. I am relieved to learn that most guests vacate the hotel early in the day, expecting to return to freshly cleaned suites in the afternoon. This, I surmise, is the reason for the eighth-floor maids' later lunch hour.

I run several errands, fetching additional bedding, newspapers, and for those few who have chosen to stay in this morning, additional pots of coffee and trays full of Cookie's pastries. The mini croissants are so enticing I fear my stomach will rumble its displeasure at not being offered one.

On my second trip to the kitchen in less than an hour, I decide that if I were staying on the eighth floor, I too would choose to stay in, if only to enjoy a croissant or two.

By noon, we have tended to all of Miss Smythe's suites and one of Clara's. Rebecca steers me back to the linen closet, pushing her cart over the thick carpet with ease.

She closes the doors behind us but continues to keep her voice low. "Clara has three suites in her charge this week, but one of them is a bit tricky."

"What do you mean 'tricky'?" I feel my left eyebrow lift.

"I believe you are familiar with Mr. Barnes?" Rebecca raises her own eyebrows.

I tuck a giggle behind an open palm. "Indeed. We had a meeting of sorts."

"Well, he tends to linger in his suite, making it inconvenient for cleaning. When he does appear, it is to chat with every passerby that happens to come his way." Rebecca pauses before adding, "When one doesn't come his way, he strolls the halls, I can only assume looking for entertainment."

"Sounds harmless enough. He did strike me as the talkative sort."

Rebecca agrees with a vigorous nod.

"So, what is the plan? Do we knock on his door and oust him so we can tidy up, or do we wait him out?" I am speaking in jest, but my quip evidently goes unnoticed by Rebecca.

"I think we should head down for a quick bite while we can, and maybe he will venture out in the meantime."

Though I do not relish this approach, since it takes me further away from what I've come here to do, I am in no position to say otherwise. "If that is what you think is best."

"I do. Besides, I'd enjoy a bowl of Cookie's soup, just to be on the safe side of remaining well."

Upon returning from lunch, Rebecca sends me to check on suite 815 while she prepares the cart with fresh linens, towels, and dainty lavender soaps that smell heavenly. She instructs me to knock firmly, announce myself, and wait. I am to repeat this process two more times if the door goes unanswered.

With the instruction firmly planted in my mind, I cross the threshold into the hallway. I get my bearings and am about to turn left toward suite 815 when Rebecca offers one more vital piece of information.

"Suite 815 is occupied by Mr. Barnes." She lifts both

shoulders in a non-verbal apology. Little does she know how fortuitous this news is to me.

I almost dance down the hall of deep red carpet, buoyed by my good fortune.

Standing before Mr. Barnes' suite, I straighten my posture and put a flat palm to the bun at the back of my head. I lift my arm and give three quick, decisive knocks. I am leaning toward the door to announce myself when it swings open.

"Well, Miss Wilson, what a pleasant surprise."

"Good day, Mr. Barnes. I have come to inquire about setting your suite right for the day." I deliver my friendliest smile before continuing, "But I also wanted to speak with you about a matter that may benefit both of us."

"Do tell, Miss Wilson. Do tell."

"I have been informed that you work in the movie business in Hollywood."

"Is that so?" Mr. Barnes tilts his chin up to examine me from beneath narrowing eyes.

"Not to worry, sir. I am not a foolish girl with unfounded, fanciful dreams. I am, in fact, a theatre actress interested in expanding my horizons to the California movie scene. I have received several glowing reviews from my recent role as Mrs. Craig in *Craig's Wife*, and I would be more than happy to share those with you."

"That won't be necessary. I feel as though I can take you at your word." Mr. Barnes' eyes travel the length of my eighth-floor uniform. "I didn't realize you tended suites on this floor. I believe the last time we met, you were wearing a different costume."

"How perceptive of you, sir. I am filling in today, as a few of the hotel maids have fallen ill."

"So, what exactly can I do for you, Miss Wilson?"

"Well, sir. If you would allow me to share my talents with you. Perhaps an audition of your choosing." I lose my train of thought when I see Miss Smythe and her fully stocked cart trundling up the hallway toward us.

I do not have time to utter another word as the cart arrives at my side.

"Apologies, Mr. Barnes. We thought it might be an appropriate time to tend to your room, but I see that it is not." Miss Smythe curtsies before setting her attention squarely on me. "Miss Wilson, we do not wish to disturb Mr. Barnes. We will return at a more convenient time."

I feel Rebecca's gaze tugging me backwards, as I imagine she wishes her hands could do. I twist my lips as a slight eye roll escapes without warning.

Mr. Barnes' smirk is hard to miss. "Actually, I was planning to go out. Let me grab my coat and hat, and I'll be out of your way."

Rebecca stops mid-stride. "We have no desire to put you out, sir."

"Not at all, Miss Smythe. I was explaining the very same thing to Miss Wilson here."

"Thank you, sir. We will have your room ready as quickly as possible."

Mr. Barnes turns to grab his coat and hat off the rack and steps into the hallway. "Thank you, ladies."

Rebecca turns away from us as she manoeuvres her cleaning cart out of his path, and Mr. Barnes leans in, whispering near my ear, "I look forward to helping you in any way I can, Miss Wilson."

Without another word, he tips his hat to Rebecca and walks confidently toward the lift.

CHAPTER 18

WEDNESDAY, DECEMBER 21, 1927

Clara

A few days in bed have done me a world of good. I am in high spirits, and the holiday festivities are in full swing at The Hamilton. While I rested at home, Ms. Thompson and the rest of the staff have extended the Christmas decorations to all of the guest floors, with pine and holly bouquets adorning every hall table. Cookie has been on an intensive baking spree, and all guest rooms are set to receive a gingerbread cookie with their turndown service each evening until Boxing Day.

These added touches make the hotel feel almost magical, and I couldn't be more delighted by the transformation. Louisa and I are changing into our uniforms as a few of the other maids chatter excitedly about the band that will be setting up in the lobby on Christmas Eve.

I catch Lou's eye and give her shoulder an appreciative squeeze. Though she was a little disappointed to relinquish her time on the eighth floor, Louisa rallied quickly when she learned Ms. Thompson had selected her for some additional duties throughout the hotel.

At the fifth-floor landing, I tell her to have a good day and continue the remaining three floors to the eighth. Even the thought of being assigned, once again, to Mr. Barnes' suite does little to dampen my mood.

I've had time to consider William's words, and I believe he is, in fact, correct. I have duties and responsibilities as a Hotel Hamilton maid, but I also have an obligation to myself to ensure I am comfortable and at ease. Though I have little idea of how to turn his wise words into something actionable, I decide to let the day unfold as it will. I will be my usual polite and attentive self, and hopefully Mr. Barnes will be nowhere in sight, though I realize that's unlikely.

Two hours later, I push my cleaning trolly in front of suite 815. I am ahead of schedule this morning, having already tended to my first two suites. I settle myself with a deep breath and raise my hand to knock. I announce myself and am pleasantly surprised when I hear no movement on the other side of the door.

I repeat my actions. By the third knock and announcement, I am confident Mr. Barnes is not in his suite. I waste no time using my master key to unlock the door. Knowing he could return at any moment, I dash around the suite in a frenzied state.

I remove the bedding, replacing it quickly with fresh sheets. I plump the pillows, fold down the duvet, and reposition the bench at the foot of the oversized bed.

Not wishing to dawdle with a trip to the laundry chute, I shove the recently removed sheets onto the bottom shelf of my cart and set about clearing the towels, cloths, and robe from the bathroom. My cart is spilling over, but I pay it no mind as I scrub the bathtub, sink, and countertop. I run a broom over the black-and-white penny tiles before getting on my hands and knees to give the floor a good scrubbing.

Unfurling a new robe, I hang it on the hook on the back of the bathroom door, and then I move about the bedroom with the duster in hand. We seldom give the rooms a chance to gather dust, but the task is part of my job, so I give every surface a cursory swipe. I follow up with an efficient vacuum before opening the curtains fully to the view of the North Shore Mountains.

I close the bedroom's double doors halfway as I exit and turn my attention to the living area. Dusting and vacuuming take little time. I place today's newspaper on the chaise lounge at an appealing angle and am about to gather a smattering of dirty dishes piled on the writing desk when I hear a key turn in the lock.

My first instinct is to freeze, as I remember the last interaction that took place in this room. Using the toe of my shoe, I try to conceal the white linens and towels spilling over my cart's bottom shelf, afraid they will jam the cart's wheels and hinder my escape.

I force a courteous smile into place and clasp my hands in front of me. "Welcome back, Mr. Barnes. I'll clear out these dishes and be out of your way, sir."

"Miss Wilson, I heard you were under the weather." He steps further into the room, placing his coat and hat on the rack as he moves toward me.

"I am much better." Though he hasn't exactly asked, I offer the well-mannered sentiment anyway. "Thank you."

"Very good to hear." Mr. Barnes steps even closer, tossing aside the carefully positioned newspaper as he sits on the end of the chaise lounge. "Don't let me keep you, Miss Wilson. Carry on."

I feel the urge to let out a rush of relief at his indifference toward me, but I clamp my lips shut and begin gathering the dishes, placing them carefully on the cart's top shelf. This dismissive Mr. Barnes is vastly preferable to the overly attentive one I've come to expect.

With the dishes nestled safely on my cart, I position myself at its handle and urge it forward. Nearing the door, I am about to bid the man good day when I turn to find him directly behind me.

"Let me assist you with the door, Miss Wilson."

"Thank you, I am fine."

Before I can stop him, Mr. Barnes squeezes between me and the suite's entrance, pausing in front of me. His breath, laced with onion and garlic, causes the hairs on the back of my neck to stand at attention.

I resist the urge to shiver, unwilling to give him the satisfaction of witnessing my reaction. There is nowhere to retreat. My back is pressed firmly against the wall, and he is blocking my movement in all directions.

I remember William's advice to stand up for myself, and I swivel my head to the side, a clear display that I do not desire to be in such proximity to this man. I clear my throat and will my voice to be steady. "Mr. Barnes, if you could let me pass. I am needed elsewhere and am already running late."

I immediately forgive myself for the white lie as well as the ill-mannered delivery of my words. Though my response to this situation may cost me the holiday bonus, even a week's wages is not worth allowing this man to accost me.

"There is no need to rush, Miss Wilson." Mr. Barnes lowers his voice and places a hand on the wall behind my head, bringing his torso another inch closer to my own. "I'd like for us to be friends. Tell me, do you have so many friends in this world that you can't make room for another?"

William's concerned expression when he asked if I had been harmed by a guest flashes across my mind. I feel the room tilt, and before it can swing completely from my grasp, I straighten my posture and meet Mr. Barnes' eyes.

"Kindly allow me to pass, sir."

I expect Mr. Barnes to stand his ground, but surprisingly, he takes a step back before striding the two paces to the door and pulling it open for me.

I push the cart forward. "Thank you, sir" is on the tip of my tongue, but before I can utter a word, he grabs me by the arm and pulls me close, planting a sloppy, wet kiss squarely on my unsuspecting lips.

Instinct takes over, and my hand flies up to connect with his fleshy cheek. With a resounding smack, the palm of my hand strikes Mr. Barnes' face. I cover my open mouth with my stinging hand. Without thinking, I have done the unimaginable. I have slapped a hotel guest.

With me at the helm, my cleaning cart sails over the suite's threshold as though it has wings. The cart teeters unsteadily under its precarious weight, but I can't stop myself from running. I already know that I will abandon the cart completely if it crashes.

Tears stream down my face as I rush past a husband and wife, strolling arm in arm toward their room. Through tear-blurred vision, I see the man give me a questioning look, but I don't stop running until I've slammed the cart against the linen cupboard's interior wall.

Feeling no safer, I pace the small room for only a few

seconds before dashing toward the back-of-house stairs. I thrust open the door to the landing so hard it slams against the wall, echoing through the stairwell like an ominous warning.

With one hand gripping the banister railing, I propel myself down each flight of stairs. I race past the second-floor landing, my arm stretched tight by forward momentum and gravity. Out of control, I careen toward the last set of stairs and crash straight into Louisa.

CHAPTER 19

WEDNESDAY, DECEMBER 21, 1927

*L*ouisa

"Clara, what the…?" Sobs rattle my sister like a twig in a windstorm. "What is it? What has happened?"

"I—I'm sorry." Clara's words are lost in a round of cascading tears.

Wrapping an arm around her shoulders, I gently steer her to the corner of the stairwell, certain she wouldn't want to be seen in her current state.

"Slow down. Take a deep breath." Clara follows my instructions, taking slow, ragged breaths. "There you go. That's it."

She shakes her head in disagreement, but I've no idea what has caused this unhinged version of my usually timid and straitlaced sister.

"You don't understand."

"Well, I certainly won't unless you tell me what the trouble is." My teasing tone does little to quell her upset state.

"I've ruined everything."

"I am sure that isn't the case. Take your time and tell me what happened."

"Oh, when Ms. Thompson finds out, I'll be sacked for sure." Clara's chin tilts up a fraction, her eyes searching mine. "And William." A guttural moan slips from her lips as though she is a wounded animal.

"What about William?" I place a hand on each of her shoulders in an attempt to steady her.

"He won't want anything to do with me now." Clara's head lolls to one side. "I really liked him, you know. Which is probably wrong, given that he is Ms. Thompson's brother and a hotel guest as well." She covers her mouth with both hands, muffling her anguished sobs.

"Clara, you are scaring me. Please tell me what has happened." I grip her shoulders now, shaking her slightly to gain her attention.

I wait patiently as she tries to gather herself. "I—I slapped a hotel guest."

At the words, I stumble backwards. "You did what?"

Her tormented expression tells me I haven't kept my reaction in check. I try again. "Start from the beginning. Please. I can't believe you would simply slap anyone, let alone without cause. Tell me what happened, and we can figure this out."

"I, he..." She sniffles, wiping her nose with the back of her hand. "I tried to avoid him, but he is everywhere. In the lobby, in the hallway, and even when he's not in his room, he suddenly appears." Clara's exasperation appears to be ruling her emotional state, causing her to ramble.

"Tried to avoid who?" I bite back my frustration at her unwillingness, or inability, to tell me plainly what is going on.

Her sheepish expression lets me know she is embarrassed to say the words out loud. "It's Mr. Barnes."

"What? Why in the world would you slap Mr. Barnes?" The accusation is out of my mouth before I can reel it in. No, this can't be right. Scenarios race through my head, none of them seeming even remotely possible for the kind man who is set to help me advance my acting career.

Clara glares at me, her eyes backlit with fire. "I tried to tell you."

"Tell me what?" Softening my tone, I rub her arms, trying to coax her out. "I am sure this is all a misunderstanding. You'll see."

"I was standing up for myself." Clara's lips twist in contemplation before she drops her head into her hands and mumbles, "He wanted to kiss me, Lou."

My head spins as I try to make sense of what she's said. This can't be.

An exasperated sigh whooshes from her lips. "It doesn't matter now. I've certainly ruined my chances at winning the eighth-floor holiday bonus, once Ms. Thompson hears what I've done. I wanted so badly to show you..." Her shoulders drop an inch further than I thought them capable of. "To prove to myself, really, that I could manage without you. You always know what to do, and I just—I wanted you to know I could handle things so you could follow your dreams without worrying about me." A distraught moan leaves her body. "I probably won't even be gifted the turkey for Christmas dinner. Honestly, I'll be lucky if I still have a job once Mr. Olson hears of it." Clara's head shakes vehemently back and forth.

Realizing that remaining in the back-of-house stairwell in tears is a sure way to escalate this situation, should someone stumble upon us, I stand a little straighter, intending to get my sister tucked out of sight. "Let's get you cleaned up." I nudge her down the corridor toward the locker room. "We have no reason to believe you will lose your job over this." Even I don't believe my words, but until I can figure out what actually happened between Clara and Mr. Barnes, my sole goal is to keep Clara calm. I guide her toward the privacy of the locker room, offering soothing words as we move.

Once there, I step into the hallway to give her some much-needed space to wash her face and fix her hair. My mind runs rampant with the few insights Clara has provided. I've never seen her this distraught, and I can't help but wonder if she has been mistaken.

Mr. Barnes has been nothing but helpful and courteous to me. Try as I might, I cannot imagine the man, who is my only hope of finding success in Hollywood, as someone my sister would have reason to strike. There must be something else at play here. I tap a finger to my bottom lip. I will simply have to figure out what it is.

Clara emerges from the locker room, still with red blotches across her tear-stained face. Her hair is pulled back in a severe and uncomfortable-looking bun. I wonder if she is punishing herself or simply trying to exert some control.

Ushering a certainty, which I definitely do not feel, into my words, I loop my arm through Clara's and begin the short walk to the lunchroom. "We'll have lunch first, and then we can sort things out. If we get there before the others, you'll have a little more time to collect yourself."

"I'm not hungry."

I ignore her protest. "I will say that you found a break in your day and decided to join us for an earlier-than-usual lunch."

Clara eyes me warily but says nothing.

"I believe Cookie's soup is still being served. A bowl will do you good."

I stop a few paces short of the lunchroom. "We need to see what happens. Let things settle a bit and then make a plan. If after lunch there is still no news of the…" I hesitate, trying to find the right word. "The incident from Ms. Thompson, then we will figure out what to do next."

"But, what if…?" Clara's voice pitches high with worry.

I shake my head. "We cannot know what is going to happen, so there is no point in worrying about it. Let's take this one step at a time. I am sure we will find a solution." I squeeze Clara's arm, then tug her into the lunchroom, permeated with the scent of chicken soup.

My mind feels as though it is running in different directions. A solution must be found. Preferably one that will put Clara at ease while also securing my own future. It is a tall order and, given my sister's current emotional state, one I must fill on my own.

CHAPTER 20

WEDNESDAY, DECEMBER 21, 1927

Clara
  I nibble at the edges of my sandwich for the better part of twenty minutes. Not tasting the meal, I finally rewrap it and return it to my locker. Though she tries, Lou is unable to convince me, my stomach knotted with emotion, to finish even a small bowl of Cookie's chicken soup.

  Deciding by herself that I am not fit to return to the eighth floor, Louisa drags me about the back-of-house corridors, searching for Ms. Thompson. Seeing the matron is not high on my list of things to do at the moment, but Louisa's rationale is sound, and without another option before me, I follow her lead.

  She's instructed me to hide my current emotional state and my true feelings over the incident with Mr. Barnes and instead force a polite demeanour into place. Striding toward Ms. Thompson's basement office, Louisa reminds me to smile before announcing, "If she knows anything about your and Mr. Barnes' interaction, it will be better for it to come out here rather than in front of guests."

I swallow, trying to release the lump that has lodged in my throat. How can I possibly explain to Ms. Thompson that I did as she instructed and kept my head down and yet it did not stop Mr. Barnes' attention? Lou squeezes my hand in solidarity, and I find myself praying that Mr. Olson is not inside. I remember his promise to never again take the word of a maid over that of a hotel guest. "I'm not sure about this." Before I can finish protesting, we are in front of Ms. Thompson's closed office door, with Louisa announcing our presence with a knock.

"Come in." Ms. Thompson looks up from her paperwork as we enter.

Lou pokes me discreetly in the side with her elbow, and I lift my cheeks in what I hope is a smile.

"Ladies." Ms. Thompson folds her hands together on the desk. "How can I help you?"

"Sorry to trouble you, ma'am." Louisa steps forward. "You tasked me with helping in the lobby this afternoon, with the bar cart and such."

Ms. Thompson confirms her request with a single nod.

"I have found myself a little behind on the fifth floor and was wondering if Clara might take my place in the lobby?"

"I see. How are you getting through your roster, Miss Wilson?" Ms. Thompson asks me.

"I have completed all three suites, ma'am. My only remaining task is to sweep and mop the back stairwell. After that, I was planning on coming to you to see what more I could help with."

"You are certainly efficient, Miss Wilson. Remind me to

add to your roster of guest suites in the new year. Clearly, you are capable of handling a larger load."

An immense sense of relief courses through me. If Ms. Thompson knew anything about my encounter with Mr. Barnes, she wouldn't be complimenting me. The thought of confiding my predicament to her dashes through my mind but is quickly halted. Mr. Hamilton himself instructed for Mr. Barnes to be treated with the utmost care, and I have clearly not done so.

Perhaps there was another reason for Mr. Hamilton's request, beyond Mr. Barnes' status. Could it be that he is simply lonely, travelling on his own for extended periods of time? Perhaps if I had given him some companionship, treated him with more of the care required of my position, I could have avoided this entire fiasco.

As soon as the thought occurs to me, I dismiss it. No, I think. William is right. I have an obligation to myself and my own comfort, even if it disappoints another. Even if it costs me my job.

Ms. Thompson continues her thought with a wave of her hand. "The stairwell isn't the most pressing of matters. It can wait until another day. I suppose we can arrange for one of the other maids to be available for any requests from your guests." She looks between Louisa and me. "Yes, that is a fine arrangement, ladies."

"Thank you, ma'am." Louisa dips into a brief curtsy.

"I will meet you in the lobby in ten minutes." Ms. Thompson dismisses us, and together we turn for the door with the understanding that, for now, my place at The Hamilton remains safe.

Ten minutes later, I am tucked into an alcove near the registration desk, doing my best to disappear into the woodwork, when Ms. Thompson arrives with instructions.

She guides me toward the far end of the lobby, where two beautiful and inviting blue velvet-covered chairs sit angled in front of the tall windows overlooking the snow-covered courthouse across the street. With the roaring fire a good distance away, in the centre of the lobby, this cozy spot has always struck me as the perfect place to curl up with a cup of tea and a good book.

Ms. Thompson's long finger points toward the potted tree in the corner. "The bellboys will bring in the temporary bar. We will need to relocate these chairs and perhaps the other items as well, but until I've seen the bar in place, I can't be sure how much room we'll need."

I follow her train of thought, thankful for the reprieve from my swirling mind.

"Once everything is in position, you will stock the bar. Everything you will need is waiting in the hall outside the pastry kitchen. The bartender will arrive tomorrow to ensure it is all in order."

"Yes, ma'am."

"You will need to use your imagination, along with some good organizational skills. As of now, I am not quite sure the glasses and bottles will all fit." Ms. Thompson cups her chin with a forefinger and thumb as she considers the limited space.

"Will the bottles be put in place today, ma'am?" I am thinking ahead to my lack of knowledge about which bottles might go where, or whether they are to be grouped by some unknown-to-me specificity.

"Not to worry, Miss Wilson. The bartender will set up the spirits closer to New Year's Eve. We only have to allow space for them at this time."

Both our heads turn as George and a bellboy I've only ever known as Mr. Jones shuffle toward us, carrying an elaborate piece of dark wooden furniture the size of a buffet table.

"Oh my." Ms. Thompson's head swivels between the furniture and the small space we have to position it in. "That is much larger than I was led to believe."

Together, we hurriedly slide the chairs and the small table that sits between them out of the way.

"Put it right here for now." Ms. Thompson directs the red-faced bellboys. "Well, Miss Wilson, it looks like we will have to roll up our sleeves for this one." Without hesitating, the matron unbuttons her long sleeves at the cuffs.

We spend the better part of an hour working through our options. Our preference is to have the bartender's back to a wall, but the sheer length of the bar makes this impossible. Using our footsteps to measure out different scenarios, we finally settle on arranging the furniture so the bartender's back is at an angle to the windows.

Once the decision is made, the bellboys move the bar into position as Ms. Thompson tuts about, saying she wished she had known about the vastness of the bar sooner, as surely she would have placed the Christmas tree in the window corner instead.

I move around to the back side of the bar's open shelving. "Maybe we can add some fabric, like a curtain, to hide the shelving."

"That is an excellent idea. I will see what we have in the storage rooms. In the meantime, why don't you get started with filling up those shelves?"

"Yes, ma'am." I slip through the door into the kitchen hall, lift a crate of glassware off the stack, and return to the lobby, careful not to bump anything in my path.

Pulling a few wine glasses from the crate and setting them on top of the bar, I realize they are noticeably spotted with water droplets. I return to the kitchen for a tea towel, determined to do everything I can to maintain my good standing with Ms. Thompson, regardless of the storm that could, at any moment, rain down on me.

The repetitive task of wiping then examining each glass in the light from the windows lulls my mind back to the events of this morning. Try as I might, I am unable to locate a potential misunderstanding between me and Mr. Barnes.

I've been cordial and polite, but at no time did I encourage the man to think I was interested in anything but being the maid who cleans his suite. At least not intentionally. Though I've seen Louisa flutter her eyelashes and draw a man's attention her way, I'm not sure I even possess the ability to do such a thing. I am neither courageous enough nor interested in such shenanigans.

Shenanigans. The word feels like a pit in my stomach. Mr. Olson said in very clear terms that he will not put up with shenanigans and that he would not again make the mistake of believing a maid over a guest. I am as a good as fired when he learns of my dreadful behaviour. I feel the sting of moisture gathering in my eyes, and I swipe at it with the corner of the tea towel.

"I heard you were back at work." William startles me from my thoughts. "How are you feeling?"

"Oh, you surprised me." I bend at the waist, buying a moment to collect myself by placing a clean glass on the bottom shelf of the bar cart. "I am feeling much better. Thank you for asking." The words are almost exactly the same as the ones I shared with Mr. Barnes, but William's interest in my well-being seems far more genuine.

"I am glad to hear it." He examines the bar. "Quite the setup. I imagine the party will be a dazzling event."

"I suppose so." I lift another glass toward the light to examine it for spots.

"Maybe you would like to go with me?" William's smile leans toward bashful.

"To the party?" I shake my head lightly. "I don't think that is a very good idea, and I am quite certain neither will your sister or Mr. Olson."

His laugh warms the room, drawing a smile from my lips. "You are probably right about that. Not that either of their disapproval would stop me if you had said yes, but I see how it might be less than comfortable to attend a social gathering in your place of employment."

I decline to reply, unsure of what to say in response to his forward comment.

My attention is pulled across the room when I see Mr. Barnes exit the lift, strutting through the lobby as if he owns the place. I duck my chin to my chest and pretend I haven't noticed him.

It is a familiar voice that jerks my head up.

"Mr. Barnes," Louisa calls in a hushed voice.

Mr. Barnes turns toward my sister, a wide Cheshire grin upon his face. Their heads bend together as they descend into hurried whispers.

"Is everything all right? You look as though you've seen a ghost."

"What?" I glance briefly to William. "I'm fine."

He eyes me with raised brows.

I return my attention to Louisa and Mr. Barnes and watch, bewildered, as Louisa places a hand on Mr. Barnes' arm while delivering one of her disarming laughs. Assuming William has followed my gaze, I am grateful for his silence.

Ms. Thompson steps into the lobby, carrying a stack of

folded fabric. Mr. Barnes gestures her over, and they chat for a minute before he tips his hat. As he walks through the lobby on his way to the front door, I lower myself behind the bar's base and busy my hands with repositioning glasses.

Louisa and Ms. Thompson exchange a few words before Louisa slips through the back-of-house door and out of sight.

"So you've seen our monstrosity?" Ms. Thompson asks her brother, inclining her head toward the bar as she crosses the lobby toward us.

A soft chuckle replaces his look of concern. "It is rather on the large side, but the good news is the bartender isn't likely to run out of anything, with the ample storage."

"Always looking on the bright side, William." Ms. Thompson directs her attention my way. "How are you getting on, Miss Wilson?"

"Fine, ma'am. The glasses needed polishing, but other than that, I think the bartender will be pleased."

"Excellent news. Speaking of being pleased." Ms. Thompson clasps her hands in front of her. "Mr. Barnes has been quite happy with your service and has requested you as his maid again upon his return after Christmas. He is leaving tomorrow to celebrate the holidays with friends and will return on the twenty-sixth. He plans to be with us right through to the new year."

"Oh." I am shocked and unnerved, with little to offer in reply.

Ms. Thompson's brows knit together at my less than appreciative response. "You are certainly putting your best foot forward. I wouldn't be at all surprised if you were to take home the holiday bonus, Miss Wilson."

"Thank you, ma'am." I have no idea what has transpired. Did Louisa manage to talk the man out of reporting me? I recognize this as favourable news, yet the looming dread of having to return to Mr. Barnes' suite steals any joy from the announcement. I don't know what the man is playing at. All I know is that I'm not fond of being his toy.

I feign a pleased expression, but when my eyes land briefly on William's, I see a question lining his wrinkled forehead.

CHAPTER 21

WEDNESDAY, DECEMBER 21, 1927

Louisa

"What a day." Though I direct the comment to Clara, I am met with a silence that feels as chilled as the wintery evening air as we step away from the warmth of The Hamilton.

Bundled from head to toe, we trudge down the back stairs and up the alley toward the glow of the electric street lamps. "I can't wait to be cozy at home with a cup of tea."

Still, nothing. She hasn't spoken to me since after lunch. Even when we met in the locker room to change out of our uniforms before walking home, she avoided my gaze.

I place a gloved hand on her coat sleeve and tug her to a stop. "Clara, what is the matter?"

"Why did you speak to him?" she hisses at me.

"Who? Mr. Barnes? I was trying to help." I am taken aback by her anger. "I thought you wanted to sort the situation out. I thought you wanted to keep your job. And I was helping you do just that. I did it for you, Clara."

A stab of hypocrisy catches me unaware. I clamp my

bottom lip between my teeth. The truth is that I also wanted to ensure that Clara's outburst, which I still don't fully understand, hadn't derailed my relationship with the Hollywood director. I could barely get through the workday, contemplating how this event might have inadvertently stomped on my dreams of Hollywood fame.

I motion for us to continue walking as a shiver runs through me.

"You shouldn't have approached him. He is a dangerous man, Louisa."

Clara has clearly lost her mind. I consider myself to be a fairly good judge of character, and the man does not seem dangerous at all. A tad over the top, yes. Overly theatrical and exceptionally friendly, definitely. But dangerous, I hardly think so. I do not, however, say any of this to my sister. I'm quite sure she isn't inclined to listen to me, anyway.

Instead, I try another approach. "The man has been nothing but cordial and helpful to me. I would have thought you'd be more inclined to give him the benefit of the doubt, given how he stepped in to help me when I fell."

Clara says nothing, but the look she tosses in my direction feels like the sharp end of a knife.

"I figured I might have a word with him and try to untangle the misunderstanding between you. When I saw him this afternoon I found him pleasant and happy to clear the air. I was ensuring all is well."

Clara rolls her eyes at me, a sure sign that I have done wrong by her, again.

"It is, by the way."

"Is what?" Clara steps over a pile of snow, grabbing hold of my arm to balance herself.

"All is well." I give her an exasperated look to rival her own as we cross the street, another block closer to home.

"How can you think that? I've thought about it all afternoon, and it was not a misunderstanding." Clara's annoyed sigh takes shape in a breath of frosty air. "Seriously, Louisa. You can't simply smile and toss your hair over your shoulder and assume that everything has righted itself."

"I'll have you know I did not toss my hair." I giggle and pull her closer. She doesn't laugh. "Maybe when we get home you can tell me what really happened, and I mean the entire story, Clara." The lift of my eyebrow goes unseen under my toque.

Clara is defeated. I can feel it in her every movement. Her downcast eyes. Her hunched posture. Even her steps are slow and weighted.

She breaks the silence with a weary voice. "Honestly, since Mr. Barnes hasn't said anything to Ms. Thompson and he leaves tomorrow, I'd just as soon forget about him and enjoy the holiday season."

"Don't think I'll forget about this." I force her to meet my eyes with a finger to her chin.

"Promise me, Lou, that you'll stay away from him when he returns. I wouldn't ask you to do so unless I was completely certain."

I consider her request but don't promise my sister anything. I can't walk away from my one and only chance to have someone important from Hollywood truly see me. Instead, I tug her forward and distract her with a more pleasant question.

"I know you've been saving it for Christmas Eve, but do you think we could dip into the hot chocolate tonight? It would be such a treat, and isn't it best to enjoy a treat when you really feel the need for it? After such a long day, I am quite sure we deserve it."

Clara agrees to my request with a quiet "yes," but I suspect it is only to ensure this conversation is finished.

CHAPTER 22

MONDAY, DECEMBER 26, 1927

*C*lara
    Yesterday morning, Louisa and I left early, trudging to the hotel to be part of a small crew of staff to tend to the needs of guests. Thankfully, hotel management saw fit to share the Christmas workday and split the maids into either a morning, afternoon, or evening shift. The five-hour shift passed quickly as we all worked together on every guest floor, save for the eighth floor, which was tended exclusively by two eighth-floor maids per shift.

    The mood at the hotel was light and festive, a welcome change from last week's angst and uncertainty. Knowing Mr. Barnes would not pop his head out and sour my day left me free to tend to my tasks with ease and joy.

    My worry melted to the back of my mind as we gathered with the afternoon shift. In a changing of the guard, so to speak, we assembled ourselves around the piano temporarily situated across from the registration desk.

    Ms. Thompson sat at the piano bench and led us all in a chorus of Christmas songs. Soon, the lobby was filled to bursting with hotel guests and staff joining to celebrate Christmas Day. The ladies from the laundry, every bellboy and porter, and even Chef himself descended into the quaint and cozy hotel lobby as we raised our voices, if not all the way to heaven, then at least to the highest beams of the double-height lobby ceiling.

After the short day, we arrived home in good spirits, with plenty of time to enjoy Christmas afternoon and an evening meal together. The turkey, courtesy of Mr. Hamilton, is sure to keep us fed for the remainder of the week. Not to mention the gift certificate to the local butcher.

On Christmas Eve, Louisa had been juggling our large, fresh turkey when Ms. Thompson surprised us with the envelope. Having assumed Lou and I would share a gift of one turkey between us, my wide eyes had darted up to see the matron's genuine delight as she'd explained. "Mr. Olson and I thought you might appreciate not having two turkeys to roast this holiday."

Now, a day after Christmas, a fresh blanket of snow lulls all three of us into sleeping later than usual. I relish the quiet of the apartment as I mull over the events of the past week. With Louisa's injury, my illness, and the bustle of the holiday season, our hotel schedules have looked like a patchwork quilt. Today is our only official day off.

Though Boxing Day has long been recognized as a government holiday in Canada, businesses such as The Hamilton never truly close, due to the nature of the services provided, which makes having the day off more special for us. The hotel will operate with a smaller crew today, and since all city and administrative work ceases, Papa, who works with the city parks, is free to enjoy the day at home with us.

I snuggle deeper under the covers, content to enjoy the restful morning.

An hour later, I am startled awake by the telephone ringing. A quick glance toward Louisa's bed tells me she either hasn't heard or is happy to ignore the offending sound. I marvel at her ability to remain still as the third ring pulls me from my bed, my bare feet hitting the cool, wood floor.

"Wilson residence." I hear Papa's gravelly morning voice as I enter the hall. "She is, but I am afraid she isn't able to come to the telephone at the moment. I can tell her you called." Papa's voice smooths into a chuckle. "I will be sure to tell her that. She knows how to reach you, then?"

I am standing in the space between the living room and dining table when Papa turns and spots me. Unsurprisingly, he does not indicate the call is for me, so I settle myself on the sofa and wipe the sleep from my eyes.

"You do. Thank you for asking my permission." I look up and find Papa's lips quirking upward. "Yes, I imagine you can expect an answer shortly. You as well. Goodbye."

Papa places the telephone's handle on its holder and slides his hands into the pockets of his robe.

"Who was that?" The question comes out amidst a yawn.

"I'll put the kettle on and fill you in." Without hesitation, he moves into the kitchen and out of sight. I hear the sink filling the kettle and cups being retrieved from the cupboard.

A few minutes later, Papa reappears with two cups of tea and biscuits smothered in butter from last night's feast.

"How did you sleep?" he places the tray on the coffee table before sinking into his usual chair with a cup of tea and a biscuit.

"Very well. I even managed to fall back asleep for a while." I stir sugar into my cup and recline back into the soft sofa. "Who telephoned? Was it Thomas? I imagine Lou is desperate to hear from him. She'll be sorry she missed his call."

Papa smiles and shakes his head. "Actually, it was Mr. William Thompson, calling for you."

I feel the heat rise in my cheeks, warming me through, all the way to my bare toes.

"He has invited you to have tea with him this afternoon."

"Oh." I have little else to offer at this news. My mind whirs with questions I'd like to ask about my father's conversation with William, but I am at a loss for how to go about doing so.

I haven't spoken privately with William since before Christmas. Our paths have crossed, but there hasn't been an opportunity for more than a cordial hello. And now, with my situation within the hotel, I'm not sure anything more would be appropriate.

"He asked me to tell you that your favourite tea house is open today and he would like to take you there."

"My favourite tea house?" I search my brain for a tea house that might be considered my favourite, given I seldom venture out for tea. Then it dawns on me. "Masao's mother has a tea house. He must have been speaking with Cookie." I look up at Papa. "I've only been there once, with her."

Papa's head bobs up and down. "He seems a good fellow. Courteous, well-mannered, and respectful."

"You got all of that from a two-minute telephone call?" Louisa stands in the hall, dressed in a silky pink robe, her hair beautiful and wild in a cascade of curls.

"Good morning." I stand to fetch her a cup for tea, but she waves me off, moving to the kitchen to retrieve one herself.

"So, what's this about William Thompson inviting you to tea?" Louisa returns, settling herself on the sofa with her feet tucked up beside her.

Papa, seeming quite pleased with himself at having intercepted the call, adds further insight. "He even requested my permission to take you out."

"I see." Louisa sips from her cup. "He is serious, then."

I am about to say otherwise, to tell my family that William and I are merely friends, when Louisa chimes in again. "I saw the way he was looking at you the day he brought me home." Her face lights up as if someone has plugged her into an electrical socket. "Is that why he has returned to Vancouver so soon after his last visit? It hasn't even been three months since he was last here, and Toronto is on the other side of the country."

"If you must know, he came to spend Christmas with his sister." I am glad to have an answer to quell her suspicions.

"The same sister who is working through the entirety of the Christmas season?" Louisa's left eyebrow shoots up, and I realize she is right. I hadn't given his reasoning a second thought, but now I see the truth. William is in Vancouver because of me.

My instant inclination is to decline the invitation to tea. There are moments when having a sister who is able to read your thoughts is less than helpful. This is one of those moments.

"Don't you dare even think about refusing the man." Louisa shifts to face me straight on. "His weren't the only eyes I noticed giving lingering glances."

"I did give him my permission, darlin'." Papa joins in, and I swear my family is goading me. If it weren't for the earnest looks on their faces, I might believe they are having a laugh at my expense. But it is pure love and encouragement they are offering.

Papa spreads his hands wide. "He is a good man, isn't he, Clara?"

I nod as the tea settles nervously in my stomach. "He is."

"Then you'd best call the hotel and tell him you'd be delighted to meet him for tea."

An hour and a half later, I am bathed and wearing a dress of Louisa's choosing. She has tidied my hair and added a soft shade of lipstick to my lips. Despite my protests, my sister has refused to allow me to wear a toque to ward off the below-zero temperatures.

"You may wear a scarf and mittens, if you so choose, but you are not messing up your hair with a dastardly toque."

I frown, knowing the smallest gust of wind is sure to do the same amount of damage when it comes to my unruly hair.

When William knocks on our apartment door, I feel as though my knees have turned to jelly. Louisa squeezes my hand reassuringly and mouths "Have fun" before Papa is inviting William into the living room, where I am waiting.

His eyes light up when he sees me, and I am

immediately grateful to have a sister who knows how to make me presentable.

Pulling his gaze from mine, he inclines his head in Lou's direction. "Miss Wilson."

Louisa's features barely conceal the mischievousness lying in wait. "I assume we can call you William now."

"Please do" is his only reply.

There is no pretense. No put-upon airs. Despite William's education and his likely affluent lifestyle, he appears exceptionally at ease in our humble apartment. This warms my heart, and when he asks if I am ready to go, I do not hesitate.

The tea house is quiet today, given that most Vancouverites are likely cozy in their homes, nibbling on seasonal treats or napping off their Christmas Day festivities. I greet Masao's mother and introduce William as another friend of Cookie's, to which she welcomes him with a low bow and a demure smile.

We sit in low chairs beside a window overlooking the street in the heart of Japantown. The scents of tea leaves and tatami mats intertwine into a welcoming grassy aroma, and I inhale deeply. With tea and *manju*, a Japanese delicacy, set before us, we remove our coats and gloves and settle into our cozy spot.

"Did you enjoy your Christmas?" I pour the tea into the little cups, steam escaping in a delicate dance.

"I did, though I must say it is a bit unusual to spend the holiday in a hotel. Even a luxurious hotel such as The Hamilton."

I consider his comment. "I imagine it would be. To be honest, I was surprised by how many guests chose to be away from home at this time of year. I thought you might have spent the day at your sister's, but I suppose she was working too."

"She was, but she usually works on holidays." William reaches for his tea, but I stop him with a gentle hand on top of his.

The gesture is forward of me, which I realize too late. He lifts his gaze to mine, and my stomach flips.

I pull my hand away and tuck it out of view beneath the low table. "Sorry. I didn't mean to… It's just that Cookie taught me the last time I was here that the reason there is no handle on a Japanese teacup is that if the cup is too hot to hold, it is also too hot to drink."

William gives the cup on the table a sideways look. "How absolutely clever."

I sense our mutual appreciation for the brilliance of such a notion.

Folding his hands together on top of the table, William's eyes meet mine as his expression turns serious. "I know I invited you to dinner and this, though very nice, is not dinner."

My first thought is one of worry. I must have misinterpreted his attention and forced the poor man to retract his earlier invitation. I am wishing to be swallowed up by the floor when William elaborates.

"As you know, I am only in town for a short time, and it feels as though the days are disappearing right before my eyes. When I learned you wouldn't be working today, I leaped at the chance to ask you to dinner. However, I was unable to find a single restaurant open on Boxing Day." He shrugs in disappointment, and I catch a glimpse of what I imagine he might have been like as a young boy.

My worry vanishes at his explanation.

"Cookie has become a dear friend to my sister, and to

me as well. When I visited her for my morning cinnamon bun—"

I can't help myself and I interrupt him mid-sentence. "Wait, you go down to Cookie's pastry kitchen every morning to get a fresh cinnamon bun?"

A hint of pink rises in his cheeks, and I decide that blushing is my favourite look on William Thompson. I boldly note to find more reasons to make him blush in the future.

"That wasn't really the point of my story, but I see I have found something else we have in common. A love of Cookie's cinnamon buns." He lifts his cup of tea, no longer steaming, and sips with a humoured expression. "My plan is to eat as many of them as she will allow before I have to board the train for home."

I laugh, an honest-to-goodness laugh, and it feels good. All of my concerns about the incident with Mr. Barnes, the precarious nature of my position at the hotel, and the appropriateness of sitting here with William Thompson disappear.

"Anyway, hence our tea date." William raises his teacup and waits for me to lift mine. "Cheers and happy Christmas, Clara."

"Cheers," I repeat before sipping my tea.

We settle into a comfortable conversation as I tell William about the first time Cookie brought me to the tea house. He asks how I met Masao, and I catch myself beaming at the memory of offering him my apple when all he really wanted was the seeds for planting.

William shares what it is like to be a lawyer and about how he came to live in Toronto. With moisture in my eyes, I tell him about the cancer and losing Mama. In turn, he confides how he and his siblings lost their parents, his father to the Great War and his mother shortly after to the Spanish flu.

Another hour passes as Masao's mother replaces our pot of tea with a fresh one. We are deep in conversation and only notice her presence when she places the hot tea in the middle of our table.

William grows quiet as I pour him a cup. I sense he has something to say but is hesitant. I can't even begin to comprehend what it might be, given the stories we have already shared with one another. I return the pot to the centre of the table and meet his eyes in the low light of the late afternoon.

"There is something I would like to ask you." His voice is soft, almost a whisper.

I lean in and give him my full attention.

"I would like to invite you to the New Year's Eve ball at The Hotel Vancouver. It is said to be the city's finest celebration."

"Oh." I sit back in my chair, my mind fixating on the word "ball" before apprehension pokes at me, reminding me of all the reasons my going to a ball with William is not a good idea.

"I've learned you are not working that evening." He searches my eyes. Hopeful. Eager.

"It is true. I am not working." My gaze drops to the table. "I—I have never been to a ball, let alone a New Year's Eve event. Are you certain I am the one you wish to take?"

"I assure you, Clara, I would not ask if I weren't certain."

"No, I suppose you wouldn't." His gentle half smile tugs at my heart, and I wish things were simpler. I wish we had met under different circumstances and I could say yes to his invitation without reservation. I am duty bound to follow the rules of The Hamilton, and yet here I am, having tea with a guest. I have muddied the water by accepting his invitation here today, and I am suddenly aware I may have once again put my job in jeopardy.

"It is such a lovely invitation. I wonder if I might have a day or two to think it over?"

William's back straightens, and I realize I have offended him. "Of course."

My hand instinctively reaches out for his. "Please understand my hesitation has everything to do with me, not you." I feel a deep red colour rising from my neckline to the top of my forehead. "I am sure you've noticed that I am cautious. My sister would call it unadventurous." I try to shrug off the insult I've delivered myself. "I am touched and honoured by your invitation. I promise to give it my full attention."

William squeezes my hand in his, signalling to me that all is well, and I am surprised to find how comfortable his hand feels in mine.

CHAPTER 23

TUESDAY, DECEMBER 27, 1927

Louisa
　　　　Clara arrived home late yesterday afternoon, clearly smitten with William Thompson. The worry lines creasing her forehead took centre stage in our conversation, which continued long past the midnight hour. Still unsettled by Mr. Barnes, my sister has somehow convinced herself that her interest in William is inappropriate and will cost her the position at the hotel she has worked so hard for.

After going several rounds with Clara, I fell into a fitful sleep with no additional clarity on the topic. This morning I woke early and with a plan in place. When I arrive at the hotel, I will head straight to Mr. Barnes' suite and get to the bottom of Clara's unease. If things go as I expect they will, I will have fixed their misunderstanding and safeguarded Clara's position, while also securing the man's trust in me. He won't be able to resist helping me find a suitable role in Hollywood once I've smoothed everything over.

Clara stumbles into the kitchen later than usual. Her face transforms from panic at having overslept to shock when she find our lunches packed and breakfast waiting on the table. My enthusiasm for the day ahead is buoyed by her perplexed but thankful expression. A simple breakfast of leftover biscuits, cheese, and warmed-up mashed potatoes is not our standard fare, but I didn't quite trust myself with the task of flipping eggs.

I gesture for her to sit and place a cup of tea, sweetened with sugar, near her plate. "You just missed Papa, but not to worry. He has already eaten, and I packed him a turkey sandwich, an apple, and the last slice of coffee cake." I stand a little taller at the mention of my morning activities.

"Did you sleep at all?" Clara scoops up a mouthful of potatoes before taking a sip of tea.

"A little." A small chuckle leaves my lips. "I expect I'll pay for it tonight."

Not wishing to divulge my morning plans, I excuse myself to finish getting ready, calling over my shoulder, "I'll be set to leave in five minutes. I need to catch up with Hazel about the new maid, so I'd like to get to work a little earlier today, if you don't mind."

We are halfway to the hotel before Clara emerges enough from her sleep-deprived state to continue our conversation. "How are things going with the new maid, anyway? Gwen is her name, right?"

"Good, I think, but it is a little curious." I swivel my head in both directions before stepping out from the street corner. "Do you remember the girl from The New Orpheum?"

"The ladies' room maid who called you over as we were leaving?" Clara asks with a questioning tilt of her head.

"That's Gwen. She showed up at the hotel a few days later. Ms. Thompson had given her a job."

"I knew she looked familiar." Recognition dawns on

Clara. "Why do you find it curious? She did ask about where we worked. Perhaps she thought the hotel was a better option for her."

We pause our conversation to bid the doorman at The Hotel Georgia a good morning.

"I suppose you could be right. There is something about the girl I don't quite trust, but I haven't been able to put my finger on it."

"How do you mean?" Clara shifts her bag to the opposite shoulder and gives me her full attention as we pass The Hotel Vancouver. Silently, I wonder if she is knowingly putting her back to the elite hotel and, by extension, her invitation to the upcoming ball.

"She is as doe-eyed as they come." I roll my eyes in mock exaggeration. "But there is also a conniving side to her that pops up like a prairie dog when you least expect it."

Clara laughs at my remark. "To be honest, I haven't given her so much as a nod hello. I suppose I should make more of an effort."

I shrug my shoulders, unconcerned. "I wouldn't worry over it. Something tells me she won't be with us long."

Our conversation stops abruptly when a snowball sails over our heads as we round the corner into the alley behind The Hamilton.

Cookie stands at the top of the back stairs, laughing with abandon. Masao is at the bottom of the stairs, with another snowball ready to launch. His face is lit with pure glee as he lobs another frozen mound in our direction.

We duck in unison before dashing forward to catch our friend. Clara holds his arms down playfully while I ply him with tickles. I am sure he doesn't feel a thing through his thick winter coat, but he laughs hysterically until tears stream down his face.

"Stop. Please stop, Miss Louisa." He can barely get the words out between giggles.

Masao is breathing hard, trying to recover himself, as all three of us climb the stairs to the warmth of the kitchen hall.

"I told you they'd get you," Cookie teases the boy before placing an arm around his shoulders and guiding him through the door. Once inside, Cookie disappears into her pastry kitchen, telling Masao to sit tight until she returns.

"Did you have a happy Christmas, Masao?" Clara asks as she unravels the scarf from around her neck.

The boy nods in earnest. "Santa brought me a train, and my grandmother gave me my own book about planting trees."

I lean forward. "Does it have a section on planting an apple tree?"

Masao beams back at me, and his head bobs in eager affirmation.

"My mother sent this for you. It is the last one of the season." Masao pulls another delicately wrapped Japanese orange from his coat pocket. "She wanted to thank you for visiting her tea shop yesterday."

Clara steps forward and accepts the orange. "Please tell her thank you for us and that I enjoy her tea shop very much. I will save this special orange for our dessert tonight, to share with Louisa and our papa."

Masao seems pleased with Clara's plans for sharing the orange, but his eyes grow big when Cookie returns with a large cinnamon bun wrapped in a napkin.

"Why don't you come with me to enjoy this treat and

we'll put your mittens and hat near the oven to dry? Then you can head home nice and toasty."

Masao waves goodbye to us as Cookie tells him that he is just in time, as she is expecting her friend, Mr. William, to join her for a treat shortly.

Hearing the news of William's impending arrival, Clara is suddenly in a hurry to get to the locker room. Normally, I would take the opportunity to tease her, but this morning, her desire to disappear works to my advantage.

"I'll be there in a bit. I have something I need to do first." I take the opposite path at the fork in the back-of-house corridor, not looking back for fear of being stopped.

Clara doesn't even question me. She waves a hurried goodbye before heading toward the locker room.

I reach the eighth floor undetected, shedding my scarf, hat, gloves, and jacket along the way. Poking my head out the door, I survey the hall to ensure no one is present before stepping onto the cloud-like carpet that, without fail, slows my steps as my shoes sink into it.

As I lift my arm to knock, I pause, questioning for the first time whether the morning hour is appropriate for such inquiries. Movement beyond the door confirms that Mr. Barnes is present and awake. I inhale deeply and rap my knuckles lightly three times against the solid wooden door.

The door opens in Mr. Barnes' typical hasty fashion. His cheerful expression greets me first. "Good morning, Miss Wilson, and a belated merry Christmas to you."

"Good morning, Mr. Barnes, and a belated happy holiday to you as well. I hope you enjoyed a pleasant Christmas."

With a wink, he stands up straight and recites in a solemn tone, "I will honour Christmas in my heart and try to keep it all the year."

"Very good." I clap my hands together. "From *A Christmas Carol*?"

"I knew that if anyone would appreciate a theatrical mention of the season, you would, Miss Wilson." Mr. Barnes bends in a mock bow. Noticing my jacket in hand, his head quirks to the side. "You are not in uniform. I take it this is a social call, then."

Before I can respond, he swings the door open wide and waves me through with an outspread arm. "Come in, please."

Stepping into the suite, I let my eyes adjust to the darkness, all the while questioning Clara's trouble with the man. I am even more certain now that somehow my sister has gotten it wrong. Or perhaps I am merely desperate for it to be so. For Clara's sake as well as my own.

Mr. Barnes walks to the window, pulling open the curtains to let in the light from the grey sky beyond. He turns on two additional lamps and gestures for me to take a seat on his sofa.

I decline his offer of coffee as he pours a cup for himself from a silver coffee pot. He stirs in two heaping spoonfuls of sugar and an ample splash of cream before addressing me again.

"So, what can I help you with, Miss Wilson?"

"I know we spoke briefly the other day in the lobby, but given the surroundings, we weren't able to talk frankly. I wanted to thank you for not mentioning the incident with my sister to the hotel's management. She remains troubled by the situation, and I was hoping to understand what transpired so I can help calm her worries."

"Ah, I see." Mr. Barnes sips his coffee. "It is good of you to look out for your sister. Not everyone has someone they can rely on."

"Thank you, sir." I can't decide whether he is dodging my question or is genuinely appreciative of my concern for Clara.

"What did your sister have to say about our meeting?"

"Very little, actually. She has been rather close-lipped about the whole thing. I assumed it was because she was embarrassed by her actions."

Mr. Barnes bobs his head in understanding. "There is little to tell, really. Your sister and I were chatting after she had finished cleaning my suite. I leaned forward to brush something from her shoulder, and her hand came up and connected with my cheek."

I marvel at the way he negotiates the words so as not to accuse Clara of anything as unbecoming as slapping him.

"In all honesty, I thought a spider had made its way inside and managed to climb onto her shoulder. I didn't wish to startle her by mentioning the thing, so I simply tried to sweep it away." Mr. Barnes' cheeks pink. "I assume she reacted out of instinct, and I can hardly blame her for that."

I lean back slightly against the sofa. "I can understand now how a misunderstanding might have occurred. Thank you for telling me. Please know that she is dreadfully sorry to have struck you. If she had it to do over again, I suspect she wouldn't overreact."

Placing his cup on the low table in front of the sofa, Mr. Barnes shifts his position to look me in the eye. His face is lined with sincerity. "Please tell her I have no intention of speaking with the hotel management about this issue. Her position at the hotel is not in any danger from me. I welcome her into my suite as my maid, and I have no hard feelings toward her."

The relief in my exhale is palpable. "Thank you. I will be sure to convey your message."

Mr. Barnes pulls his shirt sleeve back to reveal a watch. "Well, I had better get going. I have a meeting this morning, and I am sure you have more important things to do than hang around and chat with an old chap like me."

I stand, realizing that I too should be off, so as not to be late for roll call. "Thank you again, sir. I am pleased to have things settled."

He walks me to the door, and though I am itching to inquire about meeting him again to discuss my future, I begrudgingly decide that I've asked enough of the man for one day.

I step over the threshold, ready to bid him farewell and vacate the eighth floor before I am spotted, when Mr. Barnes stops me with a hand on my forearm.

"Miss Wilson, why don't you come back this afternoon and we can chat about you? I believe you were looking for some guidance about pursuing a career in the movie business? I'd be delighted to assist you in any way I am able."

A thrill of excitement rushes through me. "I look forward to it." I deliver him one of my most dazzling smiles, toss my hair over one shoulder, and hurry down the hall toward the stairwell.

CHAPTER 24

TUESDAY, DECEMBER 27, 1927

*C*lara
    Mama's watch slips from my wrist, landing on the locker-room floor with a muffled clatter. I suppress a frustrated groan and bend over to retrieve it. In my overtired state, I must not have properly secured the watch.

Pressing the clasp tightly against the inside of my wrist, I wince at the pinch of tender skin. Mama has been present in my thoughts during the Christmas season. Traditions have a way of signalling her absence in our lives. My mind shifts to William and how I shared with him my greatest loss and told him about the life we have cobbled together after she left us.

Though my dear friend Rebecca knows of my mother's passing, I haven't talked openly with her about the details or the ramifications of such a loss, not like I found myself able to do in William's company. In a strange way, our shared grief brings us closer together. If you've never known loss, you simply can't comprehend how it changes every minute aspect of your life. Every breath you take is altered without that person beside you.

I shake my head, trying to dislodge the sombre thoughts. I have enough of a day ahead of me as it is. The least I can do is start the morning in a better state of mind. I look about the locker room. Louisa still hasn't arrived. Checking my watch, I note that she has ten minutes to be dressed and standing in the roll-call line.

With my hair combed into a tight bun, I am about to go in search of her when she pushes through the door, bustling toward her locker with her uniform, jacket, and winter accessories bundled in her arms.

I take her jacket from her arms and hang it in the locker. "You're going to make us both late." I try to etch the tsk from my words, tugging her uniform from its hanger while she pulls her day dress over her head.

Her head pops into view again. "I have good news."

"About what?" I glance around the room and realize both Hazel and the new maid, Gwen, are readying themselves at their designated lockers. "I thought you were going to find Hazel."

"I went to see Mr. Barnes."

I feel as though she has punched me in the stomach. "You what?" I feel the urge to raise my voice. I specifically told Lou to stay away from the man.

"Before you go working yourself into a tizzy, hear me out." Louisa takes the uniform from my hands and begins slipping into it. "I wanted to know what really happened between you two, and he told me." Louisa places a hand on top of my arm. "I understand why you did what you did, and he does too."

I am taken aback by this and feel my world tilt slightly. I pass Lou her apron before tying it in back for her. I didn't want her to know. I didn't want anyone to know. My shame at having found myself in such a predicament is enough to make my skin crawl.

"He isn't going to speak with Ms. Thompson or Mr. Olson. You have no reason to worry over the incident at all. Your job is safe, I promise you. Everything will be all right now." Louisa squeezes my arm reassuringly.

She pulls her hair back and secures her cap in place as I consider her news. I am embarrassed that my sister now knows the full extent of my disgrace. Even so, I feel a hint of relief seep into my awareness, knowing that my job is no longer in jeopardy.

Louisa smiles broadly at me. "Water under the bridge, Clara." She glances at the clock on the wall as I realize the other maids are moving toward the door. "Time to go. I am still aiming for that holiday bonus, and you should be too."

We say goodbye at the fifth-floor landing, and I take the opportunity to give my sister a grateful hug. I should have trusted that Lou would know precisely what to do.

I climb the final three floors, and by the time I step onto the eighth floor, I am eager to get to work. With 1928 right around the corner, I remind myself of the hope that comes with new beginnings. I am more than ready to put Mr. Barnes and his advances behind me.

The morning passes pleasantly as I tend to the first two suites on my roster. I knock on the door of the suite belonging to a kind family, whose little boy favours the sweets I leave on his pillow, and am greeted by the four-year-old and his mother. She smiles when she tells me little Joseph isn't convinced I will get my gift unless he hands it to me himself. They invite me to sit on the brushed velvet sofa, and he helps me untie the ribbon and explore the basket of goodies. Inside are treats from the British grocer and a package of speciality tea.

"How did you know I liked tea?" I ask Joseph as he wriggles with delight.

I shake his little hand and then tousle his hair, before he and his mother vacate the suite so I can get back to work. As they depart, his mother turns to me and says, "You will make a fabulous mother someday."

I am almost speechless, but I find the words in time. Blinking back tears, I tell her, "Thank you, I learned from the very best."

Bolstered by the happy interaction, I am reminded that I am doing good work at The Hamilton, and even I could see myself being awarded the holiday bonus on days such as this.

Checking my watch, I note the lunch hour is coming fast on my heels. I quickly restock my cart with fresh linens, determined to finish Mr. Barnes' suite before leaving for lunch.

I feel the heavens smile upon me when I reach his suite to discover it vacant. I set to work as usual, resolved to be out of the room before his return. Though Louisa's words are a comfort, I am no less certain of the man's intentions, and I still do not look forward to being in his proximity.

Perhaps the kind thing would be for me to give him another chance and allow him to be remorseful for his actions while not losing face. He does strike me as a proud though foolish man. I am undecided about the matter as I move the vacuum carefully around the bedroom furniture. With the droning of the machine, I don't notice when the clasp on Mama's watch gives way. I am lost in the process of making tidy passes over the carpet when I catch sight of a silver shimmer, about to be swallowed by the vacuum.

I slam my hand against the off switch and pull the behemoth of a machine back with every ounce of strength my arms can muster. Though the latch is clearly broken, the watch is, thankfully, safely resting on the thick carpet. Examining the clasp, I decide better of putting the watch back on my wrist. Instead, I tuck it into my apron pocket and finish cleaning the bedroom.

Moving my cart to the living area, I vacuum first and then begin to tidy and dust. I fold newspapers back together, remove dirty coffee cups and a stale-smelling, half-drunk pot of coffee, careful not to spill its contents as I place it on the second shelf of my cart. I wipe down the writing desk, lifting a few papers out of the way as I go.

My gaze washes over the items on the desk, but rarely do I pay them any attention, aside from ensuring nothing is damaged by moisture. The personal papers and belongings of guests are not present for my entertainment, and minding my guests' privacy is one thing I remain firm on.

The Christmas floral arrangement on the desk is looking a tad sad. I move it to my cart and begin plucking wilted flowers and leaves from the bundle. I fill the vase with fresh water, stirring in a teaspoon of sugar from the coffee service. Repositioning the flowers, pine, and holly, I play with the display until it appears almost brand new.

While returning the vase to the top left corner of the desk, I spot an envelope with *Miss Clara Wilson* written in script across the expensive-looking stationary. I don't immediately reach for the envelope. Instead, I survey the rest of the items on the desk with more scrutiny. The envelope is definitely out of place. Why would Mr. Barnes leave something for me?

I wonder if this is a Christmas gift, like Joseph gave me,

or perhaps an apology. My hand reaches for the envelope and then retreats. What if it is a trick?

Several minutes pass as I turn my attention to the final tasks in the room, trying to distract myself from the envelope. My eyes continue to be drawn toward the desk, and for the better part of fifteen minutes, I pull them away each time.

With the room situated, I find myself standing close to the desk. Curiosity winning out, I lean forward and stand on tiptoe to retrieve the envelope. A muffled thud draws my attention as my fingers stretch forward. I pause and bend to scan the floor around me. Seeing nothing, I stand once more and grasp the envelope in my fingers.

Without pausing, I flip it over to find it unsealed. I press my lips together in contemplation before gently tugging the stiff card stock from the envelope and turning it over to read.

Dear Miss Wilson,

Please accept my deepest apologies over our previous misunderstanding. I would like to make it up to you by inviting you to the New Year's Eve gala being hosted at The Hotel Vancouver. I promise to be a delightful host and only wish for you to enjoy a splendid evening to celebrate the New Year.

Sincerely,
Mr. Harold Barnes

I inhale sharply and then take several slow, steady breaths in an effort to settle myself. In two days, I've received two invitations to the same ball. I would laugh at the unlikely scenario if I didn't feel the dread of an impending disaster sneaking up my spine.

With Louisa's news that all is well with Mr. Barnes, I was beginning to explore what it might be like to attend the ball with William. It isn't a matter of whether I want to go, but whether I should.

Somehow, Mr. Barnes has managed to once again insert himself into my life and make an already difficult decision more precarious. I pace the room once, twice, three times. Stopping at the desk for the third time, I slide the note back into the envelope. I then lean it against the freshly arranged vase so he is sure to know I've seen it.

With defiance as my guide, I turn my back on his note and push my cart out of suite 815.

CHAPTER 25

TUESDAY, DECEMBER 27, 1927

*L*ouisa
    I sneak up to the eighth floor. With only twenty minutes left in my shift, I am almost out of time to meet with Mr. Barnes, as he invited me to do. I am more than a little aware that Clara would balk at my decision to speak with the man. She may even cause a scene, and I simply cannot have that. Seeking him out within my work hours is the only solution I've come up with.

Having resolved the misunderstanding between my sister and Mr. Barnes, it is easy to convince myself I am deserving of this one thing for myself. Eager to talk further about how he might assist me in fulfilling my Hollywood dreams, I take the risk, leaving Gwen to restock the linen cupboard on her own.

Climbing the stairs is a breeze, with most of the maids in the hotel finishing up their day with bringing supplies from the basement storage room to the linen cupboards, to restock their carts in preparation for tomorrow. I'll have to arrive at work early tomorrow to stock my own cart, that is if I wish to have any hope of staying on schedule with tomorrow's roster. It is a sacrifice I am willing to make.

At the top of the landing, I pull the stairwell door open a fraction and peek into the hall. Seeing no one, I slip through the doorway and move toward suite 815. Several paces down the hall, I hear voices coming toward me. Stranded halfway between two back-of-house stairwells, I panic. There is nowhere to hide, and in my blue uniform, I stand out like a sunflower in a field of red poppies. I spin in a circle, my eyes darting across every surface, desperate for a hiding place to appear.

A supply closet five feet ahead of me almost blends into the wood panelling, but its shiny brass doorknob catches the light from an overhead chandelier. Thankful for the elaborate decor of the eighth floor, I dash toward the closet and tuck myself inside. I am quietly drawing the door closed as the hushed voices of two eighth-floor maids pass by.

My breathing is rapid and my uniform is stuck to my back with sweat. I take three slow breaths, just as I would before stepping onto the stage, and extract myself from the closet. Walking quickly, I am in front of suite 815 in less than a minute. I knock quietly, trying not to draw attention from anyone besides Mr. Barnes.

"I thought I heard someone knocking." Mr. Barnes opens the door wide and gestures me inside. "No need to be shy, Miss Wilson."

I smile demurely, aware the man has no idea what I've risked to be in his suite right now. "Thank you for seeing me, sir."

"Can I offer you a drink? The hotel is in the midst of preparing for the New Year's Eve party, and I've had the good fortune of testing the celebration's signature cocktail."

Mr. Barnes takes two steps toward a small tray laden with bottles of varying shapes, sizes, and colours. He lifts a cone-shaped glass with a long stem, its rose-hued contents spilling over the lip and onto the carpet as he spins to proudly display the beverage. "I give you The Hamilton Special." He sips from the glass before adding, "It's not a very clever name, but I suppose it is more about the fun of it all."

I decline the sweet-smelling concoction but comment on its pretty colour, taking a seat on the sofa when invited to do so.

Mr. Barnes sits beside me, placing his half-drained glass on the low table before us. If it weren't for his proximity to me on the sofa, I would mention the glass leaving sticky residue on the expensive coffee table.

I chide myself firmly, realizing how much like a maid I've truly become. Pivoting my attention and my body toward the man, I delve into the conversation I have come to have. "Mr. Barnes, you mentioned that you could assist me in my pursuit of an acting career in Hollywood. I am interested in knowing how you suggest going about such an endeavour?"

"Please, call me Harold. May I call you Louisa?"

I nod my assent and wait for him to continue.

He reaches for his glass and drains it in one gulp. The hair on the back of my neck lifts, but I push the discomfort away with a subtle roll of my shoulder.

Mr. Barnes stands and plucks something from the writing desk a few paces away. "As it so happens, Louisa, I have some exciting news for you." Waving a square paper card in the air, he beams like a cat who caught a canary.

I stand to gain a better look at what he is holding. Mr. Barnes bows seriously and presents the card to me.

My gasp brings a knowing smile to his lips. "An invitation to the New Year's Eve ball at The Hotel Vancouver. How wonderful." Excitement bubbles up inside me as I do my best not to jump up and down like a giddy schoolgirl.

"My plan, Louisa, is to escort you to the ball and introduce you to every director, producer, and writer in attendance. We will dine on caviar and drink champagne, and we will light the night on fire."

I leap forward and squeeze his arm in a brief but enthusiastic show of appreciation. Too ecstatic to sit, I roam around the living room of his suite, pacing from the window to the door, around the writing desk and chaise lounge, and back again. "I have so much to do. I need to get a dress and shoes, and I should make an appointment at the salon to have my hair set. Oh, I do hope they aren't fully booked."

The daylight beyond the large windows is fading into evening, reminding me of the time. My mind is humming as I think about what Thomas will say when I tell him that a Hollywood director is introducing me about town. I contemplate the cost of a phone call or perhaps a telegram, and my heart races at the thought of giving him the happy news. Maybe we will both find ourselves in Hollywood.

Harold pours himself another drink as I lose myself in the experience of my dreams coming true. Standing beside the writing desk, I let my eyes scan the papers spread across its surface. Most of them don't make sense to me, with their numbers and columns, and given my elated state of mind, I am hardly surprised at my inability to focus, though I take notice of one that is different from the rest, a piece of stationery embossed with a woman's name, set aside from the other papers at the top corner of the desk. Harold, his second drink in hand, pats the sofa and gestures for me to join him. "You have plenty of time to sort out the details, my dear."

I sink into the sofa and cross one knee over the other. Swivelling my head in his direction, I am about to thank him sincerely for the invitation when I find him stretching toward me, one hand landing on my knee while the other wraps around my shoulders.

Instinctively, I leap from the sofa and stand, fuming before his half-slumped position. "Mr. Barnes, what do you think you are doing?"

"I did you a favour, so now you do me one." The man's words are slow and slurred, and I can't help but wonder how much alcohol he consumed before my arrival.

"I beg your pardon." I cannot remove the incredulity from my voice as the reality of his intentions becomes all too clear in the dwindling evening light. "I think you are mistaken, sir."

He pushes himself back into a seated position, his glassy eyes roaming up and down my body. "This is how the world works, Louisa. Did you think you could waltz into my room and demand a full-fledged career in Hollywood in exchange for only a polite thank you?" Mr. Barnes shakes his head, a patronizing expression sliding onto his face. "Now, why don't you be a good girl? Come sit here and let me explain how a young woman such as yourself succeeds in show business." He pats the seat beside him, eliciting a shudder from my head to my toes.

"Clara was right. You are nothing but a scoundrel." As soon as the words leave my lips, shame engulfs me. I did this to myself by ignoring my sister's warning. I was foolish and stubborn. What would Thomas say? I shake the thought from my head, and Clara's face, contorted by anguish, stares at me in my mind's eye.

"What did you do to my sister?"

Mr. Barnes tries three times to raise himself to standing before he succeeds. "Nothing. All I wanted to do was give her a kiss. One harmless little kiss."

I step backwards toward the door, an accusatory finger pointed at his chest. "You stay away from me, and stay away from my sister. Do you hear me?"

Mr. Barnes waves me away with an unconcerned motion before he drives a verbal sword right through me. "You could have been famous. Now, you'll just be a maid. Nobody remembers a maid."

I let the suite's heavy door close with a thud. My eyes brim with angry tears, and I brush them away out of spite. A shadow caught between a chandelier's glow and a hallway wall catches my attention.

The shadow moves, and so do I. By the next corner, I've caught her. Skulking around the eighth floor, rather unsuccessfully, is Gwen. "What are you doing here? I thought I told you the eighth floor is off limits to fifth-floor maids."

Clearly unapologetic, Gwen stands her ground. "But you are a fifth-floor maid, Louisa."

"Argh, I don't have time for this. I have to find my sister." I stalk down the hall toward the closest stairwell. Gwen is nipping at my heels, spurring me into a run.

"Wait. Won't you tell me what he said?" Gwen is undeterred by my insistence to flee. "Will he help you get to Hollywood?"

"Stay away from Mr. Barnes. He will only bring you trouble." I holler the words over my shoulder as I reach the first floor, where the locker room is located.

Pushing through the door into the locker room, I am surprised to find it vacant. More time must have passed than I realized. I yank the door open again, only to find Gwen falling through it toward me. "Gwen, don't you have somewhere else to be?"

"Not until you tell me about Mr. Barnes. If I am going to succeed like you, I have to follow your lead. Please, Louisa. Tell me how to win his favour so I can go to California too."

"You can't." My arms flail as my bottled-up frustration lets loose. "Don't you see? Mr. Barnes is not the answer."

"You're just saying that so you don't have to compete with me. I remember what you said that first day we worked together. You told me not to let anyone stand in the way of my dreams." Gwen's doe-eyed expression morphs into one of determination. "I imagine that includes you as well."

With a nonchalant shrug, Gwen turns on her heel and storms away.

I want to call out to her, to tell her I was wrong. I want to tell her she has to believe in herself because she is the only person who won't let her down. Instead, I watch her walk away while asking myself how I've managed to get so off track. I'm no better than Barnes, wielding words like they don't matter. Shame on me for assuming that Gwen wouldn't take them seriously.

Returning to the locker room, I change into my day dress and winter wear. Clara must be waiting for me in the kitchen hallway. I'll find her, and I'll make things right with my sister.

CHAPTER 26

TUESDAY, DECEMBER 27, 1927

Clara Unpinning my hair from its headache-inducing bun, I run my fingers through it to try to release some tension. I tug my uniform over my head and step into my day dress, swapping my shiny black oxfords for winter boots with a glance at the clock on the wall. Ten past five. Louisa should be here by now.

I tuck my shoes into the space at the bottom of the locker and am reaching for my winter coat when I remember Mama's watch. Dropping the jacket to the bench, I grab my uniform and untangle it from the apron. Rifling through the pockets, I come up empty.

"Oh." Dread fills me as I realize the small thud I heard while reaching for the envelope in Mr. Barnes' suite must have been Mama's watch falling to the plush carpet. I know I scanned the floor and came up empty, so the watch must have fallen out of sight.

"Clara, is everything all right?" Rebecca is staring at me.

"Oh, I was just wondering where Louisa might have gotten to."

"I'm sure she'll be along shortly. You know Louisa. She's not usually one to dawdle when it comes to quitting time." Rebecca's amused expression tells me she is teasing, but I am aware of the truth that lies beneath her words.

I coerce a chuckle. "I am sure you are right."

"Do you want me to wait with you?" Rebecca is gathering her things and closing her locker.

"Don't be silly. You've got to get home yourself. I am sure your mother is holding dinner for you."

My friend answers with a bob of her head. "She mentioned something about turkey pot pie. To be honest, I think I enjoy the leftovers from Christmas dinner more than the original feast." Rebecca's nose crinkles in childlike appreciation of what awaits her at home.

"You'd better head home, then." I place a hand on her back and push her gently toward the locker-room door. "Off you go, and have a pleasant evening."

"See you tomorrow, Clara." Rebecca waves at me as she slips into the corridor hallway.

I pretend to pack my things and bide my time as I wait for the last gaggle of maids to vacate the locker room. My options are limited. Mama's watch is too precious for me to simply walk away from, regardless of Mr. Barnes' antics. I glance at the clock again. Twenty minutes past five.

Grabbing my jacket in one hand and my bag in the other, I head toward the door. Louisa must have finished early and is probably waiting for me by Cookie's pastry kitchen.

I reach the kitchen hall to find it empty. Leaving my coat and bag on the small table in the hall, I decide to return to the eighth floor and retrieve Mama's watch, with or without Louisa. First, I'll check my cleaning cart. Hopefully, the watch ended up there, tucked into the clean pile of towels. I climb the stairs, knowing that if I don't locate the watch in the supply cupboard, I will have no choice but to venture to Mr. Barnes' suite.

After a fruitless search of my cart, I summon my courage and knock on suite 815. I hear glass clinking beyond the door and then the doorknob being handled. I step back in anticipation and lock my hands behind my back.

The door flies open with a rush of air. Mr. Barnes doesn't so much stand as he does lean against the hinged door, swaying slightly. "Well, if it isn't the delightful Miss Wilson."

"Good evening, Mr. Barnes. Sorry to disturb you. It seems I may have left my watch in your suite. If I could—"

Mr. Barnes raises a glass to his lip, sloshing its contents. "You thought you could what? Come into my suite anytime you like to retrieve a carelessly left personal item?"

I smell the liquor as he roars his displeasure.

"And after you declined my perfectly cordial invitation to the New Year's Eve party?" He shakes his head with slow, purposeful movements. "I don't think so, Miss Wilson."

"Sir, like I mentioned before, it wouldn't be right for me to accept an invitation from a hotel guest. The hotel has rules that we maids must follow." I try to convey with a slight shrug of my shoulders that the matter is out of my hands. "If you would be so kind as to retrieve my watch for me, I can be out of your way in a jiffy so you can enjoy the rest of your evening. I believe you will find my watch on the floor somewhere near the writing desk."

"Do you think I am daft, Miss Wilson? I have no intention of returning your watch to you. Finders keepers and all that." He waves his hand in the air, more of his beverage splattering onto the carpet.

My heart sinks at the sight of the stained carpet. I taste bile at the back of my tongue, a sure sign of warning. "But sir, what use do you have for a woman's watch?"

"I am not an unkind man. You may not agree, but truly, I am generous and fun-loving and am the sort of man many young women would fight over. But not you, Miss Wilson, and because of your closed-up, timid little ways, it seems your sister thinks she can cast me aside as well. I promised her big things, and she still refused to play the game."

"Game? What game?" My brow furrows as I try to make sense of his words. "What have you done to my sister? Is she in there? Louisa!" I call her name, but this only makes the man laugh.

Mr. Barnes places one foot in the hall, the door hitting his back clumsily as it releases. "You really are quite innocent, aren't you? Ah, but I suppose that is what intrigued me about you in the first place. The chaste ones are the most fun to play with."

A shiver runs up my spine and my feet feel as though they've been covered in concrete. My focus shifts from worry over my watch to panic for my and Louisa's immediate safety. I take another step backwards and glance down the hall, willing someone else to appear.

"There is nothing here for you, Miss Wilson. You are no longer welcome. So you can be on your way and leave me to my drink." Mr. Barnes' glazed-over eyes survey me with venom.

I am praying that his words confirm Louisa's absence within his suite. Aside from barging past the man and pillaging his suite for my watch, there is little I can do in this moment. His inebriated state, though clearly disarming his reflexes, makes him all the more dangerous, with the malice running through his veins on full display.

I turn on my heel, cheeks flaming and moisture gathering in my eyes from frustration. I need to find Louisa.

Running to the stairwell, I pass two of the biggest gossips on the eighth floor. Though I note that the maids instantly bend their heads together in discussion, after seeing me running from a guest's suite at this hour, I care little about the rumour mill and more about my sister's well-being.

I cannot deny my breaking heart at the thought of losing Mama's watch to such a hateful man, but Louisa is my first priority. I fling open the stairwell door and descend eight floors before racing down the back-of-house corridor toward the kitchen hall.

I stop short at the threshold, out of breath but filled with relief at the sight of my sister and Cookie chatting quietly. Louisa is nibbling what looks to be a gingerbread cookie while Cookie watches, a pleased expression lining her lips.

"Thank heavens, Lou. You are all right?" I bend at the waist, trying to catch my breath.

"I am." Louisa's usual ready-to-humour-me reply is missing, and I read her intentions clearly. She does not wish to discuss anything of substance here.

Cookie is watching me with a questioning tilt of her head. Trying to make light of my comment, I grab my coat and bag off the table. Forcing my hands into gloves, I continue the charade as I edge closer to the back door. "I was worried my lateness had upset you. I know how eager you are to get home this evening."

The lobby door swings in toward the kitchen hall, and

George appears, waving a small piece of paper in his hand. "Oh, Clara. Glad I caught you. I have a message here for Mr. Barnes. It's from his wife, so I thought you might want to deliver it yourself."

"His wife?" I turn in Louisa's direction and watch in amusement as her left eyebrow raises high toward her forehead.

George glances between me and Louisa, realizing we are dressed for home. "But I can see you are off shift now. I can drop it by his suite if you don't think he'll mind."

I recover from my surprise at this revelation. "Thank you, George. If you could, I would be grateful." I turn toward the back door, but then I think better of sending George to deal with a very displeased and inebriated Mr. Barnes. "Actually, George." I catch him before he disappears from sight. "Just slide the message under his door. Mr. Barnes mentioned something about having an early night, and I wouldn't want to intrude on his quiet evening."

George nods in understanding before heading down the corridor to the stairwell.

"Shall we?" I ask Louisa, tugging my winter hat down tighter.

Cookie pipes up from the doorway of the pastry kitchen. "I don't know what you two are up to, but something is going on."

I am about to open my mouth when Louisa gives her a wink. "I have no idea what you are talking about."

"I'm here if you need a voice of reason." Cookie chortles to herself as she disappears into her kitchen.

The door has barely closed behind us when I wrap my sister in a fierce embrace. "I was so worried."

"It's all my fault, Clara. I didn't take you at your word."

Louisa's eyes brim with tears. "I never should have doubted you."

We take slow, steady steps toward home, knowing our conversation will be far less private once we arrive there.

"How did you know?" Lou sneaks a sideways glance in my direction. "That I was in trouble."

"He is a dangerous man, Lou. I knew it from the start. I went to his suite to retrieve my watch, and he confirmed you had been there." I drop my chin to my chest, defeated by our predicament. "I accidentally left Mama's watch in his suite. I suppose the clasp broke while I was cleaning his room. He refused to give it back to me. Told me it was my fault that you wouldn't play some game. I'm afraid to ask what he meant by that, but I am certain it is nothing good."

"He read me wrong, just like I did him." Louisa kicks a mound of snow with the toe of her granny boot. "He told me he would introduce me to those who make the decisions in Hollywood. In return, I assume he expected me to make myself comfortable in his bed."

I gasp, clutching Louisa's arm in the process. "Did he hurt you?" The question reminds me of the one William asked me. He knew that nefarious intentions were lurking in the shadows.

Louisa shakes her head. "He didn't get that far. I suspect he might have forced the issue on New Year's Eve. He invited me to the ball at The Hotel Vancouver, the same one William invited you to. The irony is not lost on me. I can tell you that much."

I stop in my tracks, tugging Lou back by the arm. "You've got to be kidding? He tried to invite me to the same ball. I declined, which apparently did not make him happy. But seriously, does the man think we wouldn't talk to one another?"

Louisa's bottom lip finds its way between her teeth. "I think it's my fault. When I went to clear the air with him about the incident with you, he told me nothing happened. He said he was trying to brush a spider off your collar."

"What? He was lying."

My sister nods, then rolls her eyes. "I believed him. Since you weren't willing to tell me the whole story, I assumed the situation was a misunderstanding. I'm sorry. I could have been much more helpful if I had listened to you in the first place."

I pull Louisa into a tight embrace. "If I had told you everything that was going on, you wouldn't have had to guess at it. I was just so embarrassed by the whole situation."

"You have nothing to be embarrassed about. This wasn't your fault, Clara. But now that we know, what are we going to do about it? I mean, we can't simply let him continue preying on maids." A glove-covered hand flies to Louisa's open mouth. "Oh my, I should have realized it at the time. Gwen."

"What about Gwen?"

"She is about to make the same mistake I did. We can't let her, Clara. She may think she is willing to do anything to become a star, but there is an innocent, inexperienced young woman inside of her. We can't let someone like Harold Barnes hurt her."

"I will do whatever I can to help, Lou, but promise me we'll get Mama's watch back in the process."

"Deal." Louisa removes her glove and sticks her hand in my direction, pinky raised.

I do the same, and our bond as sisters feels impenetrable against the likes of Harold Barnes.

CHAPTER 27

TUESDAY, DECEMBER 27, 1927

*L*ouisa
"I know what to do." I keep my voice low to ensure our conversation remains between us. Having waited two hours for Papa's soft, rhythmic snores to begin filtering through the apartment, the idea percolating inside my head is desperate to be set free. Sitting at the dining-room table, Clara and I bend our heads together, our focus on protecting Gwen from Mr. Barnes.

"New Year's Eve is our target." I stifle a yawn and count the days until December thirty-first on my fingers. Our plan will take each one of those days, along with several sleepless nights, to execute.

"Why New Year's Eve?" Clara asks in a low whisper.

"We know he is staying at The Hamilton until New Year's Eve. After that, there is no guarantee where he will be. And who knows who he will try to manipulate once he leaves Vancouver. We can't rely on anyone else. This is something we need to do ourselves, and it will take some time to put things in motion." I grab a piece of paper and a pencil from a kitchen drawer and sit down to make a list.

The pencil trembles in my hand. Going forward with this plan may ruin any chance I have of becoming a famous actress. I have no idea how far Mr. Barnes' influence reaches into the heart of Hollywood. All I know is that too many young women could be harmed by him, and I cannot sit by and let that happen.

Shaking off the awareness of what I stand to lose, I scribble our goal at the top of the sheet.

Ensure Barnes' true nature is exposed, and protect Gwen from his clutches.

Knowing a situation as precarious as this could unravel in many different directions, I bite my bottom lip and pray the hotel will not be caught up in a scandal that would cost both of us our jobs.

"George mentioned Barnes' wife." Clara's disdain is on full display as her expression twists into a scowl. "It makes my blood boil to know how terribly he has behaved toward you and me, but to think he was married all along." Her closed fist hits the tabletop with a muted thud. "The gall of such behaviour."

Tapping the pencil on top of the sheet of paper, I nod in agreement. "I met his wife."

Clara looks at me with wide eyes.

"I didn't realize who she was at the time, but she came to tour the hotel and acquire his suite reservation. It only stands out to me because it was the same day Ms. Thompson allowed me to leave early for the first afternoon of rehearsals for *Craig's Wife*. Funny how some things come full circle."

"What do you mean by full circle?"

"When I was in Mr. Barnes' suite. This afternoon when

he invited me to the New Year's Eve ball." I let my eyes roll with reckless abandon at the mention of the invite. "I noticed a piece of stationery in plain view at the top corner of the writing desk."

Clara tilts her head in question.

"The stationery was personalized, from a Mrs. Rose Oxley-Barnes." My smile feels a touch devious as I think ahead to how we can beat the man at his own game. "Rose Oxley is the daughter of the founder of a major-motion-picture company. She is Hollywood royalty. Her husband, our Mr. Barnes, is merely proof that she did not marry well."

Clara's mouth forms a long O, and I nod slowly.

"What was she like?" Clara leans forward, her arms flat against the table's surface.

"Wealthy. Socialite. Impeccably dressed. I remember she had this stole positioned just so on her shoulder. I've always wondered how women walk around with something so bulky hanging precariously from one shoulder. I am certain it would tilt me sideways." I wiggle my shoulder animatedly at the thought.

Clara slides the paper toward her and takes the pencil from my fingers. "Okay, so your plan is to somehow get Mrs. Barnes to the hotel before New Year's Eve?"

"Yes, precisely."

Clara's practical nature mixes with a bucketful of worry as she grips the pencil, turning her knuckles white. "How are you going to do that? We don't have her phone number or address, and how likely is it that she will board a train simply because a maid from the hotel where her husband is staying requested her presence?"

"She will come. I am almost certain of it. I don't imagine the likes of Rose Oxley-Barnes would take such unflattering news of her husband's activities lying down. I will try to contact her tomorrow. If she arrives in person, we are all set."

"What if she doesn't? Or what if you can't get in touch with her?" My sister's legitimate concerns give me pause.

"Clara, I think we are going to need a plan B."

CHAPTER 28

WEDNESDAY, DECEMBER 28, 1927

*C*lara   Our conversation continues the next morning as we walk to the hotel, our strides hurried by our urgent chatter. I barely feel the chill in the air as we go over our plans leading up to New Year's Eve.

I lift my wrist to check the time, only to be reminded that Mama's watch is currently being held hostage by Mr. Barnes. I remember Mama's words clearly when I think of my distaste for the man. *If you let them, people will show you exactly who they are.* How right she was, I think to myself as we pass The Hotel Vancouver.

A thought pops into my mind. Nothing in my life will change unless I start doing things differently. Something deep within me warns me not to dismiss the notion. For the most part, I am content. I enjoy sharing a home and life with Papa and Louisa, but if I am to be happy, truly happy to live my life on my terms, then I had better start figuring out what those terms are.

I've spent my entire existence following rules set out by

my parents, society, and more recently, the hotel. I realize now that I can't let people like Mr. Barnes push me around as though I have no stake in the outcome of my life's experiences. No one should be allowed to determine what is and isn't acceptable to me. Though I am deeply appreciative of the role models I have in Ms. Thompson and Mr. Olson, even the hotel's rules need to be questioned in certain circumstances.

"Lou, how long do you think this will take if everything falls into place on New Year's Eve?"

My sister knows the reason for my question without needing me to say more. The delighted smile on her face tells me so.

"There'll be plenty of time for you to enjoy the New Year's Eve ball. I am happy for you, Clara. When will you tell him?"

I tug on the hotel's back door and grin. "Right now."

We are laughing as we tumble into the kitchen hall.

"What has gotten into you two?" Cookie appears in her kitchen doorway, holding a plate with a single giant cinnamon bun.

"Nothing." We say in unison before collapsing into a fit of giggles.

"Sisters," Cookie teases as she leans forward, swivelling her head to scan the corridor.

"Looking for someone?" Louisa recovers, lifting a questioning eyebrow while peeling the scarf from her neck.

"William, I mean Mr. Thompson, should be down any minute for his morning treat. I made him an extra-large one in hopes that he will do me a favour this afternoon." Cookie puts a finger to her lips, signalling for us to keep her secret.

I recognize the opportunity and, feeling bold, step past my fear and grasp it. "I can take it up to him."

Cookie looks me up and down, assessing my current state. "Did you find some gumption in your breakfast this morning, Miss Wilson?"

I press my lips together, knowing this is likely only the beginning of the teasing from my friend.

"All I can say is it's about ruddy time, if you ask me." Cookie passes me the plate. "Don't you go breaking his heart. He is a good one, and Lord knows they are few and far between."

I steal a glance at Louisa. Beaming, she takes my coat and bag from me and says she will retrieve my uniform with her own, affording me a few extra minutes. I take the offered plate from Cookie and make my way to the back-of-house corridor, unable to tuck my smile out of sight.

On the third floor, I stride with a confidence that comes from knowing exactly what I want all the way to room 305 and knock three times on the door.

William's face lights up when he sees me. "Clara, good morning."

"Good morning. This"—I raise the enormous cinnamon bun to eye level—"is from Cookie."

He chuckles, taking the plate from me. "She must have a chore for me to do. I've noticed the pastries are bigger when she has a favour to ask of me."

Feeling amusement at the secret shared with William, I wink knowingly and say, "I promise not to let her know you are on to her."

He opens the door wider. "Would you like to come in?"

"I would, actually." I step into his room and am pleased to see how tidy it is. Though I know the maid has not yet been in, his bed is made, the curtains are drawn open, and the papers sitting on the small writing desk are stacked neatly.

William watches me as I scan the room. "I must apologize," I say, "for keeping you waiting about New Year's Eve. It wasn't my intention. Things sort of got out of hand with that problem I was having and—"

He steps toward me, closing the gap between us. His hand is on mine while his eyes search my face. "Is everything all right? It's that Mr. Barnes, isn't it?"

"How did you know?" I feel the warmth of his hand seep into mine, and in the blink of an eye, I can no longer tell where his hand ends and mine begins.

"Do you want to talk about it? I mean, I realize you probably have to talk with my sister first, but I am here to listen whenever you are ready."

"Thank you. You are kind to offer." I hesitate before deciding to give him the short version. "I am working on a way to ensure the man is put in his place, but currently it doesn't involve speaking with your sister or Mr. Olson."

William's smile reaches all the way to his eyes, and I know he is pleased and also a tad curious. "I won't say a word. From the little I've seen, the man certainly needs to be shown back to his corner. I am pleased to know you will be the one to put him there."

"I'll have Louisa's help, but yes, I've come to understand it is important to teach others how to treat us."

His head bobs in agreement.

"That's why I've come to see you this morning. I would be delighted to attend the New Year's Eve ball with you, if the offer still stands."

"Of course it does. There is no one else I would consider asking. I am very happy to hear that you will join me." I didn't believe his smile could grow wider, and yet it does, only making him that much more handsome. "What time shall I pick you up?"

"The thing is, our little plan could unfold anytime between now and New Year's Eve." I cringe a little at having accepted before giving him all the information. "I am not sure what time I will be available, but I promise you, I will attend the ball."

William squeezes my hand in his, sending a warm thrill through my body. "We will figure it out. I'll take any minute you can spare me, Clara."

"I'll be sure to save as many minutes as I can for you. I should be getting on. Enjoy your cinnamon bun." We walk to the door hand in hand, only letting go at the last possible moment.

CHAPTER 29

WEDNESDAY, DECEMBER 28, 1927

*L*ouisa
    I hang Clara's uniform in front of her locker and ready myself for the day ahead. My thoughts turn to Mrs. Rose Oxley-Barnes and what I might say to the woman, should I be lucky enough to secure a way of contacting her.

I spent all morning considering my options. I don't imagine reaching her at home is possible, despite it being the most appropriate setting for her to learn of her husband's transgressions.

First, I considered sending a telegram to Thomas in the hope that he may have a way of locating Mrs. Oxley-Barnes' telephone number. But that is a tall order, especially with only four days until New Year's Eve, and I have no desire to add the extra load to Thomas's already long workdays.

I laughed out loud when Gerald's name came to mind. The man was a thorn in my side for several weeks leading up to the opening night of *Craig's Wife*. On the day he almost ruined Thomas' production, he left us standing on the street as he headed to the train station, outrunning a gang of thugs he owed money to. Gerald has since sent me a letter informing me that he is out of harm's way. I can only assume he felt bad about his abrupt departure.

Gerald, it seems, is in California, pursuing his acting career while evading the riffraff who still seek his whereabouts. Though I have little doubt Gerald would be able to weasel his way into the inner crowd that Mrs. Oxley-Barnes runs in, I have no desire to have my own future thwarted by being linked to such a morally challenged man.

Instead, I turned to the man who has joy and kindness running through his veins. Before leaving home this morning, I made a telephone call to Mr. Johnson at the theatre. Knowing the good-natured janitor would be at work first thing in the morning, I sweet-talked my way past the theatre's office receptionist, and within minutes Mr. Johnson's friendly voice greeted me hesitantly. "Hello, this is Mr. Johnson."

Though he may not be able to put me in direct contact with Mrs. Oxley-Barnes, I am sure he will be able to persuade the theatre's receptionist to help him track down the information I need. The only thing I can do now is wait until the midday meal so I can slip out of the hotel and discover what Mr. Johnson has learned.

By noon, I am wound tight with worry over whether our plan will work. Plan B is a whole other level of brazen, and I would prefer to not have to try to pull it off. Instead, I am hopeful a simple telephone call to Mrs. Rose Oxley-Barnes will be all it takes to set things right.

A benefit of my whirring mind is the speed with which I tend to each of the guest rooms on my roster. I'm thankful Ms. Thompson decided to pair Gwen with Hazel this morning. I do not mind missing the girl's incessant chatter, which I'm sure would have come with far too many questions and elicited dagger-laced looks from me.

Grabbing my winter wear and lunch from the locker room, I trudge through the melting snow toward the theatre, snacking on my sandwich as I walk. Upon my arrival at the theatre's doors, I am careful to wipe my winter boots thoroughly, not wishing to spread dirty snow onto Mr. Johnson's sparkling lobby floors.

The whoosh of the door closing announces my arrival. I am barely inside when the kindly man reaches my side. "Miss Louisa, I did what you asked, and I am happy to say we have good news. We've managed to track down the telephone number for Oxley Pictures in Los Angeles."

"Oh, Mr. Johnson, that is fabulous news. You are a true friend, and I thank you from the bottom of my heart."

Mr. Johnson extends his elbow for me to take, and we head to the back of the theatre, where the offices are located.

I greet the receptionist and thank her for her assistance with the matter. She hands me the slip of paper with the company's name and telephone number before extracting her purse from a low desk drawer and standing to leave.

"You know," she says, "the theatre makes frequent telephone calls to California. I'm sure an extra one won't be any cause for concern." Her unmistakable wink does not go unnoticed.

"Well, that is a bit of interesting news. Thank you for the information." I smile wide as she moves toward the office door, the fresh scent of her perfume leaving a path behind her.

"I'm heading out for lunch now, Mr. Johnson, and I'm quite certain I'll be gone for at least thirty minutes."

Mr. Johnson's bemused expression tells me he was expecting this additional bit of assistance. "Thank you, Miss Carol. We'll be sure to close the door up tight once we're through here."

With a nod of her head, Miss Carol is through the door and on her way to lunch, leaving us to telephone California.

"Well, Miss Louisa do you know what you're going to say?" Mr. Johnson gestures to Carol's chair for me to sit in. "We could jot it down if it will help you."

I pick up the telephone handle and meet Mr. Johnson's eyes. "I know precisely what I am going to say."

Arriving back at The Hamilton, my delight at having completed the first half of the mission is subdued by the reality that Clara and I must be prepared in case the woman does not arrive before New Year's Eve. In speaking with a secretary at Oxley Pictures, I was informed in no uncertain terms that Mrs. Oxley-Barnes was unavailable for the remainder of the day. Leaving a message with a somewhat uppity clerical worker was the closest I could come to convincing Mr. Barnes' wife that she is needed in Vancouver.

Rather than feeding a rumour mill among the office staff at Oxley Pictures, I decided to protect the woman's privacy and instead leave my phone number along with a slightly coded message—one that I am hopeful a wife who suspects that her husband's activities are roaming beyond the bounds of a marital relationship will understand.

> To: Mrs. Rose Oxley-Barnes
> From: Miss Louisa Wilson
> Message: I am a theatre actress from Vancouver, Canada, who has become acquainted with your husband during his stay at The Hamilton. As you are sure to be aware, your husband is a busy man, so I thought it best I contact you directly to invite you to The Hotel Hamilton's New Year's Eve celebration. The evening is sure to be intriguing and informative for all. I hope you will be in attendance as your husband is awarded the recognition he has so indisputably earned during his stay. If your schedule allows, we welcome your visit to Vancouver and look forward to meeting you in person.

I trek up the five flights of stairs toward the fifth-floor guest rooms, my footsteps heavy with the weight of our backup plan. Even if the message is delivered, there is no guarantee Mrs. Oxley-Barnes will take my note seriously. Then there is the consideration of the train travel from California to Vancouver. It took Thomas several days and nights to arrive in Los Angeles from Seattle, after being shuttled from one train to another. Only a first-class ticket keeps travellers from spending time waiting in train stations along the route.

But surely, if Mr. Barnes can afford to stay on the eighth floor for weeks on end, Mrs. Oxley-Barnes can manage a first-class train ticket to Vancouver. Maybe there is hope yet.

Stepping onto the fifth floor, I straighten my apron and move toward the supply cupboard at the opposite end of the hall, where my cleaning cart awaits. As I near the lift, hushed voices grab my attention. I slow my steps so as not to interrupt what is likely a private conversation among guests. Waiting for the lift to arrive, I circle back a few feet to give the couple some space.

Ding. "Fifth floor." The lift operator I know as Mr. Tuppary is a short man with a booming voice. I swear he could be heard a floor above and below his current one.

I step forward and am crossing in front of the lift's closing doors when I glance beyond the grate and the brass detailing to see Mr. Barnes, smug as ever, inside the lift.

The grey-blue carpet feels as though it has rippled up to greet me, and I trip, falling slightly forward in my stride. I recover myself just clear of the lift, and that is when I spot her.

Gwen is tucked into a small alcove in the hall, peering down at something in her hands. My mouth is open, about to tease her and ask if she's lost her way, when she pivots slightly, her body no longer shielding the card she holds. The triumphant smile plastered across her face worries me. My eyes travel again between the card and Gwen's admiring expression before understanding dawns on me.

Gwen is holding an invitation to The Hotel Vancouver's New Year's Eve ball, and I know without a doubt that Mr. Barnes gave it to her.

Instinct kicks in, encouraging me to look straight ahead and pretend I haven't seen either one of them as I move swiftly through the hall. The swish of my skirt is the only sound thrumming through my pounding ears as the guest-room doors fly past me at an alarming rate.

There is no backing out now. Gwen will certainly not be inclined to listen to anything I have to say, now that she's got the attention she was angling for. My anger with Mr. Barnes knows no bounds, and disdain for him rises within me. How clearly I see it now, the manner in which he preys on the innocence and aspirations of young women.

Knowing all too well what I have to do next, I walk right past the supply closet and toward the stairwell. Clara needs to know. It's time to put plan B into action.

CHAPTER 30

FRIDAY, DECEMBER 30, 1927

*C*lara Louisa and I will finish our early shift by noon. With planning for the New Year's Eve event in full swing, Ms. Thompson asked if we would be willing to hand over our maid duties and help with the set-up instead. This morning, we rose far earlier than usual, with the plan to arrive at the hotel by six o'clock.

Papa, concerned about the safety of us walking to the hotel in the dark morning hours, dressed and readied himself for the day in order to accompany us to work. He walks us right up the steps to the hotel's back-of-house kitchen hall, waiting to ensure all is as it should be.

Hearing the door creak open, Cookie appears from inside her pastry kitchen, mixing bowl in hand. Papa inclines his head upon seeing our friend, taking off his hat to say good morning.

"Ah, you are just in time." Without giving us any indication of what she is talking about, Cookie retreats into her kitchen as we exchange puzzled glances.

Papa bids us farewell, not wanting to cause us a delay. I ask when to expect him home this evening. "I shouldn't be long past four thirty," he says.

I stand on tiptoe and kiss his cold cheek. "Thank you for walking with us."

He is ducking out the door when Cookie's voice cuts through again. "Where do you think you're going?"

Papa turns as she strides toward him, a box held tight between her arms. Handing the box to Papa, she beams. "I made an extra batch. Tell those fellas at the City Parks Board that The Hotel Hamilton thanks them for keeping our city streets free of snow and ice."

Papa's cheeks lift with a smile as he peers into the box. The scent of sugar and cinnamon wafts through the air.

"Aren't you the lucky one?" Louisa teases.

I see his face flush with colour, making me pause to watch him. "Thank you, ma'am." He lifts the box slightly in Cookie's direction.

"What's this 'ma'am' business? Call me Cookie for goodness' sake." Cookie's cajoling laugh stops short as her eyes drop to the spotless white floor. "Or, if you prefer, you can call me by my given name. It's Ruby."

"Thank you, Ruby." He looks at Cookie and his eyes seem to dance in the bright light of the kitchen hall.

Louisa and I exchange a look, both unsure of what is happening before us. I shuffle in place, which spurs Papa back into action.

"Thank you again. The boys are sure to devour these." He looks back at us one last time before saying goodbye and heading out the door.

Despite not being on maid duty today, Louisa and I pick up our uniforms from the laundry and head to the locker room to change.

The conversation quickly turns from the peculiar encounter in the kitchen hall to our afternoon plans for the day. I am tasked with finding a deep-blue stole for Louisa and an evening dress for the ball I am attending with William tomorrow night.

Louisa apologizes for the third time for not being able to accompany me as I shop for a dress. This is clearly troubling her, and she has made me promise to buy something less practical and more glamourous, touting my one opportunity to welcome in 1928. Her final warning hit a little too close to home for me. If I didn't heed her advice, she promised to return to the shops on Saturday morning and spend even more money to ensure I have a dress suitable for the evening.

My sister has a list of errands all her own, dividing and conquering being the only way we will have time to get what we need to set our plan in motion. After fully understanding the predicament Gwen has found herself in, we discussed the idea of confiding in Ms. Thompson and Mr. Olson in order to protect the girl. In the end, we were at a loss as to how to make Mr. Barnes accountable for his actions without proof of wrongdoing.

Fearing his word might have more sway than ours, we decided our plan was the best hope of getting Gwen out of her precarious situation as quickly as possible. Our first goal is to protect Gwen, and the decision to not intervene ahead of time weighs heavy on our hearts. Having both been on the receiving end of Mr. Barnes' attentions recently, we are more than aware of how things might go. But Gwen is still fooled by his act and would not be convinced to extract herself from the situation.

We meet Ms. Thompson in the upper floors of the banquet rooms. Tables line every wall, and Louisa and I cover them all with crisp white linens before adding a crimson, gold-trimmed table runner to each. The silver, freshly polished by Lou and Gwen, arrives on trays carried by bellboys wearing white gloves to protect the gleaming surfaces from fingerprints.

Ms. Thompson calls me to the kitchen when the flower delivery arrives, and I spend the remainder of my morning arranging flowers for varying sizes of vases. Before leaving for the day, we all gather in the readied banquet room, with candles lit and Ms. Thompson's hand on the light switch. It is a trial run for the sake of efficiency, but as the room descends into candlelight, everyone goes silent as we appreciate the beauty we have created for The Hamilton's first New Year's Eve celebration.

By ten past twelve, Louisa and I are waving goodbye to one another at the corner of Georgia and Howe. I head to Spencer's department store while Louisa takes the streetcar to our old neighbourhood near the Murray estate to meet a friend from her theatre club. Louisa knew exactly what she was looking for and whom to call when plan B became necessary.

Spencer's window display draws me close, with brilliant red and gold accents highlighting holiday outfits for the whole family. I notice a mannequin with something fluffy slung over one shoulder, so I push through the door in search of something I never dreamed I'd have a use for. A kind woman behind the candy counter offers me directions to the women's section.

My mouth hangs open unceremoniously. I am in the far corner of the women's section, surrounded by furs of all kinds. I'm not sure what I was expecting, but heads and feet were not on my list of things to watch for. I back away from the foxes and skirt a display of mink. I am about to turn tail and run when I spot a table with rectangular, coloured furs on display. Breathing a sigh of relief, I stand at the table for several minutes, deciding between two blue options.

With the stole in hand, I wander through the dresses. The racks are lined with everything from long, beaded gowns to short flapper-style dresses. A full petal skirt catches my attention, but the dress's hefty price tag makes me turn away. A gold scoop-neck with a bow is nice but a tad flamboyant for me.

An hour and a half and several trips to the dressing room later, I've settled on a peach, beaded chiffon gown in the standard flapper sleeveless style, with a V-neck suitable for showing off a long necklace. I was delighted to find it on the sale rack, leaving me enough of my budget to find a suitable necklace to accentuate my neckline.

I don't even have to leave Spencer's to find the accessory. A few paces away, I secure a simple pendant necklace that, when resting against my collarbone, dazzles in contrast to my cream-white skin. With my tissue-wrapped packages stowed in my shoulder bag, I step out into the crisp mid-afternoon air.

Feeling particularly pleased with myself, I stroll toward home, stopping at the butcher shop to purchase a small roast, Papa's favourite. Given the hour, I'll have plenty of time to make the roast for dinner. After several days of turkey leftovers, I'm certain tonight's dinner will be a welcomed treat.

I push tomorrow's activities from my mind as I load my grocery basket with potatoes, cream, and a pound of butter. Roast beef, Yorkshire pudding, and mashed potatoes are sure to put a smile on all three Wilson faces. Tonight we will feast, and tomorrow Louisa and I will do what we must in order to ensure Gwen is safe. I only wish we could be certain of the outcome when it comes to Mr. Barnes.

CHAPTER 31

SATURDAY, DECEMBER 31, 1927

*L*ouisa
After styling Clara's hair as best I can into her requested finger waves, I add rouge to her cheeks and dark lipstick, a deeper shade than she's ever worn, to complement the amount of cream-coloured skin she is baring tonight. Though I mocked her with an "ooh la la" when she donned the sleeveless dress for me late yesterday afternoon, I am quite pleased to see my sister being a tad bold when it comes to William Thompson.

Papa was invited to the Murrays' estate for a festive evening, and I am pleased to see him and Mr. Murray mending fences, now that Papa has his feet firmly rooted and his spiralling habits with the drink under control. We kissed him goodbye, wishing him a happy New Year before setting our attention on our plan.

As Clara slides into her dress, careful not to muss her hair, I retrieve the costume I borrowed from my friend at the theatre club. A travelling suit is not something I've ever had the need to purchase, given my consistent lack of travel plans, but for tonight's purposes, it will do just fine.

I paint my nails bright red, letting them air-dry before tossing the blue stole Clara purchased yesterday over one shoulder. I'll have a minute at most to be convincing, if it comes down to that. I just hope it is enough.

Peering into the mirror, Clara lets out a slow breath. "Do you think this will work?"

"I don't know. All I do know is we have to try."

"Okay, then. William will be here in thirty minutes to pick me up. I will meet you on the eighth-floor stairwell, the one closest to the lift, like we planned."

I inhale sharply, holding back tears that are threatening to spill and ruin my carefully painted face. No matter the outcome, I am proud of my sister and our plan to show Mr. Barnes that the Wilson sisters will not be exploited. Pulling Clara into a fierce embrace, I give her one final affirming nod, grab my clutch, and head for the streetcar.

A few streetcar stops later, I stroll through the front door of The Hotel Hamilton. The doorman welcomes me, and before giving him a chance to recognize me, I angle my chin in the opposite direction. Once through the door, I lean against the dark, gleaming wood of the bellboys' stand, trying to blend in with the bustling lobby crowd. Clara and I decided it best to have a lookout of sorts at the lobby level, so yesterday morning we invited George into the fold, giving him the briefest of explanations and specific instructions to be on the lookout for Mrs. Oxley-Barnes.

"Has our guest arrived?" I ask sweetly, batting my eyelashes in George's direction.

"I almost didn't recognize you, Miss—" He cuts his words off short before shaking his head. "Not that I've seen. I know you were hoping for better news."

I place a reassuring hand on top of the desk. "You know where to find me should she arrive."

I don't push my luck by loitering in the lobby. Instead, I note the time on the lobby clock as five forty-five and move swiftly to the lift, taking it only to the first floor of guest rooms. I step from the lift as soon as the grate opens, relieved at not being recognized by the lift operator. The worry of being discovered by a colleague is far more acute in the confines of the lift, and I breathe a sigh of relief as I stroll down the first-floor hallway.

I locate the nearest back-of-house stairwell and climb the remaining seven floors, my heels clacking against every tread. Cracking the door open, I peer into the quiet of the eighth floor. If I crane my neck to the left, the door of Mr. Barnes' suite is within view. Knowing this isn't the most prudent position, I steal peeks into the hall every few minutes, while listening for movement on either side of my hiding place.

We know from Clara's invitation that The Hotel Vancouver's ball opens with a cocktail reception at six thirty, with dinner being served at seven. I arrived early to avoid missing Gwen's arrival or Mr. Barnes' departure. We can't be sure what they've arranged for this evening's events.

Several minutes pass, and then I hear the lift's *ding* and the announcement of "eighth floor." I stretch my neck to gain a better view and watch Gwen step toward suite 815 in a dark blue, shimmering beaded dress that shows off her bare legs daringly. A light fringed shawl rests across her shoulders, its transparent fabric revealing her sleeveless arms and a plunging neckline.

The girl doesn't hesitate. Doesn't survey her surroundings. Heck, she took the lift all the way up to the eighth floor. I am questioning whether she is brazen or foolish when she lifts her hand and knocks on the door.

Mr. Barnes places one foot into the hall while his other foot holds the door ajar. He clumsily balances a drink, which I presume is The Hamilton Special, in one hand as his eyes roam up and down Gwen's petite frame. Her dark bobbed hair is styled neatly, and her lips, painted a deep red, smooth into a demure smile as he compliments her.

"You are ravishing, my dear."

I am unable to determine if it is Mr. Barnes' empty flattery or Gwen's much earlier than anticipated arrival time that is making my stomach sour.

"I've poured you a drink. Come in and let's get acquainted." Mr. Barnes motions for Gwen to pass through into the suite, his centre girth not leaving much space between the two. As she steps forward, sliding past with her back to him, his empty hand wanders toward her waistline, dipping low to settle on her hip for a fraction of a second.

I want to scream, to tell her to run as fast as she can to escape his clutches, but I can't. Doing so would ruin the plan. Instead, I crouch in the stairwell, hand positioned firmly over my mouth, preventing both sound and the unsettled contents of my stomach from escaping.

Assuming the hour hasn't quite reached six o'clock yet, my heart sinks with the knowledge of how long Gwen may be alone with Mr. Barnes in his suite. I have to do something. I can't simply abandon her to a fate I have no desire to even imagine.

Grabbing my stole, I race down seven flights of stairs. At the back-of-house corridors, I remove my shoes and tiptoe toward the entrance to the basement. With the evening festivities upon us, I am hoping the offices will be empty.

Reaching the cold cement floor of the basement, I slip my heels back on and move as quietly as I can toward Mr. Olson's office. Closing the door behind me, I scurry around the desk and pick up the telephone's handle. Not giving myself a moment to sit, I dial our home connection and wait for it to ring.

"Wilson residence." Clara's voice sings across the line.

"It's me. Gwen arrived early. We need to do something."

"But it's not even six o'clock." Clara's worried tone matches my anxiously beating heart.

"Still, she is already in his suite. We can't leave her there."

"Hang on. I think William has arrived."

I hear Clara set down the telephone handle, followed by murmurs from afar.

"Okay, we are on our way. But Louisa, we don't have a choice anymore. For Gwen's sake, we need to—"

"I know." I resist the urge to toss my hat to the desk so I can run a hand through my carefully coifed hair as my frustration grows. "Do what you must. I can't wait for you to arrive. I have to do something to help Gwen."

Without waiting for Clara to respond, I hang up the phone, take a deep breath, and slink back toward the lobby.

Standing in the doorway between the kitchen hall and the lobby, I stare daggers at George until I gain his attention. Lifting my arms in question, I am met with a sad shake of his head. Darn, I think as I climb back up to the eighth floor. I am out of options. Without Mrs. Oxley-Barnes' presence to call out her no-good louse of a husband for all his improprieties, I have no other choice but to push forward with plan B.

I run through the plan in my head. Knock. Perform.

Dash. I'll need to be quick and forceful in order to pull this off. Gwen is counting on me.

Given the cocktail I spotted in Mr. Barnes' hand, I am hopeful his inebriated state along with the element of surprise will allow me to slip right past him into the suite before he realizes I am not his wife. The plan is a risky one. Not only do I have to gain entrance to the suite under false pretenses but I also have to get back out, hopefully with Gwen safely at my side.

My costume, complete with travelling suit, stole, and a stylish wide-brimmed hat that shades my face, is all I have to convince Mr. Barnes his wife has arrived to ruin his good time. With any luck, my impersonation will be enough to shoo Gwen from the suite, ensuring her safety.

After I'm discovered, I'll be on my own. I may very well find myself trapped in Mr. Barnes' suite, but it is a risk I have to take. If it weren't for me and my careless words, Gwen wouldn't be in danger. Despite the warmth of my costume, a chill runs up my spine.

At the top of the stairs, I take a minute to steady myself. The change to an immediate rescue means Mr. Barnes will not be exposed as the scoundrel he is, which does not please me at all. But for now, that can't be helped. From the beginning, Clara and I agreed that Gwen's safety would come above everything else. When all of this is over, I am afraid it will come down to Mr. Barnes' word against ours regarding his actions within the hotel.

I straighten my clothes, tugging the stole into place so it lies across my right arm and shoulder, just as Mrs. Oxley-Barnes wore hers the first and only time I laid eyes on the woman. I pull on the stairwell door and step onto the plush carpet, moving quickly toward suite 815.

Positioning myself so my face is partially hidden

beneath the brim of my hat, while ensuring my red-painted nails and stole are the first things he'll see, I knock with assuredness on the door of Mr. Barnes' suite.

He fumbles for the door handle on the opposite side, giving me the advantage of knowing his position. When the door opens, I move quickly, throwing it wide with my stole-covered arm. "Darling," I drawl in my best impersonation of a woman I've shared no words with. I do not wait to be let in. Nor do I pause to appraise his surprise. I simply force my way past him, determined to get to Gwen. "I've come to join you for the celebration."

I stride into the living area as if I own the place. Gwen is lying on the chaise lounge with her arm hanging limply over the edge. My eyes shift toward an empty glass tipped over on the carpet. Forgetting my ruse, I rush to her side and notice that the hem of her beautiful dress is tugged up two inches above her knees and her carefully painted lipstick is smeared onto her cheek.

"Oh, Gwen. Why didn't you listen to me when it really mattered?" I feel the moisture gather in my eyes as I place a palm to her cheek, assessing her in the only way I know how.

The girl is unresponsive. Even the slam of the guest-room door does not rouse her. I'll never get her out of here on my own. I feel the hairs on the back of my neck stand to attention as Mr. Barnes stalks up behind me.

"Well, well, well. It seems you didn't wish to be left out of the fun after all, Miss Wilson. Or should I call you Louisa?"

CHAPTER 32

SATURDAY, DECEMBER 31, 1927

*C*lara
    William's eyes reveal his delight at seeing me dressed for the ball. I hardly give him a chance to say anything as I explain the situation and hang up the phone. We rush from the apartment, with him taking my hand to ensure I don't trip down the three flights of stairs as the slightly heeled shoes I am not used to wearing click-clack with every step I take.

Out in the brisk winter air, William secures us a taxi while I fill him in on the plan Louisa and I hatched, ending with Louisa's phone call. We are a short drive away, which is enough time for William to squeeze my hand and say, "You know we'll have to go to my sister with this?"

"I do." Meeting his eyes in the darkened back seat, I ask, "Does she know you are taking me to the ball?"

He shakes his head. "I wasn't keeping it a secret, if that is what you are wondering. My only intention was to keep you to myself for a little while."

"I suppose we will both have to be bold, then."

William tilts his head in question.

"You are merely informing your sister. I, on the other hand, am informing my boss. That comes with a risk."

"Ah, I see. If it helps at all, I don't think she'll be displeased. Don't tell her I told you, but she talks about you like a proud mother hen."

I feel my hand squeeze his and decide it is now or never. "Speaking of secrets. I have something more to tell you about Mr. Barnes. You see, the trouble I was having was due to him."

William's head snaps up in concern. "What did he do?"

"He tried to force himself on me with a kiss." I feel my cheeks warm at the bluntness of my words and am instantly thankful for the lack of light in our confined space.

"Did he succeed?" His voice is hoarse and filled with fury.

"Not in the way a kiss is meant to be exchanged, he didn't. I am saving that for someone special."

We arrive in front of The Hotel Hamilton, the lights of the hotel filtering into the back seat of our taxi. William's face is flushed with colour, yet he doesn't take his eyes off me until the driver is opening the back door closest to him.

William pays for our ride as I slide across the back seat toward the open door. Offering me his hand, he helps me from the car. Time is ticking, and though there are many things that need to be shared between us, they will have to wait. Gwen needs our help.

Strolling into the hotel through the front door unnerves me at first, but that changes when the doorman greets me with an approving smile. "Miss Wilson, you are exquisite this evening."

I offer a quiet "thank you" and do my best to keep my

wits about me as we move toward the back-of-house corridor that leads to Ms. Thompson's basement office.

William pokes his head into Cookie's pastry kitchen. "Have you seen Eliza?"

"Well, you certainly clean up nicely." Cookie steps into the hall with a teasing laugh. Her eyebrows lift toward her hairline as I come into view. "And you, Clara, are lovely."

William shifts his weight from one foot to the other before pressing forward. "It's urgent. Eliza?"

"Basement office. She headed there five minutes ago." Cookie's expression turns to one of concern. "Can I be of assistance?"

We are already moving down the corridor when William calls over his shoulder, "You might want to brew some strong tea. I have a feeling we are going to need it."

Out of sight of prying eyes, William reaches for my hand, and together we hurry toward the basement.

Ms. Thompson's office door is open wide, and we step inside to find her and Mr. Olson chatting casually, each with a small pour of something dark in a crystal glass.

Their eyes travel between William and me, dressed for an evening out and arriving with laboured breaths. It takes only a moment for Ms. Thompson to recognize there is trouble.

She stands abruptly, her legs pushing the chair back with a screech. "What is the matter?"

William gives them the short version of the story I relayed to him. Mr. Barnes' intentions are clear from his actions toward myself, Louisa, and now Gwen.

Ms. Thompson looks to Mr. Olson, a hand placed across her midsection. "Robert, I knew that man was trouble. I should have stepped in when I suspected. Oh my goodness. Poor Gwen."

Without uttering a word, Mr. Olson ushers us through the door with a guiding hand. A few minutes later, the four of us are in the service lift and climbing slower than I'd like to the eighth floor.

"What was the girl thinking?" Mr. Olson's head swivels in Ms. Thompson's direction.

I bite my bottom lip, feeling Mr. Olson's admonishment as though it's been directed at me alone. Perhaps telling him was a mistake. What if Mr. Olson believes Mr. Barnes instead of us? What will that mean for Mr. Barnes being found out? What about the security of our employment at the hotel? Worst-case scenarios spiral through my mind.

Ms. Thompson shifts beside me, drawing my eyes upward. Her pursed lips and stoic silence tell me that she does not agree with Mr. Olson's assessment of the situation.

William, sensing the discord, speaks up as the lift passes the fifth floor. "Robert, from all that Miss Wilson has told you, surely you will keep an open mind. A girl's well-being may be at risk here."

He must realize he is the odd man out, as Mr. Olson nods in agreement before clearing his throat and breaking the tension with another loaded question. "So, you two are…?" He gestures between William and me.

"Getting to know one another," William replies without missing a beat. I clamp down on my bottom lip, not from worry this time but to suppress the smile that is eager to be set free.

Ms. Thompson clasps her hands in front of her and says pointedly, "I dare say, you have excellent taste, Miss Wilson." Her lips twitch as she does her best to restrain a laugh I am certain is on the verge of tumbling out.

The lift door opens, saving me from the need to find a suitable reply. Like a herd of elephants, we storm down the hall to suite 815. Ms. Thompson pulls out her master key and inserts it in the lock. With a twist and a push, we dash into the room.

Two heads swivel at our boisterous arrival. Tears stream down Louisa's cheeks. I run to my sister, who is kneeling on the floor beside Gwen's motionless body splayed atop the chaise lounge. "Are you okay?" I smooth my hands over her tear-stained face. "Did he hurt you?"

"He didn't have the chance to." Louisa holds up the business end of a small ice pick. Her knuckles white from her steadfast grip on the cocktail accessory's handle. "But Gwen." Louisa's voice stretches high with alarm. "I'm not sure what happened. She's been like this since I found her."

Ms. Thompson kneels beside us, placing two fingers to Gwen's neck.

Louisa's words are coated with regret and marinated in emotion. "I didn't get here fast enough." Her head shakes back and forth as fresh tears gather and fall.

Ms. Thompson turns and narrows her eyes on Mr. Barnes. "What did you give her?"

Mr. Barnes, standing near the bathroom, shrugs his shoulders; his lack of concern spurs me into motion. I pivot from my crouched position to take in the rest of the room. Mr. Barnes is cradling his left hand, which I assume was injured by Louisa's ice pick. William is standing beside him, one hand latched strongly onto Mr. Barnes' arm, either holding him back or preventing him from running.

Ms. Thompson stands and moves toward the man as a fury I've never seen her possess flashes across her face. "I asked you, what did you give her?" The question roars from the hotel matron, garnering all of our attention, and I am instantly thankful she is on our side.

Mr. Barnes offers nothing, dismissing Ms. Thompson

with a turn of his head. The matron, disgust and concern emanating off of her, pivots and faces Mr. Olson. Her eyes plead with him to take action. With a single nod, Mr. Olson steps toward the narrow telephone table tucked discreetly into the room's corner, the luxury of a telephone being afforded solely to guests of the eighth floor.

"Mr. Reynolds, this is Mr. Olson. I need you to call for a doctor immediately. Suite 815. Yes, that is correct."

Ms. Thompson takes three quick strides across the room and stands beside Mr. Olson. "Robert, the police too."

"Eliza, surely we can—"

Ms. Thompson shakes her head. "The police, Robert."

Mr. Olson exchanges a worried look with Ms. Thompson. With a sheepish nod, he instructs Mr. Reynolds to also call the police. Hanging up the telephone, he runs a distressed hand through his hair, and I sense that he is coming to terms with his incorrect assumptions. It is hard to discount the facts. With Mr. Barnes' blatant disdain toward everyone in the room and Gwen's unconscious state, the only logical conclusion is that Mr. Olson has misjudged the situation.

Ms. Thompson reaches up to give Mr. Olson's arm an understanding squeeze, and I blush at being witness to the gesture.

"I know. You are right, Eliza." Mr. Olson acknowledges his error with a tilt of his head before moving to the suite's door and securing it in the open position for those soon to arrive.

I squeeze Louisa's shoulder before leaving her at Gwen's side to search the room for answers. If Gwen has consumed anything to make her so unresponsive, it will be here. I spot the empty glass and the nearly empty bottles on the small trolley Mr. Barnes had brought up for his enjoyment.

I point to the silver tray laden with the discards of cocktail ingredients. "It's this." I turn to face Mr. Barnes. "How many did you give her?"

The man says nothing, turning his nose up at my accusation. I step toward his sneering face. "How many?" I cajole my features into a pleasant smile. "Mr. Barnes. Just so we are clear, you are going to be arrested tonight. The girl is underage, under the employ of The Hotel Hamilton, and clearly unable to stand on her own two feet. As you've stated before, you are a worldly man. Surely you know that harming a girl to the point of unconsciousness isn't likely to go well for you. If something more happens to poor Gwen because we were unable to properly care for her, those charges will be much more severe."

William smiles devilishly as he meets my eyes. "As a lawyer, I can say with certainty that Miss Wilson here has made an astute assessment of the situation."

William squeezes the arm attached to Mr. Barnes' injured hand and the man hollers. "Three. She had three of your Hamilton Specials."

I want to scream at the man. Did he tell her they were punch? Did she know what she was getting into? Gwen is a petite thing with hardly an ounce of fat to spare. How many drinks did he think someone her size would need? My inner rant is cut short by Ms. Thompson's voice.

"Clara, get a clean cloth from the bathroom and run it under cold water." Ms. Thompson has regained her composure and is back in charge. "Louisa." She has to call her name twice to garner my sister's attention. "Louisa, dear. Go pour a glass of water for Miss Russell. We'll need to get her up and encourage her to drink it."

Louisa and I return at the same time. Ms. Thompson

places the cool cloth on Gwen's forehead and motions for Lou to help reposition the girl while I take a step back.

By the time they've got her sitting up, Gwen is beginning to stir. Louisa tucks herself in beside Gwen and places the cup to her lips. The glass and its contents fly across the room when Gwen pushes it away, calling out, "No more. I don't want any more."

Ms. Thompson's usual tight bun at the back of her head has come loose, with wisps of hair sticking up in all directions. She steps away, taking a moment to collect herself with a hand placed firmly against her lips. I take in the scene from beside the writing desk, close enough to be helpful but far enough away to give Louisa and Gwen some space.

A splash of colour and movement at the door catch my attention. "I see you've got quite the party going on in here." The woman at the door turns slightly and motions to someone behind her. "Let's be sure to capture it for posterity."

The flash of a camera's bulb lights up the room like a bolt of lightning, and my eyes snap closed in response. As we all recover from the unexpected blinding light, the woman I can only assume is Mrs. Oxley-Barnes steps toward her husband. "Well, Harold. It seems you've got yourself into a bit of a pickle." She tilts her head slowly from side to side, examining the man.

Gwen seems to rally at the commotion and manages to sit up with Louisa's help. The girl holds both her stomach and her head while Louisa whispers quietly to her, telling her she is going to be all right.

"What are you doing here?" Mr. Barnes' voice is pinched with irritation as he addresses his wife. A slow smile stretches across my face as the realization that Louisa's plan has worked. Mr. Barnes will have to answer for his actions.

"I got your telegram. Something about urgent business in Vancouver. Unable to travel home at this time. Really, dear, did you expect me to believe there was business in Vancouver during the holiday season? You are slow to realize I am wise to your ways." The woman winks in Louisa's direction. "My, it's like looking in a mirror. A much taller mirror, but how clever of you."

It's like watching one of Louisa's theatre productions as Mrs. Oxley-Barnes moves about the suite, asserting her role as if she is on stage in front of a large audience.

The petite woman walks toward Mr. Olson and extends a hand. "Pardon me. I've forgotten my manners in all the hubbub. It is nice to see you again, Ms. Thompson, and I presume you are Mr. Olson."

Mr. Olson inclines his head.

"I am Mrs. Oxley-Barnes. I believe we have a few friends in common." The woman leans in. "Namely, Mr. Hamilton."

Mr. Olson is about to reply when Gwen's garbled voice cuts through. "You're married?" With a look of disgust, Gwen collapses back into Louisa's supportive hold.

"Not for long." Rose Oxley-Barnes grins mischievously. "When word of your plans arrived, I packed a bag and made a quick stop at my lawyer's office on my way to the train station. Daddy was kind enough to let me borrow the Pullman to expedite the travel."

From her bag, she pulls out a large envelope. Her smile grows as she hands it to Mr. Barnes. "The divorce papers, dear. Do us both a favour and sign them tout de suite. We both know this marriage has no legs to stand on, with all your philandering and lies."

"But Rose. You can't." Mr. Barnes' demeanour changes from angry to frantic to pleading. "We were good together once. I know we've grown apart recently, but I need you. You are my everything. We have a home and a life. Don't do this to me, Rose. I'll be lost without you."

"Harold, we haven't been good together since our honeymoon." Mrs. Oxley-Barnes scans the audience assembled for the dissolution of her marriage, catching my eye in the process. "And just to be clear, I have a house and a life. You no longer have that same privilege." She inclines her head toward the door as three police officers enter. "I suspect you will be busy trying to explain yourself to these fellows for quite some time, anyway."

CHAPTER 33

SATURDAY, DECEMBER 31, 1927

*C*lara   Two police officers take hold of Mr. Barnes, freeing William to return to my side. Mr. Olson speaks with the third officer, filling him in on the events of the evening as Mrs. Oxley-Barnes watches from the corner of the room, out of the way.

I lean my head toward William. "I love my position at The Hamilton." Lifting my chin, I meet his gaze. "Honestly, I do, but you were right. No job is worth letting someone else's rules make me feel uncomfortable or unsafe. Sometimes, being a good employee means raising the red flag when something is amiss, even if you don't think it is your job to do so."

"I couldn't agree more, Miss Wilson." Mr. Olson steps toward us, indicating that the police officer would like to speak to William. "Rest assured, I will be amending the hotel policies first thing Monday morning. I've underestimated how a maid might find herself in a precarious position through no fault of her own. I want all the staff at The Hamilton to be comfortable coming to us for assistance of any kind. I won't be so quick to judge the next time, though I do hope there is never a next time. I will discuss this evening's events with Mr. Hamilton, and I promise you, we will come up with a better solution to keep our staff safe and happy. I imagine if our employees are happy, then the guests we serve will be as well."

Ms. Thompson signals to Mr. Olson that she and Louisa are taking Gwen to the basement to telephone her parents. "I will be right down. I'll stop by to speak with Mr. Reynolds first, and I'll have him direct the doctor to your office. I don't imagine this will be a comfortable or easy conversation for Gwen or her parents."

The police officer in charge tells Mr. Olson they will be in touch but that he should expect to make time for all those involved to be interviewed in the coming days. "We will remove Mr. Barnes from the hotel. Would you prefer us to exit via the back door?"

Mr. Olson looks to Mrs. Oxley-Barnes and with a defiant tilt of his chin says, "Take him out through the lobby." Checking his wristwatch, he adds, "It's nearly eight o'clock. The place should be humming with a crowd by now."

I stifle a gasp, but William, it seems, cannot hide his surprise and lifts his eyebrows in question. Mr. Olson's sober expression tells me he means business. Humbled by the events of the evening, he is willing to face the whispers that are sure to come with the police escorting a guest out the front door. He is risking his own embarrassment and possibly the hotel's reputation to ensure Mr. Barnes receives the public shaming he so readily deserves.

Mr. Barnes is placed in handcuffs. The sound of metal closing around his wrists is hard to ignore, and I feel the mood in the room grow sombre. The officers are pushing him forward to begin his walk of humiliation when I remember he still has Mama's watch.

Before the officers can take him away, I spin toward the writing desk, shuffling papers onto the floor in a hurry. This may be my last chance to find it. "It has to be here." I swipe an arm across the desk, finding nothing but dark wood beneath. My heart sinks at the thought of losing Mama's watch forever. Deflated, my chin drops to my chest as William steps toward me with concern. Moisture rims my lower lids as my eyes scan the papers scattered about the plush carpet.

Out of the corner of my eye, I catch a glimmer of silver peeking up at me. I drop to my knees and breathe a sigh of relief. "I've got it." I pluck the watch from the floor beneath the writing desk and lift it up to show William. Standing, I turn to call after Mr. Barnes before he leaves the suite and my life forever. "This"—I hold Mama's watch up for him to see—"isn't yours for the taking. In fact, none of us are."

I place Mama's watch on my wrist and try to force the clasp closed. Still broken, the clasp gives way and slips from my wrist. William catches it and tucks it into his suit pocket. "Why don't I keep this safe for now?"

Appreciation rushes through me at his kindness. Even if I wanted to, I couldn't hide the smile William's thoughtfulness elicits.

The police officer in charge raises a hand in farewell. "Thank you, everyone. We will be in touch soon. I hope you are able to enjoy the rest of your evening."

We watch in silence as Mr. Barnes is escorted from the suite. Glancing around the room, I consider the chaos one man created in all of our lives. I wonder how it is possible for one person to cause so much turmoil.

People like Mr. Barnes may shout the loudest, but that doesn't mean their words carry more weight. They are simply hiding their true intentions behind a wall of noise. I look at William, and though I don't have the answers for everything, I know without a doubt that there are good people in this world. Those are the ones who deserve my time and attention.

William extends his elbow in a gallant gesture. "Miss Wilson, I believe we have a ball to attend." I slide my arm into his.

"I believe we do, Mr. Thompson."

We stroll past Mr. Olson as Mrs. Oxley-Barnes inquires about a room for the night. "This one appears to be vacant, and I have already paid for it."

I marvel at the woman's forthright approach. I imagine she ruffles her fair share of feathers, but I bet she isn't concerned over whether her actions are deemed pleasing. I've learned from my dealings with Mr. Barnes that you will always disappoint someone, but that someone shouldn't be yourself.

CHAPTER 34

SATURDAY, DECEMBER 31, 1927

*L*ouisa
 I wave to Clara and William as they leave for the ball, and though I am happy for my sister, I feel a pang of sadness that I am no closer to fulfilling my own dreams. Now, they feel even more unattainable. Ms. Thompson stands beside me, both of us watching the merriment of the hotel's first New Year's celebration with tired expressions.

The lobby has been transformed, with low-slung chairs gathered around small, round tables. The Christmas tree apparently came down yesterday afternoon, significantly expanding the available space in the lobby. Piano music filters through the room like a bird riding a breeze of wind. An extensive bar sits in the corner near the hotel's front windows, with waiters coming and going from it in rapid succession.

Mrs. Oxley-Barnes, soon to be minus the "Barnes," steps from the lift and joins us at the edge of the fanfare. "Seems to be a quaint little party." She peers directly into my eyes. "I'll be having a drink, if anyone needs me."

I am considering her words when Ms. Thompson nudges me forward. "Go on, Miss Wilson. The woman has invited you to join her. Don't keep her waiting."

I take the vacant seat next to the woman as a waiter I've never seen in the hotel stops at our table. "I'll have a sidecar. Actually, better make that two. I feel I might be needing it tonight." She looks at me. "What can I get you? I am sure it is the least I can do, considering your assistance with my soon-to-be ex-husband."

"Just a glass of water, please."

The waiter shifts his tray from one hand to the other. "We have punch without spirits if you would prefer something festive."

"Thank you, punch would be lovely."

"Have we met before?" Mrs. Oxley-Barnes scrutinizes me from across the table.

I extend my hand. "Louisa Wilson. Pleased to meet you, Mrs.—"

She cuts me off with a wave of her hand before offering mine a light squeeze. "Call me Rose. I've never liked the double last name, but my father insisted I maintain my family name to keep from getting lost in another man's world. I think I'll enjoy going back to 'Oxley,' despite father knowing best and all that."

She studies my face. "You were the maid I met a few months ago. I remember thinking you were pretty then. I can see why he chose you." Rose pauses as the waiter delivers our drinks, placing a steaming plate of Hu's dim sum in the centre of our table. She takes a sip from her squat glass. "I assume he did choose you?"

"It seems so." As soon as the words are out of my lips, I want to pull them back. "I didn't realize he was married."

She nods and takes another sip before popping a morsel

of dim sum into her mouth. Her first glass is going down quickly.

"And," I add in an effort to clarify, "I didn't invite or accept his attention in that way."

"You are certainly not the first. I just hope you are the last." Another sip from her glass and I can see the bottom. "What did he lure you in with?"

I look at her, my jaw slack.

"He always has a play. Who was he pretending to be in Vancouver?"

"He told me he was a Hollywood director, and my dream of acting in motion pictures convinced me he was telling the truth." I feel shame climbing my neck in a swath of red.

Rose's laugh comes out like a bark, startling me. "A director? Well, that is a new one. I hate to break it to you, but Harold Barnes is nothing more than an accountant."

She waves her empty glass in the waiter's direction, and he signals his acknowledgement. Her second sidecar is on the way.

"He is an accountant for a film company, or at least he was." Another dismissive wave of Rose's hand tells me she is thoroughly done with the man. "Honey, he is the furthest thing from being in the know when it comes to filmmaking."

I bob my head in understanding as the waiter places her second cocktail in front of her.

Leaning across the table, Rose lowers her voice, concern etched into the corners of her eyes. "Is the girl going to be okay? Did he hurt her?"

I meet her halfway across the table with my own quiet reply. "She is going to feel unwell for a while, but other than a bruised ego and a whopping headache, Gwen has assured us he didn't have a chance to harm her." A soft smile tugs at the corner of my mouth. "Before tonight, she had never had a drop of alcohol. She said the drink tasted like punch." I look at my own glass, eyeing it more warily now. "She gulped two down in quick succession, and she remembers she was sipping number three when she collapsed onto the chaise lounge and dropped the glass." I shake my head, thinking about Gwen's final comment before her parents appeared in Ms. Thompson's office. "The drink spilling on the carpet was her biggest concern. I suppose she might be a keeper as a Hamilton maid, after all."

Rose sits back, relief flooding out of her in a long exhale. "I am glad. I'm not sure what I would have done if he had caused her harm. I would have blamed myself for sure." She tilts the glass to her lips.

I lean across the table and meet her eyes, determined for her to hear me. "He wins if we blame ourselves. We can't let him win, Rose."

Rose sits back in her chair, her fingers drawing imaginary lines up and down her glass. "It was you? With the message?"

The room is getting warm as more guests crowd inside, the evening nearing midnight. I decide the waiter is trustworthy and take a sip of my punch. The sweet concoction tickles my tongue.

"Yes, it was me." I fiddle with the cocktail napkin my drink sits on. "I hope it wasn't too forward of me. I was trying to be discreet."

"Oh, you were very discreet, Louisa. It took me the better part of three hours to figure out what your message meant. When his telegram arrived, I put the pieces together." Rose pushes her half-full drink to the side of the table. "After that, the decision was made."

I nod solemnly, understanding that regardless of what needed to be done this evening, Mr. Barnes' actions still cost Rose a marriage, and that can't be easy.

After a few minutes of silence between us, Rose brushes her bereavement away, replacing it with a triumphant smile. "I did a little research myself, Louisa. I've read about your recent success on the stage. Seems you might have been an easy target for my good-for-nothing soon-to-be ex-husband. But there is something I want to share with you, woman to woman.

"I don't want you to think I am successful because of my family name. My father instilled his work ethic in me. He encouraged all of his children to work hard and strive toward their goals. He is a fine example of embracing each day as a new opportunity." She leans forward and laughs. "Now that I think about it, that's probably why Harold managed to cling to me for so long. I thought that one day I would make him into the husband I wanted him to be.

"I suppose we all have our blind spots. But I built my career with hard work, determination, and belief in myself and what I was doing." She raises one eyebrow, and I do not miss the challenge laced within it. "You took a risk tonight. In calling out a man for his inappropriate actions. Many women wouldn't have done so, and certainly not with such fanfare and flare." She eyes my attire, the blue stole slung over an empty chair beside me, with an approving smile.

"It seems you also believe in yourself and what you stand for, Louisa. The question is, do you have it in you to keep believing? Hollywood may appear to be full of glitter and sunshine, but it isn't for the faint of heart. What you experienced tonight, though devastating, is all too often common behaviour in the movie business. Are you up for that?"

I square my shoulders, feeling the thrum of assuredness as it courses through me. "Yes. Yes, I am."

Rose stands, eyeing me expectantly. "You have my number. Be sure to stay in touch. Get a few more credits under your belt, and then we'll talk. We women need to stick together, after all."

She extends her hand once more to me, and I rise and accept it. She waves the waiter over and tells him to charge the drinks to suite 815.

I try to hold my tongue, even going so far as to bite my bottom lip. But I take my last chance before she walks out of earshot, knowing that if my career is going to move forward, then I have to be the one to make it happen.

"Rose," I call out to her, and she turns. "I'll get those credits."

A confident smile and an acknowledging nod tell me she's looking forward to our next conversation.

CHAPTER 35

SATURDAY, DECEMBER 31, 1927

Clara

Having missed the dinner hour, William and I are tucked behind a column in the grand ballroom of The Hotel Vancouver, nibbling from a plate of cheese and crackers he managed to convince a waiter to bring us. Taking in the elaborate decor, I am in awe of the time and effort put into the fanciful decorations, and I imagine the hotel in its natural glory would have been more than enough to stun me.

The chandeliers glow warmly, hanging from the ornate ceiling, its design as fascinating as the artwork adorning the flock-papered walls. Champagne flows like a fountain over a tower of glasses, the shimmering, gold-tinged liquid cascading from the top to the bottom. I can barely tear my gaze from its magical lull.

A band plays an upbeat tempo, and dancers fill the floor. Though we are essentially on the outside of the festivities, I am having the time of my life watching everyone. William doesn't press or hover. He simply smiles, observing me as I take it all in.

With the last cracker gone, he sets the empty plate on a tall, round table and reaches for my hand. "May I have this dance?"

"Oh, I've never…" Embarrassment warms my cheeks.

"Come." William inclines his head toward the dance floor. "It's merely an excuse for me to hold you in my arms. If our feet move a little, then we'll be doing quite well."

I take his hand and let him guide me onto the dance floor. The band transitions from the up-tempo song into a ballad. The timing is perfect. With my hand in William's, I make a wide circle onto the floor and raise my right hand into his left.

"Ah, you have done this before." He winks at me.

I let the words settle between us, then clue him in to my thoughts. "Only with my father. I used to dance standing on the tops of his feet while he moved around the room. I was little, of course, but it is a fond memory I keep tucked in my heart."

"Thank you for sharing a piece of your heart with me." William's sincerity warms me through, and I feel as though I'll never know the cold again.

"I suspect you might be winning more than one piece of it, Mr. Thompson."

We dance in silence through three more songs, our eyes never leaving one another. When the band strikes up a faster rhythm, we are unfazed, content to remain as we are, in each other's arms. Only the stilted conclusion of an unfinished song and the announcement that there is one minute to midnight tugs us from our trance.

Instead of releasing me from his arms to ready ourselves for the countdown, William pulls me closer, his warm breath caressing my cheek as he leans his mouth toward my ear. A most delightful shiver runs through me as he whispers, "Clara, may I kiss you at midnight?"

He doesn't pull back to examine my expression. He waits patiently for me to answer. I feel every beat of his heart as it thrums steadily against my own chest. The countdown begins, with the crowd yelling, "Ten!"

I startle but recover myself with speed. I have—

"Nine," the crowd yells, their excitement growing like a raging river.

—seconds to decide if I will allow William Thompson to be someone truly special in my life.

"Eight."

Someone I can safely set boundaries with and share wonderful moments with.

"Seven."

Someone who feels like home, while making me feel completely safe and comfortable.

"Six."

I feel the warmth of his breath on my cheek, and like a magnet I lean into his embrace.

"Five."

Who am I kidding?

"Four."

He already is all of those things, and I know for certain now that I want him to be more.

"Three."

I angle my chin and pull back slightly to peer into his soft, grey-blue eyes.

"Two."

I move my hands, placing them lightly behind his head. They move of their own volition, my fingers snaking among the curls at the base of his neck.

The crowd screams, "One!"

I feel the heat of a blush as I consider my words. Determine to be undeterred, I tug my bottom lip between my teeth and let my gaze fall to William's waiting lips. "Not if I kiss you first."

"Happy New Year!" The entire ballroom seems to be shouting.

His cheeks colour. I feel the strength of his hands at my waist as he inches me closer. A fleeting, wide-eyed, boyish grin draws me in as my lips press to his. As I melt into his embrace, the room and everyone in it disappear.

Minutes pass as we stay locked in one another's arms. The excitement of the bustling crowd jostles us. The band erupts into a boisterous number while confetti scatters from the balcony above us. All of it, I am sure, is stunning, but neither one of us pays it any mind.

William tilts his head back to meet my eyes. "Happy New Year, Clara."

"It certainly is." I sigh before tugging him closer for another kiss.

CHAPTER 36

TUESDAY, JANUARY, 3 1928

*L*ouisa

The newspaper calls to me for the twentieth time this morning. I avoid Clara's amused expression as I pick it up and read the front-page headline again. I am unable to get a grip on myself and instead read the same paragraphs on repeat as the details of the last few days settle.

This time, I am thankful for the graininess of the black-and-white image, if only because it protects Gwen from further scrutiny. I talked to her yesterday over the telephone after the news story landed on every street corner in the city. She is reflective and plans to take some time off work until things calm down.

The photograph shows me bending over an unconscious Gwen, though I doubt anyone who wasn't in the room would be able to tell who any of us are. The caption beneath the photo is what continues to pull me back to the article.

Louisa Wilson, a rising star in the Vancouver theatre scene and the lead actress in Thomas Cromwell's recent production of Craig's Wife, *seen here assisting an unnamed maid in the Hotel Hamilton on New Year's Eve.*

I skim the rest of the story, catching Clara out of the corner of my eye as she admires Mama's watch, now firmly attached to her wrist. On New Year's Day, William showed up with the watch and a tiny set of borrowed pliers. He sat at the dining table with Papa, sipping tea and tinkering with the watch until it was fixed.

Papa rose from the table, patted William on the back, and announced, much to Clara's embarrassment, "He's a keeper." Then, planting a kiss on Clara's head, he added, "Don't let him get away, darlin'."

Clara shifts her focus from Mama's watch to me. "You know," she says, "you wanted to be famous, and look at that newspaper. They called you a rising star. I suspect it's only a matter of time before you're on the road to Hollywood."

I consider her words while remembering my new goal of securing a few more key acting roles. When I reach out to Rose Oxley, I will be prepared for the next step in my career. The telephone rings, interrupting our simple breakfast of toast and tea. I stand and answer it as Clara finishes packing our lunch for the day. "Wilson residence... This is she. Oh, hello, sir."

Clara wanders back into the room with a dishtowel in hand.

"I see. Yes, I am available. You'll have to work around my schedule at the hotel. Yes, it is important for me to keep my position at The Hamilton." I glance in Clara's direction, barely containing an eye roll.

I stifle a huff. "I apologize that it may be an inconvenience for you, but I have no plans to leave my position at the hotel. I am quite sure you do not ask your male actors to quit their jobs in order to accept a role in your productions." I bite my tongue and don't add mention of the significant pay difference between male and female actors, regardless of whether the lead role is female.

"Unless you are prepared to cover my wages from the hotel in addition to the agreed-upon amount for the role, this is my best offer. I promise you I'll work harder than any other person on your stage, but it would not be prudent for me to exchange a steady income for a short-term stint under the bright lights."

I straighten my back, willing myself not to cave on my terms, even with the offer of a lead role within my reach. A victorious smile curves my lips upward. "Very well. Thank you, sir. I will see you on Saturday at ten o'clock. Goodbye."

I cannot stop the giggle from erupting. "That was the director of *All Soul's Eve*, the play I auditioned for. He has had a change of mind, and he wants me to take on the lead role."

"Lou, that is fantastic. I am happy for you. But what was all that talk about not leaving The Hamilton? I thought you wanted to pursue acting full time."

I shrug my shoulders at the fickle appearance of my about-face. "If I'm going to make a name for myself, I've got to start by treating each day as an opportunity. It takes time and effort to build a career in film. I've decided that since I have the time, I'm going to do it my way."

"Speaking of time." Clara glances at her watch. "We'd better get going, or we're going to be late."

Clara

Putting the last hairpin in place, I check the mirror, ready for the day to begin. The locker room is a bustle of activity, since chatter has begun to surface that the winners of the holiday bonus have been selected.

Given our rather eventful New Year's Eve, I assume my and Louisa's names are no longer in the running. Our shenanigans have created quite the stir throughout the hotel, and with yesterday's newspaper headline, I am certain we are currently an embarrassment, certainly not adequate contestants in a "best maid" contest.

Ms. Thompson enters the locker room, her presence halting the chatter. "Good morning, ladies," she says, eliciting a murmur of "good morning" from all of us.

"As you've probably heard, we have finalized the winners of the holiday bonus." Ms. Thompson flips pages on her clipboard. "I must say you all played an important role in a successful holiday season, and you are to be congratulated for your hard work and consistent attention to our guests' needs."

Ms. Thompson scans the room, meeting every face. "You did not make our task an easy one."

Restrained, nervous laughter filters through the gaggle of maids.

Recognizing the building anxiety, Ms. Thompson lifts her clipboard and begins to read off the winners' names.

"The award for guest floor number one goes to Carol Potter. Congratulations, Carol."

The locker room fills with applause as those closest to Carol congratulate her.

"Guest floor number two goes to Margaret Adams."

Another round of applause conceals Louisa's whisper in my ear. "Good for her. She deserves a little recognition in her life." Maggie's delight brings a smile to my lips. After having a challenging time settling in with the other girls, Maggie seems to have found her way, and I am truly pleased for her.

Ms. Thompson goes through the rest of the guest floors one by one, with Hazel taking home the prize for the fifth floor and Beatrice being selected for the seventh.

As the room settles back into quiet, Ms. Thompson sets down her clipboard and clasps her hands in front of her. "The purpose of the holiday bonus was to challenge you and see how capable you are as maids, colleagues, and women." Her eyes flick in my direction.

"When it comes to challenges, I must admit I had not anticipated some of the events that transpired during the holiday season."

A ripple of laughter moves through our group. Mr. Barnes and his arrest are the worst-kept secrets among the hotel staff.

"The recipient of the eighth-floor holiday bonus showed us strength of character, as well as duty to and respect for her position as an eighth-floor maid. And most importantly, she demonstrated that each of us has an obligation to be true to ourselves. Ladies, there is no rule or person that should ever invalidate what you know to be right in your heart. Following your instincts isn't always easy, especially when they tell you something different from what everyone else around you is saying, myself included."

Ms. Thompson's gaze lands directly on me. "For that, I apologize." Clearing her throat and lifting her voice an octave, the matron announces, "Please help me in congratulating Clara Wilson for her exceptional work and service as the winner of this year's eighth-floor holiday bonus."

The room erupts in applause, with everyone turning to watch me as Louisa pulls me into a fierce embrace. Lou whispers in my ear, "Look at you, little sister, setting the world on fire."

The Hamilton Special
(an almost historically accurate cocktail)

To an ice filled cocktail shaker add the following ingredients and shake lightly holding the top on tight.

- 1 oz Vodka
- 1 oz Contreau
- 1 oz Prosecco
- 1 dash of Angostura aromatic bitters
- 2 oz of blood orange soda

Carefully open the cocktail shaker (the soda and Prosecco will make it fizzy) and strain into a cocktail glass.

Slice a thin piece of orange peel and spritz into the glass before adding the peel to the rim or if you prefer into the glass as garnish.

Note: San Pellegrino blood orange soda is what is used in this recipe however the blood orange flavour was not available until 1932, hence the almost historically accurate mention above.

AUTHOR NOTES

The Hotel Hamilton is a fictional hotel, however since the story is set in Vancouver, *Cocktails Before Midnight* takes place on the traditional, ancestral, and unceded territories of the of the xwməθkwəy̓ə m' (Musqueam), Sḵwx̱wú7mesh (Squamish), and Səlilwətaʔɬ (Tsleil-Waututh) nations in Vancouver, British Columbia, Canada.

Electric Christmas lights were still a novelty in 1927 with most family homes either going without or still embracing the somewhat scary (to this author), tradition of using candles on the boughs of their holiday tree. Department stores and the like, embraced the brightly lit strings of colour to attract shoppers into their stores during the holidays.

Thomas Edison created the first strand of lights in 1880 and he displayed them outside his Menlo Park, New Jersey laboratory. The first string of electric lights created specifically for a Christmas tree took place in 1882 when Edward H. Johnson, a partner in the Edison's Illumination Company, hand-wired eighty bulbs in red, white, and blue.

AUTHOR NOTES

He took his strand home and wound them around his Christmas tree. The lights, at the time, were cost prohibitive and required the services of a wireman (today's electrician) to install. In addition, many people were still wary of anything electric in the early 1900s so the demand for electric Christmas lights took decades to become what they are today.

When it comes to long distance telephone calls, I was unable to confirm the availability of telephone communication between Vancouver and Toronto in 1927. However, in 1918 Montreal and Vancouver were connected via telephone for the first time so I reasoned that with another nine years of advancement, it would have been likely that both Vancouver and Toronto had long distance ability.

Louisa's search for Romaine Fielding and his untimely death are indeed inspired by real events. Mr. Fielding did visit Vancouver seeking "a second Mary Pickford" in 1916. He was a Hollywood actor-writer-director and he was on the search for fresh talent. He ran advertisements in the papers for a contest to find his next leading lady then proceeded to interview contestants, choosing seven finalists to film. My research indicated that he repeated this scouting venture in several Canadian cities. Mr. Fielding passed away on December 15, 1927.

The New Orpheum Theatre opened in November 1927. It was the fourth theatre to be called The Orpheum in Vancouver thus when it opened in 1927 as a Vaudeville and Photoplay hotspot, it was called The New Orpheum. The theatre still stands today and features everything from rock concerts, to silent movie nights, to the Vancouver Metropolitan Orchestra. It is a stunning building and definitely worth the visit should you find yourself in

Vancouver. They also offer Orpheum Tours should you wish to delve a little deeper into its history.

The Vancouver Police Department has been in existence since 1866 and has a unique history all its own. Though I haven't delved into the shadier side of things, and trust me there seem to be plenty of them, the officer's death, Constable Ernest Sargent that I mention in the story is a very real and very sad bit of fact. He was only twenty-five years old with three years on the job. The city was on high alert for a known-to-police criminal who was later arrested in Victoria, charged and tried for the death of Constable Sargent. Unfortunately, the man was found not guilty of the crime.

Though Motion Picture Magazine was a real publication, my mention of what was written within its pages is a creation of my own. The magazine may very well have written about the golden years of Hollywood, but I was unable to confirm those mentions.

Train travel from Los Angeles to Vancouver was a research rabbit hole for me. I spent weeks scouring railway company historical notes, train enthusiast sites and more before asking for help. Reading train timetables and connections is far from easy reading, especially when one person's travel can occur on multiple different railroads with several stops and layovers. Thankfully, John from Parks California answered my questions and confirmed that first class tickets, especially with a private Pullman car, was achievable in 2-3 days from Los Angeles to Vancouver. He also confirmed that those with lower class tickets took the milk run and ended up waiting for hours to days in train stations as they made their way to their intended destination. I should also mention that by 1927 train travel

AUTHOR NOTES

was beginning to fall out of favour as the automobile became more reliable and affordable.

    Mrs. Rose Oxley-Barnes is, without a doubt, a fictional character. I did however, take inspiration from an interview I read of one of the founders of Paramount Pictures. I was inspired by the man's inclusion of both his sons and his daughters when it came to working and creating. I infused Rose's family life with a similar strong work ethic and a passion for creating. Though the timing of the interview did not coincide with the story's timeline, I was able to confirm that Hollywood Royalty did exist in 1927.

    Though the word "assault" has existed in a legal sense since the 1580s as in the use of menacing words or actions, we continue to see this type of power play in today's world. It is a nasty business when one person attempts to hold power over another in a threatening manner. Being on the receiving end of such things is far from easy and sadly, it often comes at a cost to the individual being assaulted. My hope is that, through story, we will be reminded that every individual has a right to protect themselves. Setting boundaries to ensure one's personal and physical safety takes courage and determination. If you or someone you know is in an abusive situation, please reach out for support in your community.

    To learn more about the research that goes into my novels, subscribe to my author newsletter by visiting my website at tanyaewilliams.com and you will receive an eBook copy of At the Corner of Fiction and History, facts and follies that inspire the stories.

ACKNOWLEDGMENTS

Writing a novel is challenging. Writing a series is, for me at least, ten times more challenging. I owe a debt of gratitude to my editor, Victoria Griffin for keeping me on the straight and narrow with this novel and The Hotel Hamilton series as a whole. Thank you for clarifying in three little words what I was trying to say in a draft full of thousands.

All of The Hotel Hamilton covers are a result of a photo shoot with three amazing people who helped me bring my vision into reality. Thank you to my husband, Dave for his photographic genius and continual patience with my requests. Thank you, Emily for being the most delightful and photogenic model I could have ever wished for. Thank you to my dear friend, Kari for supporting me in every way and also thank you for politely asking strangers to kindly step aside so we could get the shot.

Thank you to my cover designer, Ana Grigoriu-Voicu for taking a photograph and turning it into another stunning cover. I am grateful for your talent and ability to truly capture the essence of a story.

Thank you to the amazing Brianne Matheny for helping me stay on track with the characters, setting, and more.

Thank you to my beta readers Kelsey Gietl, Kate Thompson, and Diana Lesire Brandmeyer for their continual support, understanding, and keen insight into story. Readers can thank Diana for her nudge to have William ask Clara for a kiss at midnight.

I am forever grateful for the people in my life. I am lifted up, supported, inspired, and spend a great deal of time sharing a laugh. Many of them are authors and I continue to be in awe of them. Thank you, Michelle Cox, Carla Young, and the Pencil Dancers.

Thank you to the ladies of The Eleventh Chapter. So much talent in a small group of authors. I am honoured to walk among you. Thank you, Jenn Bouchard, Kerry Chaput, Jen Craven, Maggie Giles, Caitlin Moss, Sharon M. Peterson, and Colleen Temple.

To my HNS After Party friends, thank you for hanging out each month and enriching my life along the way. Together, we grow, we laugh, we learn, we mourn, we support, and we cheer one another on. I am so grateful to know each one of you.

Huge thanks to my advance reader team for reading, catching typos, and supporting me and my books in so many ways. I value each one of you and thank you for your continual support and interest in the stories I write. Any book I write doesn't feel quite real until I hand it off into your capable and welcoming arms. Thank you!

To my newsletter family, thank you for opening my

emails, answering my questions, and being just as excited as I am when a new cover, new story, or new goal is reached. Your support means the world to me.

Friendships change and shift as we move through our lives. Whether it is due to a change in location, outside obligations, parenting, marriage, and more, we are often tasked with adapting our relationships as our lives morph. True friendships ride the tide of change and show up with a smile and a hug whenever they are needed. Thank you for evolving with me, Kari, Donna, Tammy, Irene, and Judy.

To my family, thank you for your love and support. For cheering loudest and celebrating each milestone along the way. Knowing where I came from allows me to spread my wings creatively and that is a gift I am forever grateful for.

This novel is dedicated to my great Aunt Irene who lived a full life all the way to 101. She never let a conversation end without telling me how proud she was of me, even when she was no longer able to read the stories I wrote. I will miss her family updates, fun sense of humor, and our lengthy phone chats. I will always remember her saying things like, "I had better get to the salon before someone turns me upside down and tries to use me as a mop". Rest in peace, Aunt Irene. We will remember you, always.

To Dave and Justin, thank you for your love, support, and daily dose of comic relief. Thank you for not saying anything but simply sorting it out when I've worked well past the dinner hour. Thank you for letting me talk nonstop as I attempt to sort a story out and thank you for loving me wholly, despite my many shortcomings.

And to you, dear reader, thank you for taking the time out of your day to read Cocktails Before Midnight. I hope the story made you smile, laugh, think, and feel while exploring your own thoughts about power and personal boundaries.

ABOUT THE AUTHOR

A writer from a young age, Tanya E Williams loves to help a reader get lost in another time, another place through the magic of books. History continues to inspire her stories and her insightful view into the human condition deepens her character's experiences and propels them on their journey. Ms. Williams' favourite tales, speak to the reader's heart, making them smile, laugh, cry, and think. Cocktails Before Midnight is Tanya's eighth novel.

ALSO BY TANYA E WILLIAMS

The Smith Family Trilogy

Becoming Mrs. Smith

Stealing Mr. Smith

A Man Called Smith

The Hotel Hamilton Series

Welcome to the Hamilton

Meet Me at the Clock

Cocktails Before Midnight

A Vintage Vineyard Novel

Growing into Greatness

Stand Alone Titles

All That Was

Made in the USA
Coppell, TX
16 October 2024

38729289R00163